SEA OF SORROWS

TIL KINGDOM COME
BOOK 1.5

ABIGAIL BRIER

THE DAWN ISLANDS
MONSV
WESTERN DOCKS
NAUTOI
TABRANA
KEINOPAI
PRISON ISLE
SEA OF DAWN

TH FISHING VILLAGE
EASTERN DOCKS
SEA OF DAWN
ETS
ORIANA
CASCATA
BRISTOL

BLACK SEA
ORO
USHOLK
VALLEY OF THE SHADOW
EDMA
INK VALLEY
DEAD WOOD
NORTHERN WOOD
THE
BRUNES
OZANNA
VESTELE
SUNSTONE FOREST
ADULLAM
BRINLAND
HOLLOW COVES
DAWN PRISON
SEA OF DAWN
THE DAWN ISLANDS
TABRANA
ORIANA

THE ISLES OF VOLCANIA
ESWEN
REMONT
CRYSTAL SEA
ARRESIA
Z.W.

for those who are drowning and cannot breathe, may you find the breath of life everlasting

ISBN: 979-8-9897181-3-9 (e-book)
ISBN: 979-8-9897181-4-6 (paperback)
First Print Edition 2025

SEA OF SORROWS

ABIGAIL BRIER

PROLOGUE
DEATH'S LULLABY

Cove's heart of stone threatened to pull her downward into the depths of the sea. The colorless night fought for her soul as the waters churned around her. Grains of disrupted sand scraped her legs, and her increasingly panicked, shallow breaths offered no relief against the saltwater that poured into her lungs, as if its sole mission was to wipe her from existence. She blinked against the salt in her eyes, searching for any sign of shore in the endless night.

She fought the darkness that coaxed her to join it in death, but her flesh was weak from hours of treading the water. Her strength was quickly waning, her legs nearly useless against the raging sea. There were no visible ships on the night horizon to signal, and she knew there would be no land for miles. The ocean was lapping at her ears, lulling her into death with its eerie song, and she coughed as she fought to keep her mouth above the waves.

Her parents' killers had pursued her too, and she had

nowhere to flee but into the inescapable rip currents. Because her parents had been willing to die for the Light within them, Cove was all alone. An orphan. Her parents were dead, and at only twelve years old, she was about to meet the same fate. This wrathful sea was going to swallow her whole.

No.

She pushed her body upward, struggling to stay afloat.

Breathe. She gasped for air, but it could not fill her.

A wave crashed over her head, and she was pulled back under, sinking further beneath the surface with each passing second. The stars above were like embers in the sky, winking out as she was separated from their light by a dark and cloudy haze of ocean water.

Swim.

She kicked her feet as her hands reached helplessly for the air above, but only the tips of her fingers broke the surface. Her chest involuntarily heaved, inviting the sea to nest in her lungs. She tried to force it out, but a retching motion overcame her, and more and more water entered in with each panicked gasp.

I cannot do this anymore.

She gave into her weakness, allowing her body to be pulled further beneath the weight of the sea.

Yes, you can. Swim.

Her fatigued arms moved wildly, seemingly out of her control, until she had broken the surface once more. She choked on the salty waters and begged for relief, but her lungs were waterlogged. On her own, she was dead. Within minutes, she would fall unconscious, and her body would be left to rot a hundred miles beneath this surface, watching ships sail overhead until the world went up in flames. There was only one who could save her—the very one who must have given her life—and she deserved none of his mercies.

She choked the near silent words into the night anyway. "My life is yours," Cove said in surrender. It was a desperate plea as she kicked with all the might she had left. The waves crashed over her, and she bobbed above them once more. She yelled into the vast wilderness with all the breath she had left. "I give it to you!"

She gasped, and into her lungs entered the breath of life. The darkness within her melted away. She coughed as her lungs cleared and the Light of the Father swelled within her tired body, pouring from her chest in a strange and steady rhythm. The glow seemed to hover over the face of the waters, shining like a beacon amid the dark sea. She squinted against the light as the strange power shifted around her, keeping her body level with the surface. The sea began to calm, and slowly, she relaxed, letting the Light guide her way, just as her mother had always told her it would. She floated on her back in the now-gentle, rhythmic waves, breathing in pure, replenishing air and listening to the soothing beat of her heart.

I am going to live. He saved me. I am alive.

She drifted through the waters, resting and marveling at the galaxies above, until the silhouette of a sailboat with tattered sails formed on the horizon before her. The distance between them closed quickly, and before Cove knew it, the sailor and his wife were pulling her up onto the deck by her tired arms.

"I'm Ahlia," the woman said, unable to take her curious eyes from Cove's new, glowing mark. Cove brought her fingers to where it was illuminated at her collarbone.

"And I'm Marinos," said the sailor from behind her. "We saw your. . .*Light.*"

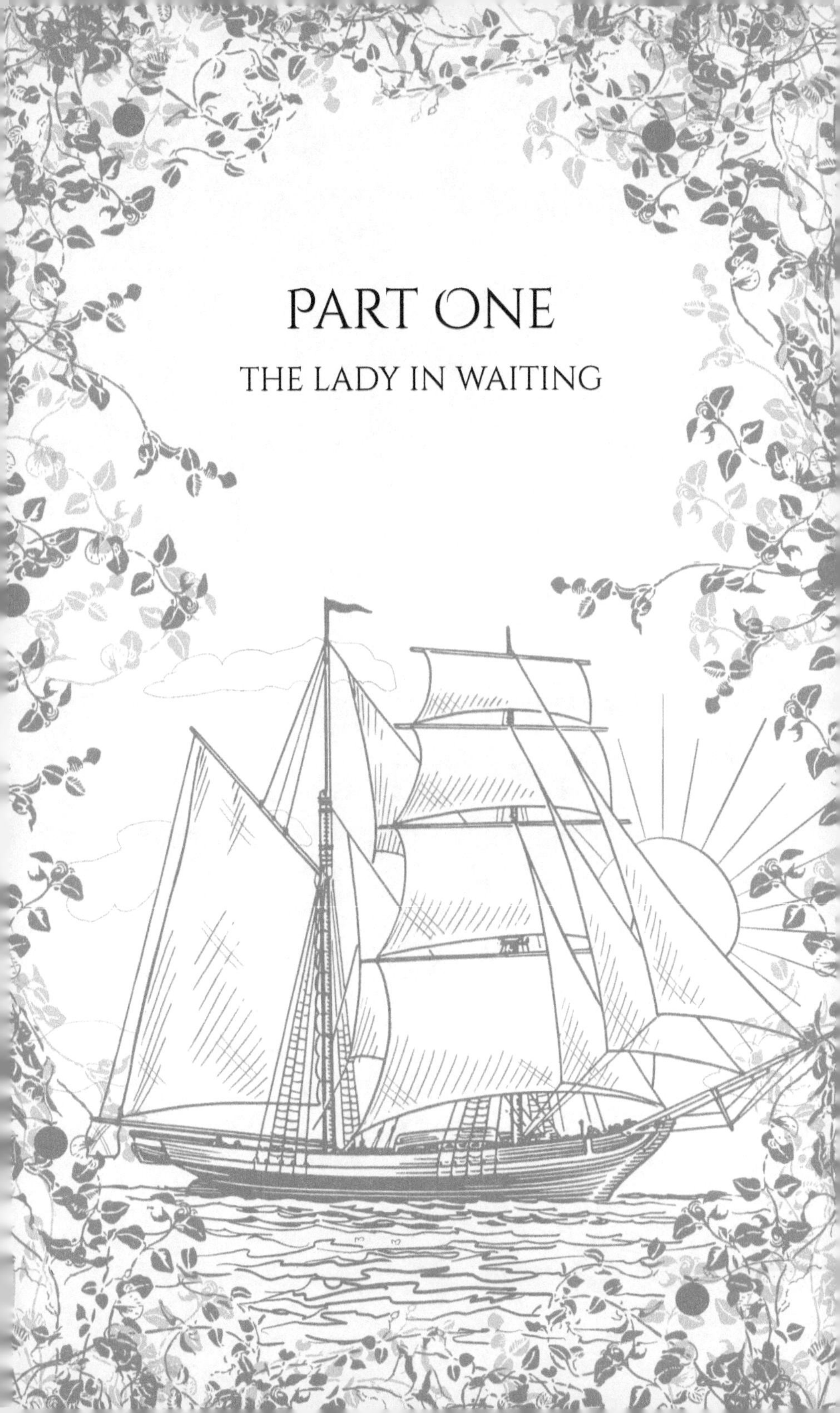

PART ONE

THE LADY IN WAITING

CHAPTER I
A GARDEN OF SECRETS
COVE

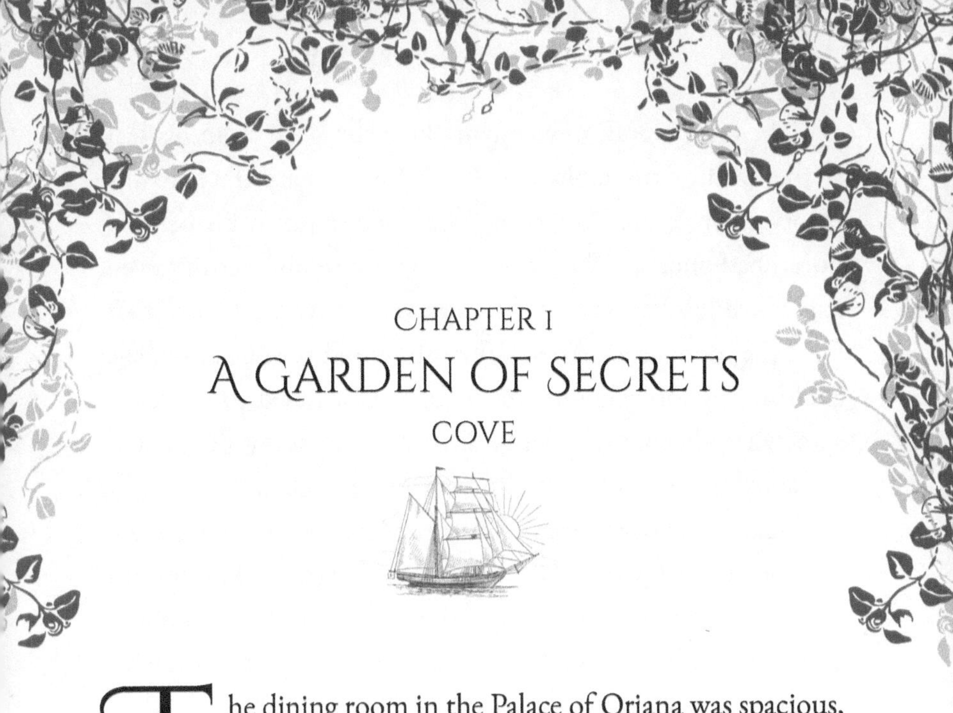

The dining room in the Palace of Oriana was spacious, and a stormy breeze sent the ivory curtains billowing along the edges of the colonnades, but no amount of fresh air could calm Cove's nerves in anticipation of the conversation the night would bring. She watched the flickering of a hundred candles' flames, allowing herself to be momentarily captivated by the warm glow that danced across the walls and ceilings and illuminated the feast that was set before her.

"You have not eaten much, Cove," King Sebastian said inquisitively. Cove blinked, remembering she was in a room with him and the princess. She sat up a little straighter, forcing herself to take a bite of bread. When the crumbs fell into her lap, she blushed and brushed them from the folds of her blue gown then pulled a cotton napkin from the table.

Beside Cove, Princess Mina of the Islands of Oriana and Tabrana looked up from her plate. "Father, must you always pry?"

The once blond, now-graying king shrugged from his seat at the head of the table, and Cove saw his gaze travel to the empty chair across from him, where she assumed his beloved queen had once sat. Wrinkles shifted around his chestnut eyes, and Cove blinked through the unwanted wave of grief that filled the room around her. When she could breathe again, she could not ignore the unfamiliar Light that called to her from somewhere beyond the king. She felt it pursuing her, but it remained unseen as the king answered his daughter.

"Can I not worry about you girls?" he asked with a cough, looking between Cove and the princess. He covered his mouth with a handkerchief, and Cove did not miss the specks of blood that clung to the cloth before he quickly tucked it into his jacket.

Cove allowed her gaze to sweep to the side for only a moment, assuring that the king's daughter noticed too, before speaking. "You have not eaten much either, Your Majesty," Cove said. His eyes fell to his untouched plate. "How have you been feeling?" The king chewed on the inside of his cheek for a moment and wiped the corner of his mouth with his thumb.

"No better, no worse. But tonight is not about me, dear Cove. Your mother and father should be here any minute. I am sure they were only delayed by the storm," he said, though Cove knew he did not believe his own words. The skies were clearing now, and the two moons were making their appearance among a million stars, shining silver against the blue night. Mina's brown eyes matched her father's, and they, too, gave Cove a look of sympathy. She took Cove's hand beneath the table, squeezing once.

In Cove's service to the princess as a lady, the two of them had become like sisters, and their close relationship had earned

Cove high favor from the king. She had dined with them daily over the past four years and had shared in much conversation. With the onset of his illness, the king had begun treating her more like a daughter than his daughter's lady, but Cove was careful with her trust, and to her, King Sebastian was just another unpredictable man to fear. Outwardly, he was kind, but he was also a king, and those in power would sit at the feet of darkness if it meant protection for themselves and their reign. After the death of her parents and seven grueling years with Marinos, she knew better than to trust so easily when so much was on the line.

How long are we to wait? Cove thought. Her adoptive parents were over two hours late, and the king had given the order to begin eating without them over an hour ago. Beneath the king's mask of indifference, Cove knew he was growing impatient. She could feel the irritation he kept hidden beneath. His only tell was the slight tapping of his fork against the table.

Respectably, he had a distaste for Cove's parents without even knowing the truth about them. The truth was, they had worked to secure her a position as one of Princess Mina Sanchez's ladies-in-waiting, not because it would benefit Cove, but because of the money she would have access to if she were to marry a wealthy man. When Marinos and Ahlia had plucked her out of the sea those years ago, their schemes and ideas had begun churning. Marinos and Ahlia had never loved her—they had seen her for all she was worth to them, and that was money.

Now she sat here, in the midst of royalty, bearing shame for the tardiness of her father. The king's familiar servant came forward with more wine, filling each of their glasses and offering Cove a reassuring smile that settled just beneath his blue eyes. She returned it and took a nervous swig.

After a few moments, when yet another bottle had been emptied, and Cove was sure the ailing king was longing for his bed, Marinos waltzed in, unaccompanied by her mother. Cove refrained from rolling her eyes and held her chin high, hoping for an explanation that did not make her look poorly in the sights of the King of the Dawn Islands.

"Your Majesty!" Marinos exclaimed as if they were old friends, hands held high as he approached the head of the table. He plastered on a pleasant smile. Cove cringed at his slurred speech, watching closely as the two men hugged, and she wondered when Marinos had grown comfortable enough in the presence of the king to be his drunken self. Perhaps his dependence on the rum had grown insurmountable—too great to be ignored for just one evening.

"Your palace always amazes me, Your Majesty." Marinos worked to flatter the king, selecting a silver spoon from the table and examining it. "Such beauty, from the gardens to the architecture, to even the silverware." He held the spoon up high, eyebrows arched as if impressed, and set it back down.

"It's lovely to have you dine with us this evening," the king said with a nod of thanks.

Mina sat rigid in her chair next to Cove and gave her hand one more squeeze as Cove rose to greet her father.

"Father," Cove said with a dip of her chin. Marinos surveyed her slowly, taking in the expensive clothing and golden bangles around her arms, and then he took her hand, clasping it between both of his.

"Daughter, how nice it is to see you." Cove was grateful, at least, for his attempts at civility before the king. "Your mother sends her best. You know how she is. Afraid of sailing," he muttered. Cove gave him a tight-lipped smile, pulling her hand away and turning back to her seat.

Yes. Married to a sailor and afraid of sailing, though they lived on a boat for the first fourteen years of their marriage.

Cove found little solace, little room to grieve, in the two long years she spent at sea with them on that small boat. They rarely docked for more than a week at a time, and when Marinos did decide to stay ashore for more than a few fleeting hours to sell nets of silver herring to the local markets, Cove was not allowed out of sight. She stayed close by, usually arm in arm with Ahlia, practicing language and song in preparation for the work Marinos had planned for her. While at sea, Cove threw nets and worked the long days away. She never practiced using her gifts of Light. She would not have even known what her gifts were if weren't for the times she lost hold of her emotions, the loss of control awakening her otherwise subdued power. Marinos and Ahlia allowed no practice out of fear of what she could accomplish, and because of their knowledge of that condemning power in her veins, Cove never rebelled.

She was not surprised Ahlia had not come to dinner. Cove had been a lady to the princess for nearly five years now, and neither the king nor the princess had laid eyes on her *mother* once. They were likely beginning to believe she was completely imaginary. Marinos would not risk bringing his wife here. Not when her distinct Volcanian attributes made it obvious that she was not Cove's true mother. It would raise questions, and though Marinos was clearly lacking in manners, he did not want to paint a horrid picture of himself. *The sailor who found an orphan girl and recognized her not as a daughter, but as an investment—for the money she could make him.* As far as anyone in the palace knew, Cove was conceived and raised at sea by Marinos and his peculiar, *afraid-of-sailing* wife. Not even Mina knew the truth about Cove's childhood and the deaths of her biological Ember parents. Cove refused to recount such atrocities.

"You are growing more beautiful by the day, Cove. You look just like your mother," Marinos said. Cove raised a brow and smiled faintly, clenching her jaw so tightly she thought her teeth may crumble.

"It is good to see you, Father," she lied. "I hope you have been well?"

He nodded, glancing at Cove's already-picked-at plate. "My apologies for the delay, Your Majesty," he said to the king. If Cove hadn't known better, she'd have thought he was completely sober. "I appreciate you giving my daughter the opportunity to serve the princess." He looked at Mina with a grin before he downed half his glass of wine. Cove felt the blood rush to her cheeks.

His hands were dirty, and his tunic was covered in rain, sweat, and seawater after his short sail from Tabrana. He had at least tried to comb his hair to the side, but it was greasy, and he looked as though he had not shaved in weeks.

"How have you been performing? Much singing, I hope?" he asked, blue eyes glassy as he shoveled his first bite of food into his mouth.

Cove refrained from working her jaw. Instead, she closed her eyes for only a moment before sucking in a deep breath and looking directly at her father. "I have other duties in the palace that do not involve singing." He knew these things. He knew that her position as lady to the princess was one secured by friendship and not by anything he had done.

Cove was fourteen when she met Mina. After her first two years at sea, things changed. She started working on the shore. Marinos shifted from selling fish in Tabrana on occasion to selling on the island of Oriana multiple times a week. Almost daily, Marinos would temporarily dock and deliver nets of herring to the local island markets nearest the palace, where the noblemen and women walked the streets in luxury gowns and pearls. Ahlia no longer accompanied them off of the boat, and instead, she bartered with the merchants while Marinos set Cove up to entertain, a small woven basket at her feet to collect coins from the wealthy.

Cove sang her mother's songs on that street for weeks, chest aching with every note, until the day Princess Mina threw a gold ring in her basket with a smile and welcoming conversation. Her brunette hair and the gems at her throat had shone in the island sun. With that gold, Marinos saw opportunity. From that day forward, he encouraged Cove to nurture a friendship with the princess, realizing what good it would do him.

Cove played into his scheme, not to use Mina for her wealth, but because she craved friendship. She needed time away from Marinos, and only when Cove was walking the streets and chatting with Mina, was she allowed out of his reach. Cove and Mina became fast friends. It was an effortless friendship, held together by laughter and hours of long walks through the gardens and down the beach while Marinos secretly trailed behind. Cove particularly loved when Mina would bring her in through the palace gates where Marinos could not follow. Just the little bit of distance gave her the ability to breathe a little deeper.

When it came time for Mina to select two ladies on her

own fourteenth birthday, she invited Marinos and Cove to the palace for selection, and Marinos's luck fell into place. Cove stood amid fifteen other girls, all hoping to be hand picked by the king for the two available positions as the princess's ladies in waiting. Cove assumed the king had only selected her as a lady for his daughter because he had felt pity on her. Marinos bore no title of nobility and Cove should have been the same: nameless and unimportant. But the king had willingly gifted her a title, only because his daughter had insisted.

Marinos paused his eating and balanced his elbow on the table, waving his fork in the air with a piece of meat dangling at the end. "You haven't been singing? Not at all? How do you expect to make a living wage?" The tone of his voice hardened. "You must work for your stay, Cove. His Majesty is doing you a big favor here." Cove cringed at the memories of long years spent practicing an array of different skills, bettering herself so that she could earn coin. All for his benefit.

The king shifted in his seat, but before he could speak, Mina's steady voice rang through the dining hall. "Cove works very hard, Marinos. She attends to my needs all day and is also the greatest friend I have. To me, having a relationship is much more valuable than *money*." Her tone at that last word was brief and curt, like an accusation. "But I make sure that she is well-cared for." The princess smiled graciously, refusing to break his stare.

Marinos smiled at Mina as he closed his teeth around the fork and began chewing a piece of meat. "Well then, I guess that is all that matters." He turned back to Cove. "Though, surely you could continue working for Her Highness while singing on the side."

Cove narrowed her eyes at him. Her love for the art of song

came from her mother and the memories of the lullabies she would use to sing her to sleep. Although she had wished to keep that one last sacred piece of her mother to herself—to preserve what remnants she had left—Marinos had exploited it for profit.

"Cove's kindness is what earned her a place in our palace. She is my friend. That is the sole reason why you are eating here, in our dining hall, with your daughter who bears a title despite the fact that you do not," Mina said with her pointed chin held high.

The king cleared his throat uncomfortably. He was a peacemaker, never taking sides in an attempt to avoid any conflict. Cove thought that trait was quite peculiar for a king—cowardly. It made him unpredictable, and to Cove, untrustworthy.

"Cove will have the opportunity to sing next week. I was going to ask her to perform at the upcoming ball. She will be paid well. If, of course, she accepts. She will not be forced," King Sebastian said. Cove took a deep breath and turned her attention to her father. She disliked singing for an audience, did not enjoy the hundreds of eyes watching her, the attention of men whom she did not know. Balls were miserable enough, fending off proposals and trying not to be noticed in a way that could mean death if her lightmark was discovered.

But because Marinos was present, she looked to the king and said, "I would be happy to entertain your guests, Your Majesty."

"Wonderful!" Marinos said, clapping his hands together. The loud noise startled Cove, and she flinched in her seat.

The king smiled at her, and at her side, Mina's eyes dropped to her plate. "Marinos, you are welcome to join, of course," the king said. Cove stiffened as she stopped the quarrel from pouring from her mouth.

"Gladly. I will be there. Thank you, Your Majesty. And what is this ball in celebration of?"

The king's throat bobbed, and he coughed into his napkin once more, hiding the blood better this time. "Nothing in particular. I just enjoy hosting parties."

Marinos hummed, enjoying the last of the food on his plate.

The king's statement was a half-truth. News had not yet spread across the island, but both Mina and Cove knew what this ball would entail. King Sebastian of the Dawn Islands would soon die from the illness that plagued his body, and with his death, the fiery-spirited Mina was to take the throne. Both girls allowed the king privacy on the subject and did not push or prod, but this ball was likely the day he would announce that he was dying—and that his only heir would begin her reign.

Marinos took his napkin from his lap and wadded it up, placing it on the table. He motioned the servant over, ordering him to clear his side of the table. *A poor fisherman, here to live like entitled royalty. But only for the evening.*

Cove watched the gentle servant who had been serving the king for all her years here. Like Cove, he seemed to be favored by Sebastian. He was not treated as a lowly servant but was visibly appreciated for his service. It was not quite friendship, but there was a whisper of pride in the king's eyes when he looked upon him. The servant quickly cleared Marinos's place and turned to Cove, dipping his head to ask permission to clear her place as well. His loose curls brushed atop his eyebrows, and Cove nodded and watched him carefully as he turned to take the mess out of sight.

Marinos smacked his palms against his knees, drawing everyone's attention except the servant's, who was on his way out of the room.

"Well, daughter, I must get back to your mother. Would you mind walking me out?" It was typical for him to arrive and stir up strife for her, scarf down his meal, and leave. But Cove wanted him gone, so she rose and grabbed her shawl from the back of her chair at once. Though she was already covered up to her neck in a sweeping fabric, she placed it over her shoulders. The extra layer brought her some comfort against the darkness of night. Begrudgingly, she took Marinos's arm.

"Thank you for dinner," he said to Sebastian and Mina. "It was delicious." Mina was twirling a silver utensil in her hands, chestnut eyes watching Cove closely for any sign she needed saving.

Cove mouthed the words, *I'll be okay.* Mina nodded from behind the long table and dropped her eyes to her lap. The warmth from the candles shone against her brunette curls, illuminating the iridescent pearls in the thin golden headpiece Cove had gifted her four years ago on her fifteenth birthday. Cove offered her a tight-lipped smile and turned on her heel to lead her *father* toward the docks, where his sailboat would be waiting.

The two of them walked through the portico and remained silent until they reached the bottom of the steps outside of the palace where Marinos could be sure they did not have company. They were nestled in the privacy of the palace gardens, hidden away from the many light stone buildings of the surrounding village. The thick green vines that covered the island and trailed up every column rustled in a gentle ocean breeze. Cove released Marinos's arm, and he turned toward her, eyes flashing with quiet rage. She stepped back, but he caught her arm in a strong grip and held her there.

Here comes the most dreaded conversation of the night.

"No daughter of mine will remain unmarried past her twentieth year. You marry by the end of summer and earn me a decent bride price, or I will reveal your little secret," he spat, shoving his finger into her collarbone where Light graced her skin beneath her clothes.

"By the end of the summer?" Cove echoed. She was accustomed to his constant deceit and blackmailing, but she thought she had more time.

"By the end of the summer, or you'll be in chains on a ship to the trades in Oro. Or maybe dead, depending on who gets to you first." Cove swallowed. The smell of rum was heavy on his breath, but he was sober enough to get his point across. "Six months should be plenty of time to trick a man into marrying you. At this point," he paused, surveying her up and down, "you must be actively avoiding proposals. Not anymore. Find a wealthy husband and start paying your dues. You're late on this month's pay."

"If you didn't keep raising my *dues*," she said through gritted teeth, yanking her arm from his grasp, "maybe I could afford to pay them on time."

"Or maybe you should work a little harder. Use your voice. It will make the money until you wed. Your job is to marry a wealthy man, one with his own estate, providing me with a steady flow of income. You cannot remain a lady to the princess forever. There is much better money out there." Cove would voluntarily keep this position forever, even if it offered no pay at all, as long as it kept her far from him. A paid position as a lady to the princess was not typical. Marinos did not realize how lucky he truly was.

"I am just to steal from my husband each month to pay you hush money?" Cove's heart pumped wildly.

"Either that, or you'll be with the others of your kind." Spit landed on her cheek. Cove could feel her face heating, and she willed the waves within her to calm.

"How do you expect me to marry and survive when my husband finds out I am lightmarked on our wedding night?"

"Perhaps you can make him care for you as you have your precious princess. You have such a strong will to live." Marinos shrugged. "But in the end, it is not my problem."

"Not your problem until I am killed at the hands of my own husband and your monthly wages stop coming. What will you do then, when you have no means of survival?"

"For your bride price, I am asking more than what you would sell for in the trades. That would be enough for me, if that marriage was sure to bring your death. You have been an investment for me, Cove. Your death would be the reward. I live comfortably on your payments, yes. But I have my own money. I am still a working man, daughter."

"Not a man," she spat, trying her best to look down her nose at him, though he was a head taller than her. "Something smaller. Something *less*."

The bones in the back of his hand cracked against her teeth. She wiped the corner of her mouth and stepped forward once, enticing him to try again. He only held out an open palm and waited silently.

After a few seconds of listening to the ocean waves crash around the island, Cove pulled the silver coins from the folds of her dress, counting them as she placed them into his palm.

"More," he said, wiggling his fingers. Cove clenched her jaw tightly.

"More? This is my whole month's wages. I have nothing left."

"Your jewelry. It is gold, is it not?" he said.

Cove stepped back. "The princess gave me these. I cannot."

"You can. And you will. Or," he flipped a coin over in his hand, tracing the image on the interface, "I will turn you in."

Cove ripped the bangles from her arm and shoved them into his free hand.

"That will be all," he said matter-of-factly as he carefully examined them. "I must be getting back to your *mother* in Tabrana now. You are safe with that little mark of yours for at least one more month," he said in disgust before he turned and left her there. She stared after him for a few long breaths as her hand found its way to her collarbone.

Cove wiped the blood at her mouth, and as she turned on her heels to head back to Mina and the king, she saw the king's servant watching from the colonnades above. Her heart began thrumming in her chest.

How much had he seen? How much had he heard?

Cove kept her head down, slowly ascending the steps to where he awaited her at the top. She swallowed her fear, avoiding eye contact with him as she followed him back to the dining hall. His hair was a darker blond than hers—more golden. He opened the door, and she walked through, briefly examining his face for any sign that he had heard her conversation. There was nothing. His face was completely stoic until they stepped into the light of the candles. It was then she saw a flicker of emotion in his eyes. *Anger.*

His glare followed her across the threshold. It was unfortunate that one of her abilities was to involuntarily absorb the emotion in the room, because she could *feel* the hatred rolling off of him as he stood at her back.

He knows my secret. He knows I bear the Light. He is going to turn me in right here to the king.

Cove kept a read on his emotions and did her best to keep her split lip from the light, but Mina and the king were arguing and had not noticed her return anyway.

"You must marry, Mina. You are to be Queen of the Dawn Islands. You will need a man to rule beside you," the king said. *What?*

"I need no man," Mina argued, crossing her arms.

"And I thought I needed no woman. Your mother, Mina. . .when we married, I did not believe I would need her—but we became partners. You will want someone by your side in your reign."

"Maybe. But I want to marry for love, Father. And I will not find that in the Prince of Edmaria."

Edmaria? A kingdom of darkness. A kingdom who participates in the Ember Trades.

Cove stood silently, the servant's rage continuing to burn hotter at her back each second. It was a tidal wave so strong, Cove could not ignore it. Her cheeks flushed.

"Just meet him once, Mina," the king said, placing a kiss on his daughter's forehead while she sat at the table. "I am not saying you must accept his proposal. But you must consider it."

An alliance between The Dawn Islands and Edmaria?

The king ruffled Mina's dark hair and then nodded to Cove. She ducked her head before he could notice her split lip.

His gaze hovered on her for a moment longer before diverting to the servant behind her. Cove stiffened, but the servant stayed silent, and the king only said, "Goodnight, girls. Get some rest." For a moment Cove saw something like sadness in the king's eyes as he looked past her, but amid the mixture of emotions in the room, it was hard to tell if she had just imagined it.

As the king and his servant exited the dining hall, Mina looked to Cove. They stared at one another for a moment, unsure whose issue to address first. Mina's proposed marriage to the Prince of Edmaria, or the fact that Marinos was still a lousy excuse for a father. Cove offered no encouragement in the moments it took for the servant to trail the king out of the dining hall. She only held her breath, worrying about the most dire of issues at hand. Someone else knew she was an Ember in a world that would have her dead.

When the door shut behind the servant, and a visible shutter echoed through Cove's body, a crease formed at Mina's forehead. The princess rose from the table and walked toward her, taking Cove's chin in her hand and lifting it softly.

"A weak excuse for a man," Mina muttered. "Why do you bother keeping in contact with him? He is worthless. The title my father gave you is not tied to him. You can be free, Cove."

Cove swallowed and blinked back a tear. She would never be free.

Mina continued, her eyes resting on Cove's once-bangled wrists. She huffed, realizing Marinos must have taken them. "I will not pry for information, but you say the word and he will be dealt with." *Dealt with*, as in taken to prison or killed. Besides Marinos, Ahlia, and now the king's servant, Mina was the only one on this island who knew Cove's secret, and Cove knew it was safe with her. But even if Marinos were killed before he was given the chance to tell, Cove's mother would be left alive, and she would avenge her husband by making sure Cove's life was a short one.

"He cannot be dealt with, Mina."

The princess's eyes softened as she realized. "He would turn you in. His *own blood,* for being an Ember? He would sell you?"

Cove glanced nervously around the empty room and nodded slowly. She was not his blood, but if she were, she was sure he would treat her the same. Mina shook her head, face wrinkling in disgust. "We can kill him. We can do it ourselves."

I do not want to be a killer. Cove had witnessed death—*killings.* She had watched her mother's chest rise and fall one final time. She knew the grief that accompanied such things. She wanted no part in any more death, even if it was deserved. Even though Marinos and Ahlia had wronged her in every way, she did not wish to lose another set of parents. "I am not getting you wrapped up in this, and I will not hurt my only family."

"My father and I are your family," Mina said sternly. "Family does not hurt family, and Marinos is hurting you."

Cove smiled sadly, taking Mina's hand. "Even if my father deserves to die, my mother does not." Perhaps that was a lie.

"And?"

"She would choose my father over me every time. She would avenge him, and my secret would be out. Killing him and leaving her to talk would make it all meaningless." Mina did not know Ahlia—did not know the horrible things she had said to Cove on that night in the middle of the sea those years ago.

"Even if it was revealed that you are an Ember, my father and I could protect you. This is our kingdom."

Cove scoffed. "We both know it does not work like that. Embers are hunted all across Arresia, no matter the state of the kingdom. The Dawn Islands are not as safe as they once were." Mina did not want to admit it, but the king had lost his way after the death of his queen six years ago and had allowed the darkness to take root in his kingdom. The Dawn Islands were in a state between complete dedication to the darkness and allegiance to the Light. The Embers were already in hiding, and soon, Cove feared the islands would be lost in total shadow.

"My father can protect you," Mina said.

"You cannot tell him," Cove reminded her. Cove appreciated the king's kindnesses, and sometimes, she even considered him to be the closest thing she had to a worldly father, but she could not trust him with this. She had never seen him stand for evil, but she had never seen him stand against it either. He thought he was keeping the peace, but sooner or later, he would have to choose a side in this war.

To a king that did not know the Light, the darkness would seem more appealing—more likely to win. A king always craves power, whether he is a peacemaker or not. And because true power belongs to the Father of Lights, it was very easy for greedy men of prestige to fall to the darkness in opposition to the Light.

"Mina, remember, this must be kept between us. Your father may think he cares for me, but if he knew the truth. . .Mina, he is surrendering to the cries of his people. They want a

Black Temple to worship in. You have seen him calculating. The foundation is laid. He is trying to make a way. He does not realize the darkness he is entertaining. And now, he is considering an alliance with Edmaria—a kingdom who would sell me into the trade in an instant. This is a dangerous road that will lead our kingdom to ruin." Cove took a deep breath.

Mina wiped the sweat from her brow with the back of her hand and began fanning herself.

Cove paused, giving her a sympathetic frown. "Mina. There are two princes of Edmaria. Which one is your father proposing you marry?"

The princess bit her lip. "Andreas." Cove's heart plummeted into her stomach. A marriage with the eldest prince would result in not only an alliance, but the merging of their kingdoms when Andreas became king at the end of his father's reign. Arresia would no longer be seven kingdoms but six.

"I cannot marry him," Mina said. Panic filled the room around them. Cove took her hand.

"You will not have to. There is still time to convince your father to reconsider. It takes three weeks to sail from Edmaria. We have time," Cove said unconvincingly.

Aside from a few coughing fits, the king was quiet at dinner the next evening. Princess Mina sat across from him at the long table, and Cove sat between them both, awaiting the entree. Cove's throat bobbed against the uncomfortable silence that filled the room. Mina's anger with the king was palpable, and with every passing minute, Cove fought to defend her mind against it. She could not allow the emotions of the room to overcome her and stir up her power.

She shifted in her seat. The air seemed stickier than usual. She crossed and uncrossed her ankles beneath the table, wordlessly begging for the princess to say *anything* at all to her father, but the silence persisted until the princess had cleared her plate and stomped out of the dining hall.

As Mina's irritation exited through the doors with her, Cove inhaled and adjusted the folds of her dress, finding any excuse to avert her eyes from the disappointed king. Thankfully, the servant that had followed her to the gardens was nowhere in sight this evening, his place filled by a woman Cove had seen scrubbing the floors of the hall outside her chambers just last week. A familiar face, but not one who knew her secret. She took a deep breath. *At least something had gone right tonight.*

"Cove," the king said. She blinked, painting a pleasant smile on her face before looking up at him.

"Yes, Your Majesty?" There was a twinkle in his eye as he shook his head at her proper manners. She knew she was not required to address him by title at their nightly dinners, but in this moment, it seemed the right course of action.

"It is quite obvious my daughter is unhappy with my decisions." He sighed. The skin beneath his eyes sagged, and his hair was thinning. He was worn—from the illness, yes, but also from the weight of carrying this kingdom. "I am only doing what is best for her—what will be best for her when I am gone." Cove swallowed and dropped her eyes to the bright red lobster on her plate. "She is not ready to rule this kingdom on her own," he explained. "And the islands are in need of strength more than ever. War is brewing." He massaged his temples.

War is here, Cove thought. *It has already begun—and it will rage until all seven kingdoms are overwhelmed by it.* She kept her back straight against her chair.

"An alliance with Edmaria would bring us the strength we need," the king continued. "Mina would not have to worry about the war with them on our side. And in the grief that will follow my approaching death," he suppressed a cough, "she would have the freedom to mourn. The islands would be cared for and so would my girl."

"But," the king added. "I do not think an alliance can bring comfort to her in the way that your friendship can. Your friendship healed her after the passing of her mother. Promise me you will care for her in my passing too—that you will be here for her."

Cove nodded. Mina's friendship had healed something in her, too. "You and I are all she has. You know I will take care of her, Your Majesty," she promised. But it would not be within the confines of an alliance. Because this alliance with Edmaria, it could not happen.

The king smiled softly and breathed in a shaky breath, as if a weight had been lifted from his shoulders. "I've always been fond of you, dear Cove. You remind me of my sister, Vevila," he said, wiping his mouth and handing his plate to the servant. "I did not always agree with her choices," he muttered, "but she was always good to me."

Cove focused on stilling the nervous tapping of her fingers. She had heard little of Mina's Aunt Vevila—whom Mina had never met—but Cove did know one thing. Like her, Vevila was an Ember.

Embers were those who followed the Father of Lights and were filled with his Light, which was made manifest through unique gifts and abilities meant to benefit his Kingdom. Cove was aware of no others like herself in all the world, though she knew they existed.

A piece of Cove wanted the king to tell her all about Vevila and her life as an Ember, but Cove knew how the story ended, and she longed for a peaceful night—one where she could rest instead of being tormented by the anxieties that would come with hearing the king speak of his distaste for people like her. She felt like a liar in his presence, a thief of his respects. He would not hand his respects over so readily if he knew—would not so confidently leave his daughter in broken pieces for Cove to mend back together.

"You would have loved her," the king said with a shrug. "Her voice was exquisite. Perhaps the two of you would find yourselves singing duets here on the islands. That is, if she had never married Arne Ozanne and gone to rule at his side in Ozanna."

"I am sure she was lovely," Cove said.

"I never supported that alliance," he muttered.

Cove did not support *this alliance*.

"It only set us back," the king said. Cove said nothing, only fixed her eyes on the silverware in her hand. Who was she to talk politics and alliances with a king? She did not belong here, where she could not speak her mind.

The alliance the Dawn Islands had entered into with Ozanna had been strong for years, but after Queen Vevila's death, King Sebastian had chosen not to continue the alliance through the reign of his Ember nephew, Gerrin. Cove suspected King Sebastian sided with the darkness out of fear. When Degare and the Delle Witches suddenly attacked Ozanna nearly twenty-two years ago, Ozanna fell quickly.

None of Ozanna's other allies had made it in time to prevent the fall of the kingdom. Now, Oro ruled in its place, and Cove thought maybe it was the heart of every darkness in Arresia.

"Edmaria is strong. Ozanna never would have stood a chance against it," the king said.

What about Oro? Cove wanted to ask. *Could Edmaria stand against its shadows, if Oro decided to rise up against it?*

"This is the best deal for my girl," the king reiterated with sorrowful eyes. "And for you, Cove. You'll take care of her, and you'll be taken care of." He would never promise such things if he knew of the Light she bore. "I trust you'll stay by her side. Even when you marry, you must remain at her side. Where she goes, you go."

The princess was Cove's best friend, and she would follow her anywhere. The two of them would stay side by side, but both of them knew that this was an alliance that could not come to fruition. For the sake of all the Embers in Oriana and Tabrana, and for the sake of Arresia and its seven kingdoms. The islands could not become territory of Edmaria.

CHAPTER 2
CHANGE ON THE HORIZON
COVE

Shadows will plague every kingdom, but my Embers shall never know a time of utter darkness, for my Light is within them. Furthermore, there shall always stand at least one kingdom in Arresia that serves me, and seven kingdoms there shall always remain. Some will fall dormant, some will breed darkness, and some will be ruled by it, but never shall seven become only six. New may replace the old for a time, but the old will rise again—bringing the Dawn; ushering in eternal Light to all of Arresia.

Cove lay awake most of the night, trying to remember the prophecy from the Light Scrolls that she suspected the kings of darkness were working to stop. She had never been able to study the Light Scrolls as an Ember. She had not laid her hands on them since that last day in the cottage by the sea with her parents. Coincidentally, the last prophecy her mother had read aloud to her was the one her mind circled tonight.

Never shall seven become only six. That passage had to be the one the serpent's eye was on. Perhaps Edmaria believed that if they were able to declare a prophecy false, it would elevate their power above the Light.

New may replace old for a time, but the old will rise again. . .

Cove's mind settled on the abandoned kingdom of Ozanna, and of Oro—which had taken its place. She could see no end in sight for King Degare of Oro's reign, as his power was only growing, but she had hope that the old would rise again, carrying the Dawn on its back. The world around her may be blind to the darkness, but Cove had been given the Light to see. Sometimes she felt so isolated on this island, where she seemed to be the only one with such Light.

She groaned from where she lay in her massive bed and pulled the linen covers over her head. Soft rays of orange sunlight were beginning to stream in between the towering columns that lined her chambers. Miraculously, even after she had nearly drowned as a young girl, the blue waters that surrounded the island had become a comfort to her—a reminder of the new life she had been given. The sparkling sea was radiant, and perhaps if she did not have a glowing mark on her skin to showcase her allegiance to the Light, she would venture down to the waves and take a swim. But with the many sailors going in and out from the docks, and the armada's recently increased training regimen, Cove would stay near the palace, covered up, and drawing no attention to the mark that could get her sold into Oro's trades and killed.

So far, Princess Mina had been successful in wrapping the king around her finger—at least in ensuring he did not participate in the Ember Trades. But that did not mean the islands were safe for those gifted by the Light, especially not with the king proposing an alliance with Edmaria. With or without an alliance, the darkness already dwelt here and had many followers. Only when Mina became queen, and she and Cove could slowly coax the Embers from hiding, would the fire ignite bright enough that the people who worshipped darkness would tremble and forget they ever had the upper hand. First, the two of them had to figure out how to sway the king from the alliance with Edmaria.

Cove sat up, peering through the veils that surrounded her on all sides, and looked to the golden framed mirror that hung on the wall adjacent to her bed. Slowly, her fingers found their way to the mark just below her collar bone. It glowed softly, a luminous blue forming the outline of a wave.

The people in the palace thought Cove to be quite modest and assumed her unique style of clothing was something she had brought with her from the neighboring island of Tabrana. But the truth was, that Cove wore dated, high-neck gowns, often with flowing sleeves, to hide this very mark. She dreamt she would one day be able to proudly bear the mark without fear of death, but for now, she would hide—until the Father called her out of the shadows and into the Light.

Cove rose and sauntered to the vanity, pulling a robe over her shoulders. She had recently taken an interest in studying ancient languages, and a stack of a dozen books currently cluttered the space. She shoved them aside before sitting in front of the mirror. She began unraveling her braids from the night before, leaving her light blonde hair in waves that flowed to her lower back. As she combed through a few tangles, she hummed a melody. Her mother had learned it shortly after she had become an Ember, and although Cove had not yet shared in that Light, her mother had taught it to her anyway.

There was a skitter on the balcony, and Cove turned to

watch a dove as it landed on the limestone rail with a message tied to its leg. She allowed the ocean breeze to caress her skin between a few shaky inhales before rising to meet the bird in the pink and orange hues of the early morning. She took the message in her hands, and as she said a silent prayer over the ripped parchment, the dove swooped low to where the palace met the sea. Hesitantly, Cove unfolded the paper.

Your time is running out, Daughter. Perhaps your saving grace is on the ship that sails toward your beloved princess.

The threat seemed to travel across the waters, and Cove gripped the rail between trembling fingers, unintentionally tunneling her power into the waves below. They crashed ragefully into the palace walls, sending a mist swirling into the humid morning air. She watched as the dove flew west, toward her father's home in Tabrana, and then her gaze fixed on the ship that dawned on the horizon, flying the flag of Edmaria.

No. It is too soon.

Cove became dizzy. It had not even been a week since Sebastian had told Mina of the proposal. They were supposed to have two more weeks before the prince arrived. The scene seemed to unfold like a nightmare before her, and her breathing became unsteady as she spiraled into a dooming panic. She willed the anxiety away—envisioned herself redirecting its waves that had her surrounded. She focused on the promise that was spoken with every beat of her heart and took comfort in it. She was here for a *purpose*. She was here, filled with the hope of the Light that so many did not yet have. That fact was generally the origin of her anxieties—when she could feel the darkness of the emotions of those around her and could do nothing to tame them. It was a curse to feel so deeply in a world of such unbearable pain.

Cove inhaled and counted the slowing beats in her chest. She remembered the innumerable breaths she had been gifted for the Light's purpose. She remembered the life she had surrendered and the newness of life that she had been given. Cove dared look back to the orange horizon, toward the incoming darkness that would require much trust in the Light. She pulled her robe shut as more ships came into view, heading straight for the docks.

Why had they sent an entire fleet?

The door to her chambers swung open, and a frantic, familiar voice sounded through the room. "Cove? Cove!" Cove pushed the white chiffon fabrics to the side, leaving them to ripple in the wind behind her as she rushed into her chambers from the balcony. Mina's eyes were frightened, like those of a mouse fleeing a serpent, and as Cove gripped her hands, her robe fell open slightly. Mina's brown eyes traveled to that glowing mark; the one that would condemn Cove in this kingdom. Then, Mina looked to the ships on the horizon and shook her head.

"I know. I know, Mina," Cove said, trying not to let the princess's tangible fear send her into a spiral.

"I will not marry him. I cannot. Not if it puts you in danger." Mina's eyes were fixed on Cove's lightmark as she paced around the room, mind reeling. Her own long robe dragged behind her. The silk was the color of the wisteria that bloomed across the island and was lined with expensive lace.

"Relax. We have kept my identity a secret thus far. Even your father is not onto me. I can protect myself, Mina. And I know my secret is safe with you." Cove tugged her robe back over her lightmark.

Mina forced a smile. "Always." A crease formed between Mina's dark brows. "But how will you keep it a secret from your husband? You will not be able to. The Edmarian prince and his lords are here to claim brides and ally our kingdoms. When your husband of darkness comes to realize that you follow the Light. . .you will be killed. The Dawn Islands will fall to the shadows."

"The Islands have already fallen, Mina. I cannot freely walk the streets. They have the foundation laid for a *Black Temple*. Your people worship the darkness and the ancient witch goddesses in hopes for strength and power against the Light. I have never been safe here, not truly." Cove said nothing regarding her future with a husband. She had already voiced her concerns to Marinos, but she would be left to deal with them herself. Perhaps she could convince a man to love her enough that he could overlook it, since she doubted she would ever find another Ember in this kingdom.

Embers were lightmarked, which usually made it hard to hide from those who would have them dead. The new trades in Oro were an Ember's biggest threat, where hundreds of Embers were sold every quarter and killed for their gifts. At the trades, Shades, or those who worshiped the darkness, paid the King of Oro to murder Embers using his spelled weapon. Upon the death of the Ember, their power was then transferred to the killer, turning the power to shadow and making the Shade a Despiri.

A knock sounded at the door, and again, Cove pulled her robe taut over her satin gown. "Come in," she said.

A servant entered quickly, eyes immediately finding the

princess who stood by Cove. "Your Highness! I hoped I would find you here. His Majesty has been asking for you, and we have been searching all over." Cove's gaze slid down to the white fabric that was draped over the servant's arms while Mina stared in silence.

"I shall prepare her to meet Prince Andreas of Edmaria," Cove replied, swiping the dress from the servant. "We'll be in the princess's chambers. Send for Lady Celeste—she and I are to meet with the two lords in the prince's company. Tell His Majesty we shall meet him in one hour in his throne room."

The servant nodded and Cove ushered her out, quickly turning back to Mina. "I won't let you be forced into marriage," Cove insisted. "We'll find a way."

Mina was growing more anxious by the second. "Maybe I'll like him," she muttered. "Perhaps I could inspire him to protect Embers and his father would follow suit. Perhaps we could strike a deal, and the islands could remain separate, even after he is crowned King of Edmaria. I could spend time in both kingdoms and could make them safe for you." Cove tried to remain hopeful for Mina's sake. She nodded.

"I doubt it, though," Mina continued after watching Cove for a moment. "Edmaria's goal is more power. And besides, I hear Andreas is like his father, who abused his mother." The Queen of Edmaria had mysteriously disappeared years ago. Mina never believed that she had run away as they had claimed. Cove was skeptical, too, though accusing a king of murdering his wife would land her at the chopping block as quickly as the mark at her collarbone would. Mina's face crumpled in disgust. "I suppose I am lucky then, that I am not to marry King Idris." Surely Mina's father would allow no such thing.

"If Andreas is like his father, I'll help you out of the

arrangement. I promise," Cove assured her, and she meant it. She would do anything to ensure that the prophecy of the seven kingdoms came to pass. She would not let the hope she had found in the Light be taken.

Cove looked through the colorful pastels of her wardrobe and settled on a blush chiffon dress that she knew would clash horribly with her skin tone. She looped her arm through Mina's, and their bare feet smacked against the stone as they scurried through the palace to Mina's chambers.

"Sit down over there, I'll do your hair once I get into my gown," Cove instructed Mina as she slipped behind the dressing screen. A breeze whispered through the room, bringing with it the smell of salt and citrus.

"You sent for me?" Celeste asked as she stepped through the door. "I was enjoying my morning of solitude, but your scrawny little servant interrupted my bath." Cove peeked at Mina from behind the screen. She was rolling her eyes into the mirror of her vanity as she painted her lips. Celeste's mother had some sort of deal with Mina's father, and because of it, he had ensured she had a spot as one of Mina's ladies—despite Mina's unending complaints about her miserable company. Celeste was the voice of reason that Sebastian thought Mina needed, but Cove saw Celeste's uncanny ability to manipulate as a problem.

Cove adjusted the neck and sleeves of her gown then stepped out from behind the screen, motioning for Celeste to tie the back. "The prince is docking as we speak," she explained.

"The Prince of Edmaria? Maybe the Dawn Islands will finally become relevant among the seven kingdoms. That is, if you go through with the marriage," Celeste retorted.

"I have a right to be picky about my future husband," Mina said tightly.

"I don't know why you wouldn't want to marry him. His kingdom is far more powerful than ours—the fact that they are even considering an alliance with us is. . .well, it is surprising. And you are to be queen soon. Your father will not live much longer, and you'll need a consort—"

"Enough, Celeste," Cove demanded. Mina's cheeks reddened, and she adjusted her position on the stool.

"Your gown is in my wardrobe," Mina said. "The sage green one on the left. I picked the fabric especially for you. To match your eyes." Cove gave Mina a speculative glare, and as Celeste wandered over to the wardrobe, the princess snickered and whispered low, "I must be sure she looks her best. The sooner we marry her off and she goes on her merry way, the better."

Cove gave her a wry smile.

The infinite sunlight of the Dawn Islands was beginning to shine between the tall, open pillar windows of the palace, and the sea glistened blue beyond the sheer fabric that served as a veil between the balcony and the bedroom. Celeste grabbed Mina's white gown from the bed and carried her own in her other hand. Cove moved swiftly across the room; her sun-kissed skin seemed to shimmer like droplets of water beneath the golden light.

"How shall we do your hair?" she asked Mina, humming quietly as she snatched the flowing gown from Celeste. The king had requested his daughter wear white, symbolic of her readiness for marriage. Mina cringed as Cove held the gown before her. Cove much preferred the blush of her own dress against Mina's bronze skin, the tones of which matched the pink dawn skies of her beloved home. For herself, Cove would always choose the blue of the Crystal Sea—if she was dressing to impress. But today, she would avoid the attention of the lords of Edmaria at all costs—because as an Ember, she could never accept a marriage proposal from a man whose kingdom would sell her for a handful of gold serpents. She could not keep lying, and another rejected proposal would anger her father. Her Light was becoming more and more difficult to keep concealed.

The princess's gown moved with the drapes in the soft winds that flowed through the palace. It was a beautiful dress, made with only the most luxurious fabric. "I do not wish to go," she stated once more, waving her hand at the ivory dress.

Cove frowned. "Just be your outspoken self, and I can assure you, Andreas of Edmaria will run the other way."

Mina tried to hide her smile. Celeste sat in the crook of the windowsill, examining a book Cove had left there a few days before. "You'll need to wear your hair up. I hear the prince appreciates a slender neck."

"Down it is, then," Mina said as Cove helped her step into the gown and placed a kiss on her cheek before selecting a few strands of hair to place into a small braid.

Celeste crossed her arms. "If you won't listen to my advice, fine. But at least take into consideration the good this marriage would do for our kingdom." Edmaria was a rich, desert country with a strong royal family and many connections on the continent of Ozanne—the largest continent in all Arresia. But Edmaria was a kingdom of darkness, and though the islands had already fallen, Cove could not allow them to fall any further. She would not allow them to be absorbed by Edmaria—to lose their status as a kingdom. Seven kingdoms had to remain, but if prophecy had spoken it, well. . .then Cove guessed she should not be worrying.

As Celeste stalked out of the room, Mina and Cove exchanged a quick knowing glance before bursting into laughter. "Could she be anymore insufferable?" Cove asked.

"Not in the slightest," Mina said, pinching her cheeks in the mirror, encouraging blood flow just beneath the skin. "She is just bitter because she is considered an old maid." Cove and Mina were both nineteen, and Celeste was almost twenty-four. "Mid-twenties and still unmarried? Of course, I suppose that could be me too, if I had a choice in who I marry."

Cove dropped her gaze and finished tying Mina's braid with a pearl tassel. Most of Mina's thick brunette hair remained down. The braid swept across her head and was woven around the thin golden hairpiece of pearls that Cove had gifted her. It was the only thing Cove had left of her past—and it was the only thing of value her adoptive father had not taken. It had only remained in her possession because they had not known it was tucked away in her dress the night they had pulled her from the sea. In the princess's possession, Marinos could never steal it. And it was all Cove had to give to the woman who she would one day call Queen. To the woman who she hoped could bring the Dawn Islands back out of the darkness.

"Your father did say this betrothal to Andreas would be your choice." Cove's encouragement was forced. "Perhaps you should not worry so much," she added.

Mina glared at her, chestnut eyes like daggers. "Whether it

is Prince Andreas or someone else, I will be forced to choose my husband based on status sooner or later. As my lady, in a sense, you will be forced to do the same."

"Yes, well at least you need not worry about your husband selling you into the trades on your wedding night," Cove muttered, and the princess fell silent.

Her face softened as she peered at Cove, perhaps seeing the bit of anxiety that had begun festering there. Mina Sanchez, the Princess of Oriana and Tabrana, rose to put her hands on Cove's shoulders. "I love you, sister." She tucked a lock of Cove's hair behind her ear. "I swear to you, when I am queen, I will make the Dawn Islands safe for your people again."

THREE FOR THREE

COVE

"So, we are in agreement then? Dissuade them from asking for our hands in marriage. If they propose, we shall deal with it then," Mina reaffirmed.

Cove nodded, breathing deeply as they walked in step to the throne room. Celeste joined them, her gown the perfect shade of green against her pale complexion and black hair.

"Well, one of the three of us will be getting a proposal for sure," Cove said under raised brows, admiring Celeste's beauty and nudging Mina's arm. Mina grinned.

"I get first choice on which lord, Cove," Celeste said.

"Take them both if you wish," Cove muttered.

As the three of them stopped outside of the doors to the throne room, Cove squeezed Mina's hand in a gesture of comfort. *Together.* Cove paused as the male servant with curly blonde hair opened the doors. For a small moment, his mysterious gaze locked with hers. Her secret seemed to haunt him, and she swallowed nervously before his attention followed after the princess, who was now a few steps in front of her.

Cove hurried along, and the three of them strode into the throne room together. Mina's chin was high, and the train of her gown dragged the floor between Cove and Celeste, who closely followed her. Cove felt the servant walking at her back and could not help but watch as he circled around to the dais beside the king, awaiting orders.

He acted as though it pained him to be in her presence, as though it strained him to keep his eyes from her, as if his mind was flooded with curiosity about the spat she had with her father. *What had he heard? And more importantly, what would he do about it?*

The ill king, clad in ivory and gold, slowly rose to his feet to greet his daughter with a smile and a kiss. He slightly turned to the side to introduce her to Prince Andreas of Edmaria, who stood with his arms crossed and gaze locked not on the princess, but on *Cove.* Shadowmarks crept from the back of his hand and up his arm, telling Cove all she needed to know about him. He had killed an Ember and was now a Despiri.

Cove averted her eyes, quickly focusing on the servant just beyond the prince's cold stare, but she could feel Andreas continuing to study her, intrigued. She reluctantly allowed the emotions within the room to be welcomed into her clouded mind, hoping to read into the prince's intention. Desire was the most prominent of all his emotions, but there was a whisper of curiosity that kept her from relaxing completely. *He does not know of your Light. How could he?* Cove shifted silently on her feet.

At this moment, she saw her unique ability to read emotion as a helpful tool, but generally, it was overpowering, inducing anxiety and uncontrolled fear. She did not look at the prince again but kept her head down, focusing on the shifting emotions of the room. *You're safe, for now.* Cove had chosen the blush gown that did nothing for her skin or hair for a reason, but in this room with two other desirable women, perhaps her true curse was that she was the one men longed for.

"Prince Andreas, my daughter, Mina Sanchez. Princess of Oriana and Tabrana. Soon to be *Queen*." Cove looked up at once to watch as the attention was brought to her princess, only to find that the two lords that stood close by were curious about her too. She ducked her head again until the heat had left her cheeks.

The prince surveyed Mina as she curtsied. "Your Highness, it is a pleasure to make your acquaintance," she said. Prince Andreas's eyebrows lowered as he watched her and turned to the king. His dark hair fell just below his ears, and the sides swooped into voluminous, windblown waves.

"You have no son? No heir besides this daughter? If I am to marry her, I must be assured of my position as king. And your illness shall take you quickly, as you claimed when you sent for this arrangement?"

The king stiffened, as did Cove and Mina. *Why had the king shared the details of his illness with Edmaria? Did that not put the islands at risk?* "Do you come to my kingdom and question my integrity?" King Sebastian asked.

The prince looked to his lords, seemingly having a silent conversation.

"No, Your Majesty. I just want to be sure we are on the same page in terms of this agreement. When entering something as precious as marriage, honesty is of utmost importance." Cove could have sworn the prince was looking directly at her as he spoke. "If we wanted to, Edmaria could take the islands upon your death, and I would have no need to marry your daughter. You are lucky we do not want to risk any losses of our armies right now—no matter how minimal they would be."

King Sebastian's fists clenched on the arms of his throne, and Cove's hands grew clammy. "Be careful how you speak to me in my own kingdom. Here, you are under my jurisdiction. King trumps prince." The king's face hardened in a way Cove was not familiar with, but Andreas grinned knowingly.

"There's the king my father said was buried deep inside. Quiet until you feel threatened. What exactly is it you are expecting out of this alliance, Sebastian?"

Mina's throat bobbed, and the king spoke again through tightly clenched teeth. "My daughter shall need a strong consort beside her, one who will not allow our kingdom to fall to the Light. I assume I can trust you with that."

Cove was not surprised at the comment. If the Light was not within you, you are of the darkness, and Cove knew no one else with a lightmark. Not even the princess. She bit her cheek, and held on to the hope that Mina's reign would be better than her father's had been for the Embers.

Andreas offered the king a sly smile and let out a chuckle. "Of course not, Sebastian. Your kingdom will remain in darkness," Andreas said with a shrug. Cove tried to glance at Mina, but her friend's face was unreadable. "And I will not solely be consort to the Queen of The Dawn Islands, but rather we shall rule as King and Queen together—over one kingdom." Cove held her breath as he continued. "Your islands will become a territory of Edmaria. Your people will be well protected, and your men will be trained by the Edmarian military. We will ensure your people's survival. We will ensure that the Embers' *god* has no chance of fulfilling whatever prophecies bring them hope."

"Very good then," the king said. Cove glanced at Mina, watching the look of betrayal that flooded her face as she witnessed her father's true colors. *He would surrender the islands' status as a kingdom so easily?* King Sebastian turned to the two Edmarian lords. "Lord Yarris of Tarbank and Lord Arlo of Ambridge," he paused, gesturing toward Cove and Celeste. "Lady Celeste and Lady Cove. My daughter's ladies." Both men's stares lingered on Cove, and the king smiled at her. Though he did not truly know her, he was the closest thing she had to a father here in Oriana—or anywhere. She knew he truly wished a good life for her, so long as he did not discover the Light dwelling beneath her skin.

His smile seemed to say, *You'll be married in no time. Your father will be pleased.*

Cove ducked her head but was careful to say nothing in response to the king's introduction. She stayed silent and allowed both men to kiss her hand while Celeste seethed at her side. Andreas and Mina were engaging in conversation, and Mina's hands were twisting nervously in the folds of her gown. This alliance was exactly what they had feared.

Cove watched as Lord Yarris finally turned to Celeste and was met with indifference.

Lord Arlo looked down at Cove. "Perhaps we could take a walk, and you could show me around the palace grounds?" Cove nodded, and his grin widened, revealing a set of yellow teeth. She gave him a tight-lipped smile in response.

The prince turned to Lord Arlo. "A walk sounds joyous. Perhaps we could all go. I would love to visit the grounds where the Black Temple is to be built." Mina looked to Cove, whose heart was pounding, and for a split second, her own fear was reflected in her friend's eyes. Cove collected herself through a series of deep breaths.

"I'd be happy to show you around. My father can join us," Mina suggested, collecting herself and looking to the king for salvation, but he winced at the invitation. The king's illness had taken a toll on his joints and his ability to partake in his usual strolls. The hundreds of winding steps through the kingdom had become impossible for him to travel, and he rarely left the walls of the palace.

"My dear, I am just not feeling up to it today. You'll be a fine host. Show our guests around and I'll see you for dinner."

Dinner? Cove thought. *We are to spend the entire day entertaining these men?*

"Yes, Father," Mina said. "Get some rest."

"Before we go, fetch us some water would you?" Andreas said to the servant behind the king. "The humidity in this kingdom is unbearable." The servant did not move a muscle, only kept his eyes where they most always were: on the king, awaiting instruction at any moment.

"Hey! You!" Andreas called to the servant, snapping his fingers loudly. Still, the servant did not move. Cove watched carefully, the way the king slowly rose to his feet as Andreas, fuming, took a step toward him. Sebastian planted himself between them, though pain clearly ricocheted through his body upon standing.

"He is deaf, Prince." Cove looked at the servant at once.

"Deaf? What good is a deaf servant?" Andreas asked. The king's hands were shaking, and he braced himself on the arm of his throne.

Deaf? Cove thought. She took a deep breath. *There was no way he had heard her conversation in the gardens then. She was safe. But how had she never realized he was deaf?* She realized she had not paid much attention to him at all until she was concerned that he knew her secret. She could not even remember his name.

"He takes orders from me just fine. He is a master at reading lips. We have even trained him to speak—with the help of a Despiri from Oro."

How could a Despiri have helped him learn to speak and read lips? Perhaps they had the ability to speak into one's mind, Cove thought.

Cove's heart sank to her stomach as she watched the servant carefully and realized he was very capable of knowing her secret based on her interaction with Marinos alone. She could have sworn his deep blue eyes darted to her for a split second.

The room began spinning, and pressure built in Cove's ears as it always did when she dove beneath the surface of the sea, searching for that little bit of solace in a world full of noise. Finding no comfort, she took a clumsy step back and Arlo's hand found her arm, keeping her upright. The servant's narrowed gaze found hers for another moment, and Cove saw his mind turning as he recognized the panic that was beginning to creep onto her face.

He knows my secret. She pulled her arm free of Arlo's and tried to calm her breaths as the conversation continued around her.

"Why waste the time?" Andreas spewed in disgust, surveying the servant.

The king turned slowly to the side, where Cove's secret-bearer stood. "Elias, our guests would like some water."

Elias.

Cove felt Mina's worried eyes on her as she recognized the panic that was setting in. Cove needed to sit down. To Cove's surprise, Elias spoke clearly in response to the king, his voice even and steady. "Yes, Your Majesty." He nodded and exited the room, coming back a few moments later with seven glasses of water. He served the king first and then handed Andreas a glass. Though they were the same height, Andreas looked down his nose at him and slowly took the water. Cove could feel the hatred radiating from the prince. *Or was that coming from Elias and his hatred for her, an Ember?* Andreas adjusted his suit jacket, and Cove saw it coming before the prince even moved an inch.

Andreas tipped his glass toward Elias, the water sloshing toward the servant in an attempt to ruin his clothing. But the water moved in a way Cove recognized as unnatural. It seemed to turn in the air, too quickly for the common man to notice, splashing onto the front of Andreas's trousers instead.

Did I do that? Cove thought. She had not felt herself lose control. But then she noticed the faintest flicker of a mischievous grin on Elias's face, and his eyes flashed to hers for a moment, seeming to plead with her. Andreas cursed and threw his glass, sending it shattering across the floor. Mina flinched beside her, but in all the commotion, Cove did not tend to her princess—she could only watch Elias.

Had he just manipulated water? She was nearly positive she had not done it, though this morning on the balcony, the sea *had* begun rising involuntarily at her distress. Perhaps she was going mad—losing control without even feeling the power leave her.

"Your Highness, I will go fetch another glass," Elias said apologetically. "And perhaps a towel."

Andreas was fuming, but Cove watched after Elias as he exited the room.

"When I am king, I will not bother with such incompetent servants," the prince spat, surveying his trousers. Cove could not read Sebastian's face, but amid the mess of emotions in the room, she'd bet his was the indignation growing hot and heavy on her neck. After Elias delivered the towel and had provided the guests with water, he turned to Mina and then Celeste, serving Cove last. His eyes were the deep blue of an incoming storm, of the clouds that rolled over the depths of the ocean, bringing rain and thunder and sorrow.

"Lady Cove," he uttered as he offered her a glass, eyes piercing hers. She took it, watching the small droplet of water that danced in the air above the rim of her glass. As it caught the morning light, Elias's brow ticked, and as he turned from her, the droplet joined the rest of the water in the glass. She raised her chin, taking a deep breath.

He keeps a secret of his own. . .I am not alone in this kingdom.

"Shall we be going, then?" Mina asked. Cove blinked and turned to Arlo, who was waiting impatiently for her to take his arm. She stole one last glance at Elias, who paid her no further mind. Mina watched Cove carefully, likely noting the vanishing queues of that once impending attack of anxiety.

Cove breathed tightly and followed Arlo's lead, walking behind Mina and the prince. Cove focused on the short train of her friend's white gown as they exited the throne room and navigated the outer hall lined with pillars. The palace sat far above sea level, and cascading from the front gates of the palace grounds were hundreds of winding steps that wove through gardens of citrus fruits and vines that bloomed purple all year round. The aroma of wisteria and salt merged with the citrus in the air. The sun was growing hot, and Prince Andreas shielded his eyes against the bright limestone of the palace steps, looking to the distant ocean waves at their right.

"Is your kingdom not the hottest in Arresia, Your Highness?" Mina asked, heeding his obvious disdain for her islands.

He scoffed. "My kingdom is made up of desert sands and hot, dry air. Moisture does not soak my clothes the minute I step into the day," he quipped, plucking the center of his sweaty tunic from his chest as they walked below an arbor and into a lavish garden. Andreas paused to survey his surroundings, and the rest of the group followed suit. Mina adjusted the folds of her dress while Cove picked an orange fruit to twist in her nervous hands.

Yarris and Celeste came down the steps close behind, and he quickly chimed in. "Edmaria is not as you hear of it in storybooks. There *is* desert, but it is not only sand and dry air. We have an ocean and sometimes a nice breeze that touches the south. The nights can grow chilly, and we have forests and winter in the southwest of the kingdom. I think there is something for everyone in Edmaria." He smiled at Celeste as he spoke, and she offered one back.

"Are you trying to convince them to return with us? As if they would have a choice in the matter?" Andreas asked. He spoke with crudeness—as though the princess were not standing right there. "The king is obviously desperate. He is *dying*. We shall take our brides as we wish." Cove's cheeks heated as she shot Mina a look.

I promise. She tried to convey the words with her eyes. Cove would not allow this marriage to happen. King Sebastian had said it himself. It was Mina's choice. She could refuse. She only had to give him a chance.

"I am sure I would love Edmaria," Celeste said in response as she smoothed the waistline of her fitted gown. Cove ground her teeth as she tried to focus on the orange citrus in her hands. Celeste continued. "I find the Black Sea quite interesting." Arlo grinned, and Cove felt his gaze shift to her, but she continued turning the fruit over with her fingers.

"Ah, yes. We not only border the Crystal Sea, but the Black Sea as well. We are close enough to travel to the Ember trades in Oro. That is, if you are brave enough to cross the unpredictable waters." Cove's heart sank to her stomach as she attempted to steal another glance at the princess.

"Or the Valley of the Shadow, correct?" Celeste asked, intrigued. She twirled a handful of her black hair around her slender finger.

Yarris nodded. "I've been through it twice. I won't make the Spring or Summer Trades, but I am going my third time in the autumn. The King of Oro is hosting another ball before those trades—to celebrate the Ember Trade anniversary. I hear the King and Queen of Ozanna may be involved in whatever he has planned."

Arlo perked up at the names. "I think he'll rob them of their power in front of an audience. To show just how powerful he is with that staff."

"Is the staff why you allied with him?" Mina asked

innocently. "Because it is better to have him on your side than against you?"

Andreas grunted. "He is not as powerful as he thinks, Princess. And we have no formal alliance as far as I am concerned, only similar interests." Mina bit her lip, lifting her skirt to take a few more steps in the direction of the temple grounds. Andreas began to follow, but instead he turned on his heels, locking eyes with Cove.

"You do not speak much, Lady Cove," Andreas said. She stiffened. "What do *you* think of Oro? Of the Ember Trades?" Cove squeezed her thumbnail into the fruit.

"You value a lady's opinions now? Just not when it pertains to marriage?" she asked. He raised a brow at her remark, and she continued, "I think I shall visit someday and see them for myself." It was the best she could do, and thankfully, Andreas seemed pleased with her answer.

"Yes, well, I plan to attend in the summer, if I make it back in time." He flashed his hand at her, showing off the shadows that had staked their claim on him. "I killed my first Ember during the first trade last autumn. Eagerly, might I add. Some hesitate when it is time for the kill. What a joke," he said, chuckling in a way that made Cove want to run the other direction. "I accept power as it comes to me, and I do not let emotions get in the way. I have no reservations when it comes to ending the power of those who threaten my own." Cove held her tongue as her lightmark became itchy beneath her gown.

She shifted her shoulders as the six of them continued through the gardens, descending to the grounds where the temple was being constructed by two dozen men. Massive work horses pulled carts of black stone the king had purchased from

Edmaria. Cove had never ridden a horse before and just seeing the beasts in action intimidated her.

"Glad to see our gift to you is being put to use," Prince Andreas said to Mina, nodding at the mounds of rock that would soon make up the temple floors and walls.

The princess forced a smile, and Cove watched her closely before speaking to the prince. "You *gifted* the islands the materials to build this temple? It was not purchased?"

"Yes, we gifted it, Lady Cove." The prince held out his hands in pride.

"To what advantage?" she queried, trying not to sound too argumentative on the subject.

He shrugged. "What good is your kingdom to us without one? How else are you to worship, so the witch goddesses will reward you with power? Why else do you think your islands are so weak? If I didn't know better, I might assume your kingdom to be undecided in the war. There is no temple for worship, but there is also nothing stopping me from taking the Embers that hide here. There is no protection for the gifted ones. I thought it was time the darkness established itself here, for good."

He should not care about such things yet. Not before a treaty has been made.

Cove felt Mina's heart sink beside her. "And why does any of what we do here matter to you?" Mina questioned.

The Prince of Edmaria smiled. "I thought we would share this news over dinner, but since you are asking, the deal has been made."

"Deal?" Mina asked, stepping forward. Cove moved with her, and the crashing of sea waves seemed to echo in her ears as she reached for Mina's hand, working to separate her from the prince.

Andreas closed the distance between him and Mina and shot her a sly smile. "You and I are to marry," he sneered.

Mina's breath hitched, and Cove tugged on her arm. "The king—" Cove started.

"Agreed to my terms before I ever left Edmaria." Andreas turned his attention back to Mina and tilted his chin. He was enjoying this.

She was supposed to have a choice.

Mina was silent, and her face was growing more pale by the second. "If you'll excuse me, Your Highness," Mina said as she ducked her head and grabbed Cove's arm before retreating down the steps, failing to finish her sentence.

Cove turned to Celeste, gathered her wits for a few grueling seconds, and then looked back to Andreas. "Please continue the tour with Celeste. She'll be a wonderful host. We'll join you for dinner."

Cove raced behind the princess through the vines and flowers, the clean smell of citrus stinging their noses as they put as much distance as possible between themselves and the Prince of Edmaria. Cove needed to feel the water on her skin, to allow it to calm her. *What was the purpose in any of this? Of this life in a kingdom who hated her?* Her heart was racing, and she could feel her power beginning to rise and simmer.

"Did you know?" Cove asked when they got to the shore. The wet sand squished between her toes as she poured her fear into the ocean, and the tides crept up to meet her feet.

"Know what?" Mina's brows sank in the middle. "Of course I did not know, Cove. He lied to me." Mina's eyes fell to the sand. "My father lied to me," she repeated, this time in a whisper of shock.

Cove ran her hands down the sides of her face. "I'm sorry," she said. Mina watched her, brown eyes worrisome, her dark hair whipping in the ocean winds. "I'll find a way. I'll make sure you do not have to marry him."

"We cannot pretend this is only about my happiness in marriage. This is about your *life*, Cove. If I marry him, he will start hunting Embers here," she whispered. "I have been able to quell my father from partaking in the trade thus far, but when he is gone. . .Cove, I do not think Andreas will listen to my counsel. You *will* be hunted." Tears welled in Mina's eyes.

Cove nodded. "I will think of something. Just to have you on my side, Mina, is everything. Thank you."

CHAPTER 4
BLOOD OR NO BLOOD
MINA

It was every little girl's dream to be a princess. It was every little girl's dream to marry a prince. But Mina was not a little girl any more—she never had been. She had been forced to play a role the entirety of her life. The perfect daughter, the poised princess. A woman of grace, taught by the queen herself—before she died. Before she had left Mina and her father bereaved. Mina had watched the grief consume her father in the years after her mother's illness and eventual death, and she had often wondered if he, too, would leave her.

He promised he would never leave her. He promised he would always keep her safe.

But he had broken both of those promises. He was ill, and he was leaving her. *Soon.* And now, he had lied to her, had all but sold her to a prince of darkness. Perhaps this was his way of keeping her safe, but he was wrong about this alliance. This alliance would be Mina's bitter end if it meant her best friend lost her life.

"Maybe your father will change his mind," Cove offered from beside her, where they now sat in the sand, knees hugged to their chests.

Mina shook her head. "He won't." Her father had kept the peace in this kingdom for as long as he could. It was time to choose a side, and he had pondered long enough on what that side would be. He was to die soon, and he was leaving Mina with what he thought would be the safest alliance. One of power. One where she did not have to make the difficult decisions.

The blue sea stretched before them, and the wind rushed through Cove's icy blonde hair, tangling the ends where they swept across the ground. The hems of their dresses were stained with watermarks, and wet sand clung to their skirts. They would need to change before dinner. Mina knew Cove found the sound of the waves calming. But to Mina, their continuous crashing only reminded her of the two islands she would soon hold in her hands as she tried to keep them from being flooded beneath a sea of darkness. There was a looming responsibility that she would soon bear on her shoulders alone. She would be expected to respect Andreas as king whilst trying to protect her kingdom—to preserve its people and the last of the Light that sat beside her now. Mina saw that the Light was good, but she did not trust in it like Cove did. She did not believe it was strong enough to ever overcome the darkness. But for Cove, she would keep that hope alive.

"I cannot believe my father lied to me," Mina muttered. Cove glanced to the side at her, blue eyes offering no surprise, only sympathy, as if the lie was to be expected. "You think he's an evil man, don't you?" Mina asked hesitantly. Hesitantly, because she cared about Cove's opinion, and Cove's judgment was usually right. The only thing Mina ever doubted Cove on was her choice to serve the Light so loyally, when doing so could get her killed.

"He is doing what he believes is best for you," Cove said.

"But?" Mina propped her cheek on her hand and watched Cove's softening expression.

"He doesn't care about Embers because none of this directly affects him. Light or darkness. None of it matters to him, as long as he keeps what he perceives as peace for himself. As long as he ensures a lasting reign for you."

Mina knew she was right. "He has all but given my reign to Edmaria." Her beloved islands, Oriana and the quaint Tabrana she loved to visit, would soon be under a reign where she had little control. She peered out at the sea and blinked as she turned to Cove. "What if his choices did directly affect him? He loves you because I love you. You are like a daughter to him. I know he will protect you."

Cove shook her head. "I am not blood. Your safety is his priority. Protecting me and risking being known as an Ember sympathizer, that could put the islands on what he sees as the losing side of the war. I would become too great a risk for your reign."

Mina shook her head. Her father cared for Cove in a way that not even Mina understood. He felt pity on her when he saw the way Marinos treated her, and he felt gratitude when he realized the grief she had pulled Mina from after the loss of his queen. When Mina's mother died, Mina had no one. But a year later, Cove was singing that beautiful song outside the palace gates—a song the queen used to hum as she brushed Mina's hair. From that day forward, they were bonded, and Mina's grief had started to shrink. Mina knew her father hoped Cove could save her again when it was him she laid to rest. Mina knew he would protect Cove, if not because he loved her, because he loved Mina.

"Blood or no blood, you are my sister," Mina finally said.

"Enough, Mina. He would not see it that way if he knew." Mina stiffened, surprised at Cove's sudden shortness with her. She knew Cove had a distrust toward men, especially after all she had been through with her own father, but it hurt that she could not see Mina's father as Mina did. She did, however, appreciate Cove's honesty, and the fact that even though no one in the palace would dare speak to the princess in such a tone, Cove was comfortable enough with her to do so. When Mina was with Cove, she could almost separate herself from her duties long enough to catch a breath—long enough to catch a glimpse of the man Cove seemed to think the King of the Dawn Islands was.

Mina was silent for a long moment, and she watched as she trailed her fingers through the soft sand between them. "I'm sorry," Cove said. "But I cannot afford to trust so easily. My life is on the line." Mina took Cove's hand in her own and leaned in to rest her head on her shoulder.

"Would you ever have trusted me?" Mina asked, lifting her head from Cove's shoulder to look at her. "Would you ever have told me, if I hadn't seen it for myself?" Mina nodded toward the hidden mark at Cove's collarbone, remembering the day Cove had moved into the palace. Mina had marched right into Cove's chambers to find out why her new lady had refused the servants she had gifted her. As Mina had stepped into the room unannounced, she saw Cove trying to lace her own corset, and in the mirror, she had caught a glimpse of that tiny glow.

Cove's eyes fell, and Mina knew her answer.

"I would not have told you," Cove said. "But I am glad you know."

CHAPTER 5
MONEY IS POWER
COVE

As the three of them sat in the dining hall, Cove could not help but relive the disaster that Marinos had brought to the table just last week. The evening, though not stormy and not yet dark, felt the same, like the walls might close in on her, and her entire life might be uprooted. Elias stood against the wall, facing the king. Cove tried her best not to stare, but her eyes were drawn to him, and she could not stop herself from stealing a few glances. *Soon, the two of them would be actively hunted by more than just the Ember mercenaries. This very kingdom would sell the two of them out for the promise of gold and power.* She looked across the table to the princess, who had her elbows on either side of her plate, and her cheek propped against her fist, the other hand's fingers thrumming wildly on the table.

"Mina," said the king. "Did your mother not teach you manners?"

Mina sat up straight, placing her hands in her lap. "I do not recall our lessons involving how to handle a marriage proposal from a man you have no interest in. Or how to handle being told that you were lied to and that you have no choice in the matter." The king's ragged face showed a whisper of surprise that she knew of the deal he had made without her, but he spoke calmly, as if he had no regrets about his decision.

"You must think about your kingdom, dear. When I am gone, the islands will be your responsibility. You know your mother's and my story. It is the same as many others. We royals do not marry for love. Your aunt, rest her soul, was much like you when she was paired with Prince Arne of Ozanna." The king smiled with his eyes. "Vevila wanted nothing to do with the man, but she quickly came to adore him. Once they met, they could not marry soon enough. We may not get to marry for love, but many find it in such arrangements."

"Don't get your hopes up, Father. Aunt Vevila had an easy choice. Arne Ozanne was not filled with darkness. He was a good man from all I have heard. His kingdom was thriving, and the only active war was with the witches."

"And look at his kingdom now. Crumbled. Non-existent. He and my eldest sister both dead because they chose the losing side. That is not a mistake that I will make, daughter." He was beginning to take a stand with the darkness, leaving his once persistent ways of peacekeeping behind.

"They were shipwrecked, not murdered," Mina argued. Cove stared forward with her head down, avoiding the family quarrel. She was familiar with the story of Arne and Vevila's failed journey from Ozanna to the islands for Sebastian's coronation.

Sebastian leaned forward in his seat. "We will not let our kingdom be on the losing side. Do you hear me?" Cove shivered at the unfamiliar sternness in his voice, and Mina nodded silently, keeping her eyes on the fingers that now fidgeted beneath the table in her lap. The king muttered under his breath, "The darkness has proven time and time again that when you are on its side, it leaves you alone."

Cove swallowed her words, avoiding the urge to correct his statement. The darkness tried to stifle all Light, and if one has no Light within, why would it bother? If someone was already doing works of darkness, feeding into its power, it may as well leave them be. But the darkness was limited, and Light's power was infinite. There would be a time when all Arresia would finally see the danger of separating themselves from the Light.

After a long moment of uncomfortable silence, Cove shifted at the sound of Mina's voice. "I do not understand, Father. How could you agree to this? I am not ready to wed."

"Mina, I do not wish to hear it. I have your best interest in mind. He is wealthy and very powerful. You'll be obtaining rule over another entire kingdom. The alliance with Edmaria will ensure your safety when I am gone. I have been too relaxed when it comes to the strength of the Dawn Islands. The Edmarian military, along with the Black Temple, will ensure your reign lasts." *Did he expect her to go there to worship?* Cove straightened in her seat.

"What does strength matter, when you've allowed our kingdom to fall to the darkness? Who would come against us? King Auden of Remont or Queen Adira of Eswen? They rule the only kingdoms of Light left, but they are weak and you know it. Soon, they'll fall too." Cove tapped her fork on the table as Mina continued. "You are proud that you have sided with the darkness? I cannot even look at you. I wonder if Mother would feel the same."

Sebastian looked down at the table, his fingers curling and

uncurling around his silverware as he fought the urge to yell. It was unlike him, and Cove wondered if the sickness was beginning to creep into his mind. "I have kept the Dawn Islands out of the trades at your request—to make you happy, Mina. I have given up riches and alliances—"

Mina cut him off. "You may not participate in the trades, but you do nothing to stop them. There are no consequences for the citizens of Oriana and Tabrana who choose to hunt and sell Embers. When there are no Embers left, why will we need an alliance with Edmaria? Who will fight against us when we are all the same? When we are all kingdoms of darkness? Would we all not just ally and become one, anyway?"

He took a deep breath and motioned for Elias to bring the wine.

Mina spoke freely now, knowing that her father would never reveal that she showed sympathy for the Embers, but that simple known fact made Cove nervous. *What if the king started to wonder who had made his daughter soft?*

"Just because each of the seven kingdoms will soon be in darkness, Daughter, does not mean there will not be a need for war. Power will still be sought, and one kingdom will always be on top."

"You should have allied with Oro, then, if you wanted to ensure a strong military alliance," Cove declared, gaining the courage to speak her opinion to the one father figure she had on these islands who would not willingly hurt her. *Unless he knew of her secret.* The king's brow raised and she cleared her throat. "Degare will be the one to land on top." *This alliance is useless.*

"Is that so?" Andreas asked, rubbing his hands together as he walked in, flanked by his two lords and Celeste. The entire room tensed as he pulled out a seat across from Cove, instead of taking the one Elias had pulled out for him across from Mina. Elias's jaw set, and Cove straightened and nestled into the back of her chair, glancing at Mina. Mina's chest rose and fell, but she held her chin high. "What makes you think Edmaria will not prevail against Oro? Degare is a weak man," Andreas said.

Cove thought about her response for a moment and decided that Andreas quite enjoyed the discourse. "I do not know much about Degare, but last time I checked, the entire world travels across seas to attend his trades. He is the only one with a Despiri army, he has a bloodstone weapon, and it is his kingdom that Edmaria sells their Embers to." Andreas raised his chin and folded his hands on the table then looked to the side at King Sebastian.

"Speaking of selling Embers, shall we discuss the details of our alliance?"

Cove's eyes shifted to the king, and she awaited another inevitable surprise. The king sat in silence for a moment and looked to his daughter as he took a deep inhale.

"Father," Mina warned. "What is he speaking of?"

"Mina, it is time Oriana and Tabrana are involved in the trades."

"*Involved* how?" Mina said through gritted teeth. Andreas leaned back in his seat, watching the argument begin to simmer, and smirked as he began listing the details of the arrangement.

"Mina, you are to be my wife in one month's time. The upcoming ball is to celebrate our engagement. Everyone will see how happy we are together. The Dawn Islands will begin participating in the Ember Trades. You will sell to Edmaria, and we will handle shipment to Oro."

Embers truly were going to be hunted on these islands then. When would the raids begin? To what measures would the Edmarian soldiers go to find the gifted ones? How many families would they destroy in their quest to extinguish the Light?

"So that is what is in it for you." Mina scoffed. "It is not only power. You'll sell our Embers to Oro and make a profit." She looked back to her father for a short moment.

"Money *is* power, Princess," Andreas said as he fixed the collar of his jacket.

Cove looked to Mina, to the king, and then to Elias. Each of their faces were pale and gaunt—each for different reasons. Elias's eyes were on her, then the storm in his gaze shifted to survey the other faces and moving mouths in the room as he tried to keep up with the conversation. Celeste was grinning at Yarris, and Cove guessed they were already holding hands beneath the table.

How am I going to stop this? She thought of her ability to not only *feel,* but manipulate others emotions. *Maybe I can stop the alliance by swaying the prince in the other direction.* She pushed the thought out of her head. She had no skill in using that gift—could not even control her *own* emotions. Emotional manipulation was a gift she did not want to touch, and she had never used it willingly. Cove knew the risks of exposing herself while trying were too great, and she did not know the strength of such a gift anyway. Though she had wondered if it was possible she had unknowingly manipulated the king to choose her at the selection of Mina's ladies, or if she had caused Mina to desire a friendship with her in the first place. *Were such things possible with this power inside her?* She studied Andreas, wondering if it was worth the risk to find out. But she knew if the Despiri prince before her knew anything about this world of Light and darkness, his mind would be guarded against such attacks, anyway, and the truth about her would be revealed.

"Well, are we going to eat or not?" Andreas asked, raising his hands and an empty glass. Elias filled it immediately, then retreated to his place at the wall across from the king. His face was now unreadable, but Cove dared to fish through all the emotions in the room, struggling to determine which was his. *Was it the worry? The anger? Or were those just hers?*

Servants piled into the dining hall, placing a plethora of savory dishes across the entire length of the table. But once again, Cove found herself with no appetite.

CHAPTER 6

YOU ARE NOT ALONE
COVE

Cove lounged on Mina's bed as the princess paced back and forth across the expansive chambers. The walls of limestone towered high above them, arching into the vine-covered ceiling. Gowns of every color filled the massive wooden wardrobe, and servants continued to deliver more. The day was hot, and there was no breeze to wind through the chambers.

"I'd bet the prince is enjoying the weather today," Cove muttered. She would hate to be in his presence and hear his unending complaints about the sticky air and the unbearable heat.

"He shall have to get used to it if he is to marry me and dwell here as my consort until he is crowned in Edmaria," Mina quipped, thumbing through the different options of gowns to wear to tomorrow's ball, where she would be pretending to celebrate her engagement to Andreas.

Cove sat up on her elbows, watching the servants scurry in and out until they had delivered the last gown. "So many to choose from," Cove said, hopping to her feet and striding to stand next to the princess. "How ever will you choose?" she said sarcastically, rolling her eyes at Mina.

"It is too hot to try them all on. I'll get them all sweaty before the ball. Maybe I'll just wait until tomorrow."

"Tomorrow will be just as hot. We are entering into the hottest week the islands see all year. But the evenings will be better," Cove suggested.

"My evenings are full of dinners with Andreas," Mina muttered.

"Mornings?"

"Full of strolls."

Cove hummed. "Afternoons, then?"

Mina gestured around, as if to show that her afternoon consisted of little more than looking at marvelous gowns that had been designed specifically for her.

"Perfect. Tomorrow afternoon we shall have a little getaway. Calm your nerves before the ball, and perhaps come up with a plan."

"A plan?"

"I *am* still trying to get you out of the marriage." She did have a plan, just not a very good one.

"It is hopeless, Cove."

Cove was silent for a moment and opted not to mention what she had in mind. Mina read the discouragement on her face.

"Spending the day with you tomorrow sounds nice. Perhaps we shall go swimming?" Mina offered with a sly smile. Cove returned it. "In the privacy of the bath house, where you'll be able to release some of that pent up *energy* you are seeming to lose control of."

Cove narrowed her eyes at the princess.

"Don't think I haven't noticed. The ocean has seemed awfully angry lately, and I saw how you welcomed Andreas with that glass of water yesterday." Cove began to deny it, but when she remembered the kindness in Elias's eyes, she fell quiet. She would keep his secret as if it were her own.

"I *have* been itching to use my gifts lately," Cove admitted. Staying hidden meant never using them, never practicing, and never using her gifts meant the power built up inside of her until she could not control it. She had also found her gifts of water manipulation to be heavily influenced by her emotions, and that made control even more difficult. Especially when she was constantly being flooded by the emotions of those around her.

"Perfect. Tomorrow we'll meet at the bath house. We shall have it to ourselves. I'll make sure the servants give us solitude. They should understand—they have been driving me mad with all this talk of the ball and their extravagant plans. All the ridiculous decisions I am to make. Why don't you just pick a gown for me?"

"Me? Choose your gown?"

Mina shrugged. "And then you can wear any of the other ones you'd like. We'll have it tailored specifically for you. . .to cover your mark." Cove glanced at the dresses—none of which would cover her mark in their current state.

"That sounds lovely, but. . ."

"You'll be singing at the ball; I should think you'll need a gown. Our measurements are nearly identical. I'll just have the seamstress adjust the neckline on me and then pretend I have changed my mind."

Cove pondered for a moment and gave in, "Okay." Her

response earned her a grin and a little nod from the princess before she began thumbing through the gowns.

"Why did you agree to perform anyway? Your anxiety will be out of control."

"Thanks, Mina. That's encouraging," Cove mumbled as she fanned out the skirt of a pastel gown.

"I just know how you hate singing for an audience. I mean, I've only heard you a dozen times in the years since I have known you. Most of those were when Marinos was forcing you to sing in the streets, or the few times you've sung at my father's celebrations. The other two were when you were on your balcony and thought no one was listening." Cove shot her an incredulous look. Mina shrugged. "I just hate that you feel forced."

"It will be fine," Cove said, pulling another gown from the lot. She had not had much of a choice when it came to her father's wishes. She hated the feeling of everyone's eyes on her, more than anything. As if they would see right through to the Light within her. "It will be fine," she whispered again.

It had to be fine.

After Cove had selected the dresses, she stepped out of Mina's chambers and into the winding hall, the sunlight shining between the columns and painting her skin. The seamstress slipped through the door behind her. Cove's anxiety was beginning to fester, and she paused for a moment to admire the beauty of the ocean. It was all around her, within reach, and she longed for it. To be a part of it. To be beneath it. To feel the power seeping from her skin and merging with the waters around her as the Light within her told it what to do and where to flow. She desired the peace it would bring to her restless thoughts.

You walk in the Light now, it would whisper. *Do not be afraid of the shadows that come your way.*

She took a deep breath before turning to collide with a firm body. She backed away quickly, apologizing under her breath. Her eyes trailed up the sun-kissed arm that steadied her until they met the stare of the king's servant—Elias. He watched her mouth intently as her apology spilled out and then he spoke softly, "I should be the one apologizing, Lady Cove. I am terribly sorry to sneak up on you."

He released her arm and put a few feet of distance between them as a few servants walked by carrying linens and florals in preparation for the ball. Cove noticed the stack of white fabrics he had dropped and bent to retrieve them.

"No, let me," he insisted, looking around, as if to be sure they were not being watched. She looked over her shoulder and adjusted the skirt of her dress as he collected the tablecloths from the ground. "Conversing with a man will not look good for you. Not when you are to be married to Lord Arlo."

Cove waited for his attention to fall back to her lips before she continued. "It is the princess who is to marry, not me. Arlo has not proposed."

"I am certain he will," Elias said.

"I should hope not," she muttered. If he proposed, she would be in quite the predicament. Especially with her father breathing down her neck, pushing her to marry. She glanced back out to the sea, willing her anxieties to rest.

"You will not accept?" Elias asked.

Cove's eyes locked on his for a long moment as she decided

what level of trust she would grant him. "I want nothing to do with him," she finally replied.

Elias bit his bottom lip, as if contemplating his next words. He sighed, and his next words flowed out in a low whisper. "I saw you with your father in the garden."

Cove went rigid, remembering the way he had watched her that night. "And what did you see?" she asked timidly.

"I know he is forcing your hand in marriage." He looked over his shoulder again, surveying the empty hallway. They were alone. She watched his throat bob. He leaned in closer, and she tilted her chin up to hold his gaze. "I know he is threatening you. I know he has something over you." His deep blue eyes were like the calm before a storm, watching her carefully. *Curiously.*

"And do you know what that *something* is?" Cove asked quietly, tucking her hair behind her ear before crossing her arms to still her shaking hands.

Elias clenched his jaw. "I believe I do." His voice was deep and gentle, like the ocean that licks the shore.

Cove took a step backward but held his gaze. "And what are you to do with that information, Elias?"

"Nothing," he said quickly. "I mean, I would never tell. I will guard your secret with my life."

Cove narrowed her eyes and looked down the still-empty hall behind him. "Why?"

"You know why," he whispered, his eyes dancing between her gaze and her lips.

"Say it." She needed to hear him say it, to know that she was not alone. To confirm that she was not crazy, and that she *had* seen him manipulate water in the same ways she could.

That after all this time, she had found another Ember in this kingdom.

He interpreted the words on her lips and scanned the long hallway once more before he spoke beneath his breath, "Because I am an Ember, too." Something like relief—comfort like she had never known—rushed through every pore of her body. She wished she could bask in it forever. Elias smiled softly. "You are not alone, Cove. There are more of us." He spoke almost too quietly for her to hear.

Her heart fluttered in her chest. "More than just you? More Embers?"

He nodded, and before she could ask anything else, she heard voices echoing down the long hall. She tapped her ear in warning, and he backed away from her, becoming the picture of an honorable servant transporting linens—not the male who had just been oddly close to a lady with a title, watching the movement of every curve of her lips, revealing secrets, and uttering words she had only ever dreamt of hearing. His eyes surveyed her one last time, following the length of her hair to where it fell at her hips.

Cove swallowed, turning her head just enough so Elias could still read her words, but any onlooker would assume her to be peering out at the sea.

"Meet me in the east gardens tomorrow, just before noon," she said.

CHAPTER 7
BREATHLESS THREATS
COVE

Cove usually woke at dawn, along with the first hint of light pouring into her chambers. But this morning dawn had come, and she had not yet fallen asleep. Her mind turned all night with thoughts of Elias and the other Embers he had mentioned in Oriana. *Where did they hide? How would they survive when the islands were to begin participating in the trades and the king's guard began infiltrating their homes along with the solo mercenaries who already hunted them?*

Embers in Oriana went into hiding years ago, when persecution began with Degare's hunt. But here in Oriana and Tabrana, the threat that an Ember would be taken and sold into the trade had once been quite low. It was more likely that an Ember would be enslaved or taken to work in the mines—which was more popular in other kingdoms than the islands. The occasional mercenaries traveled through, hunting Embers and trying to make a profit off them, but the king's guard enforced nothing of the sort. Now, hundreds of the island soldiers would be scouring the cities and villages for Embers—and the lightmarked would have nowhere to run.

It was just before noon, and as the sun climbed to its peak, Cove rolled out of bed. She brushed out the soft waves in her hair, adding a few small braids, and stepped into a chiffon gown of muted blue fabric. The neckline was high, and billowy sleeves draped from her shoulders to her wrists with three thin, golden chains lined with pearls hanging the length of each arm. Her platinum hair hung down to her waist, and she quickly put her favorite pearls into the piercings in her ears to match the new bangles she wore at her wrists.

She looked in the mirror above the vanity for a moment, breathing deeply and pinching the skin on her cheeks until they reddened just enough to bring some life into her tired face. She opted for no shoes and exited via the balcony off her chambers, toting the small bag that held her robe and dry undergarments for after her swim in the bath house. Cove descended to the gardens below by a private staircase and wandered nervously through the winding paths until she reached the eastern garden, where Elias awaited her.

He stood with his back to her and she could not help but admire the strength he held beneath his linen shirt. He was reaching for an orange fruit from the droopy branches of the tree above him, and as he reached, she saw the faint glimmer of a lightmark beneath his untucked shirt, trailing up his back. Her breath caught in her throat. *He should be more careful.* She stepped forward, inclined to touch it, but quickly stopped herself. He turned abruptly, and she remembered he did not have the ability to hear her approaching.

"My apologies, I—" she started.

He smiled brightly and she couldn't help but pause mid-sentence to reciprocate. "This is for you," he said, extending the fruit toward her. She dipped her head in thanks, taking the fruit and tracing a thumb over its tough skin. Because she had been isolated, she knew little about Ember community etiquette, but one thing she knew, and had learned from her parents, was that the offering of fruit was a sign of trust and friendship.

Trust did not come easily for Cove, but she had been up all night thinking, and she had decided to try with Elias. She reached around him and plucked some fruit from the branch. "And this is for you," she said, sure to speak toward him so he could read her lips.

He waved a hand as if to refuse. "I cannot accept," he said.

"And why not?" Cove asked.

"I am a servant, My Lady. I am not to eat from the king's gardens."

"What kind of silly rule is that? I am a friend of the princess, and I say you may eat it." She raised her brows and he shyly accepted the offering, but she was not convinced he would partake.

"Thanks for meeting me," she said.

"I had nothing better to do," he said with a wink. "The king is resting up before the ball this evening, so I have the day to myself."

His eyes remained on her lips, and she felt her cheeks heating—though she knew he did not stare out of desire. "So, Elias. Tell me how you came to be an Ember servant who works directly for a king who would have your head if he knew of your secret."

"I am more interested in knowing your story—of how the

princess knows your secret, but her father does not." Cove felt her body tense. *How did he know Mina knew?*

"You share first, and then I will think about it," Cove said, twisting a lock of hair between her fingers. He smirked and tossed his fruit into the air, catching it swiftly and taking a bite, right through the tough rind. Cove hid her grin as he chewed and forced himself to swallow.

"No wonder they peel these things," he said. She laughed loudly then, and he mirrored her smile.

"Okay, Cove," he said, clearing his throat. "Have a seat." He gestured to the stone bench that sat beneath a trellis covered in flowers that smelled of sweet honey. She sat slowly, setting her tote down and letting the skirt of her gown spill onto the ground around the bench. "You ask the questions, I'll answer."

Cove hummed, pretending to think for a moment before she began prying. She had pondered all night on what she would ask him. "You are deaf, yet you speak so clearly. The king said you learned with the help of a Despiri from Oro."

"Not a Despiri," he said with a twitch of his lip. Cove studied him for a moment in silence and then it clicked. "An Ember?" He ran his fingers through his hair, and she admired the way it swooped just above his brows in a mess of golden curls.

"But the king—he told Andreas it was a Despiri," Cove recalled.

"You cannot believe everything the king says. He can be as deceptive as any other ruler." Cove raised a brow, nodding in agreement, though she felt in a sense that she was betraying Mina. "But he probably does believe I learned with the help of a Despiri. It was an Ember from our own kingdom. The king's wife, Queen Leora, is the one who set up the lessons. And King Sebastian. . .he would not have approved if he knew it was an Ember."

"So, she lied to him?" Elias shrugged in response. "Why would they bother? I mean, why you?" Cove asked. When Andreas had asked the king why he would bother with teaching a man to speak when there were other, less costly options, for servants, Cove had been curious too. Why Elias, of all the men who could serve the king? "There are plenty of other servants who—"

"Who can hear?" Elias finished her sentence for her. Cove's cheeks flushed, but Elias let out a small scoff of laughter. "My mother was the queen's servant and healer. They became very close friends. When I was born, it took nearly two years for my parents to discover my condition. My mother was distraught, and even as a healer, she could find nothing to help me. The queen promised her she would help her in any way she could—to make sure I could work as any other man and provide for myself and my family. To live a normal, comfortable life. Seven years ago, the queen found an Ember able to teach me through mind speaking." Just as Cove had considered. "Today, I am paid well for my service to the king."

"So, Leora, was she a follower of the Light? Was she an Ember?" Cove had never met the queen, and Mina had never mentioned her mother being gifted, but she did speak of her often. Mina had explained how much her father had changed since her mother's death, as if Queen Leora had served as some sort of guiding light, keeping the king from wandering too far into the shadows. Cove wished Leora was still here, if only for her ability to reason with the king.

"I believe she was much like her daughter. Neither friend nor foe."

"Mina is my friend. She knows of the Light—"

"But does she have it within her?" Elias was quick to cut her off, and she recoiled. His eyes fell to her lips while he waited for her response. Cove was silent, so he continued. "To be without Light, is to be in darkness. She can be your friend and not a friend of the Light." Cove knew where this conversation was going, but she did not want to talk about it. She did not want to consider that Mina could ever be a threat. "Look, all I am saying is. . .be careful. The Despiri *know* of the Light. Degare and Andreas. . .they both know of the Light. Yet, where do they stand? Anyone who chooses to separate themselves from it. . .if they are not on the Light's side, if they don't carry it within them, they side with the darkness whether they admit it or not."

"Mina does not. Mina plans to make the islands safe for us again."

"I hope she does. Truly. But when things get bad—and they will with this alliance—she will have to choose a side. All or nothing. She cannot remain in the shadows between." Cove turned the orange fruit over in her lap, watching it glimmer in the hot sun. "Just look at the king. He is choosing the darkness as it grows around him. He is conforming with every new shadow. While Leora was alive, Embers were not persecuted so severely. As the world gets darker, so does he. Because he has no Light to guide him. What if Mina did not have you to protect from the darkness? Would she still fight to protect the Embers?"

Cove folded her hands in her lap and changed the subject. "You speak quite fluently—you've only been able to speak for seven years?" Elias watched her for a few seconds before accepting the abrupt change of topic.

"It comes easily now, but I could speak to some degree before. My parents taught me lip reading and what certain words meant, but it was difficult to translate without the context or sound. My life has become abundantly easier since my lessons began."

"You said there were more Embers here on the islands. Your teacher is one of them?"

"My teacher has since passed. Peacefully, in old age. But yes, there are others." He sat down next to her and took the fruit from her hands, beginning to peel it for her. She watched the way his hands moved through the motions. "There is a rebellion. There are many. Some have different end goals, but we all have similar interests."

"What do you mean? Are they not all Embers, hoping to usher in the return of the Light?"

"Not every rebellion is made up of Embers. Some only want to end the trades because they fear the power the Despiri are gaining. The kingdoms' leaders are growing hungry for more and more power. They steal food from their subjects and tax them heavily to fund the trades. Even if the people do not care for Embers, the royal armies are tearing apart villages looking for them. They are killing and killing, and there is no end. Soon, the same will be happening here. The people are beginning to fear what will become of Arresia. They do not realize it is the Light they need to turn to, they just know that the darkness is growing." He tossed the orange peel to a nearby seagull and handed Cove the fruit.

"Here, in Oriana, is there a resistance? Embers?" Cove had always wanted community. Had longed for it. She had been an outcast even in her childhood before she was lightmarked, and after she was orphaned, she was always alone. To see Elias sitting before her, to somehow trust him after only a short conversation, to feel the Light within him instead of the darkness that surrounded her each day. . .She took a deep breath. "Where are they?"

Elias flinched, and she felt a pang of sadness rolling off of him as he realized just how lonely she was. He had sympathy for her. She straightened, trying to shake the feeling of humiliation that came with being pitied. "If they are here in Oriana, I want to join them," she said.

Elias shook his head. "It is too dangerous. I have contact with them. . .but we work in the palace, Cove. We cannot know their location."

"You do not know their location?" He shook his head. "But you work for them, right?"

"I provide them with information on things that might affect their safety." He tipped his head back and forth. "Like the alliance with Edmaria."

Cove stiffened. "Do they have a plan?"

Elias watched her for a moment. "They have no plan. But you do."

Her heart became like a stone that fell into the pit of her stomach. "What?"

"I have seen the anguish in your eyes as I watch you sit between the man that is to be your husband and the prince that is to bring your demise. You have a plan."

Cove's jaw set. She could not truly consider such a plan. "It is not a very good one, and I have no clue how to execute it."

"Maybe I could assist?" he asked, doing a quick scan of the gardens and raising a palm to coax some water from the nearby sea. It swirled like a storm in his hand, spiraling and then dissipating like rain.

Cove tilted her head, trying not to gawk. What she would give for that amount of control. . .to be able to practice freely and openly so she could master her gifts. To learn how to stop them from happening against her will so they could instead be a carefully managed tool. *Where had he found the solace to do so?*

"I do not think you would want to be involved in what I have planned," she said as she watched the last drop splat on the ground. "It is crazy enough that I have not even mentioned it to Mina."

"Let's keep it that way," he said, turning his body toward her. "Tell *me*." Cove studied him.

"You do not trust her," she stated dryly.

He shrugged, pulling another fruit from the tree and keeping it for himself. "I thought we had already established that. Do not take offense. I don't trust many."

Neither do I.

"But you trust me?" she asked, crossing one leg over the other and placing her hands atop her knee.

"You're different," he said coolly as a dimple formed at his cheek.

Why? She wanted to ask. But she knew exactly what he was talking about. The invisible tether that seemed to stretch between them. The pull. It is what caused her to watch him so closely during dinner, and it is probably what caused him to follow her out the doors and into the gardens that night with Marinos. A sort of curiosity. A desire to know more. A tug from the Light within them.

She paused for a moment before continuing, "It is

probably not doable, but the prince has decided to remain on his ship until the wedding, anchored at the eastern docks. If I—we—could muster enough power to carry their ships out to sea on a current. . ." Her voice trailed off as she realized what she was saying. The murder she was plotting. She did not want to be a killer, could not stomach the thought.

"We could shipwreck them," he finished for her. Cove bit her lip, waiting for judgment from him that never came. She had been given the idea at the dinner table, when Sebastian spoke of his sister and Arne Ozanne's death by shipwreck. It would appear to be accidental—a freak accident. There would be no suspect, and Andreas would be dead. Cove doubted that King Idris of Edmaria would wish to continue with an alliance after the death of his eldest, and King Sebastian would likely die from illness before the opportunity to continue with an alliance was given. Mina would be queen, and it would be her decision alone. Through her reign, Cove hoped the Embers would find refuge in the Dawn Islands.

"I know it is a big operation. But they are planning to begin loading Embers onto the ships soon. . ."

"We need to do it before they have the chance," Elias said. She did not know how she would gain the necessary control of her power to carry out such an elaborate plan, but having Elias as an ally would be a good start. Cove took a deep breath and hid her shaking hands in the folds of her gown. Elias's eyes shifted to her lap and said, "We can discuss this later. I'm sure we will find more time to chat. The deal was, though, that I could ask you some questions after you had asked yours."

Cove blinked at him. "I believe I said I would *think* about it."

"Ah," he chuckled, rubbing his hands down the tops of his

legs. "I tell you all this and agree to help you sink a fleet of ships, and I don't get to learn a single thing about you?"

Cove rolled her eyes toward him. "Okay, you can ask me one question," she said, holding up a finger between them. "One." His lip tugged upward.

"I don't know how I will ever narrow all of the things I wish to know about you down to one question," he said. "But I'll take it."

"So, what will it be?" Cove asked beneath raised brows.

He did not hesitate. "What is it your father requires of you for your freedom?"

She rolled her shoulders. "Really? Out of all the questions you could have asked?"

He raised his hands in innocence. "You gave me no limitations on subject matter."

She chewed on her lip, but she did not remove her eyes from his. "He is rabid with greed. He requires a bride price." *And continued payments until her death, which would be an untimely one if she were to marry Arlo.*

"I figured as much. But what exactly is it that he demands? What will put an end to his threats?"

"My death, maybe," she said, looking to the sky as she laughed. He did not laugh with her—his mouth lay flat.

"And a marriage to Lord Arlo, that would be enough for him? As long as his pockets are filled? You'd walk free?"

"Free until Lord Arlo sells me into the trades the moment he sees my mark," she muttered. Elias's jaw ticked.

Cove cut him off as his mouth opened to speak once more. "You already used your one question." Cove knew there was nothing that could end her father's threats and she did not want to talk about it. Only when she was no longer breathing, when she had met the demise Marinos thought she deserved, would he be satisfied with all she had given him.

If it was truly only money he was after, Cove guessed it would be enough just to sell her into the trades. To Marinos, Cove was a possession. He craved money, but he also craved the power found in the secrets that he held over her. It was about the pride he gained when he saw the fear he could place into her. He was in it for the long run. He hated those of her kind, and tormenting her served as an outlet for him.

"You don't deserve this," Elias said under his breath.

Cove shrugged, feeling uncomfortable beneath his watchful gaze, and brought her hand up to shield her eyes against the sun that had peaked in the sky. *Mina.* She jumped up, startling Elias. "I am late, I need to get going. I have plans at the bath house with the princess." He struggled to interpret her words as she turned about, and she was about to repeat herself when he put them together.

"Let me walk you there," he offered. She thought for a moment and glanced around the empty gardens. She nodded in agreement, and he collected her bag from the bench, then ushered her toward the pools on the opposite side of the island. Elias watched their surroundings diligently as they walked, looking out for anyone who may report their suspicious whereabouts.

Cove could not imagine living without the ability to hear, but he had adapted well, and it did come with some benefits. She supposed it could earn one some separation from having to hear the horrid stories and legends that sounded through Arresia. But to know he would never hear the ocean, the voice of his mother, the sound of his lover's melody while she sang freely and openly in the kitchen. . .

Cove swallowed nervously as they continued down the hundreds of steps to the bathhouse that bordered the sea. In the heat of the day, sweat had beaded on his brow. "What happens to you if you reject Lord Arlo's proposal?" Elias asked, ignoring her one-question rule. "Your father will turn you in?"

Cove was silent for a long moment, and a part of her wanted to tell him everything, but she kept her answer short. "Yes."

"And if you had the choice, would you marry? Someone else, of course. Not him."

Cove had not allowed herself to dwell on the hopes of such things for long, but she had given marriage enough thought to know that a marriage like her parents' was something she desired. "If I had the choice, and I found a man who knew and loved every part of me, yes. I would very much like to marry and move far away from here," she said. "Somewhere where Embers are free and safe and together." So she would never have to be alone again. She watched him intently, but he stayed silent.

"Does such a place even exist?" she asked when his eyes had found her mouth once more. He stumbled over his feet, as he could pay little attention to the uneven stone path ahead while reading her lips. She could not help but reach out to touch his elbow in an attempt to steady him. He smiled, glancing down at the graze of her fingers.

"It will, one day. We Embers have a lot of work to do. But the Light will return," he said.

How can he be so sure? How did he remain so hopeful and filled with peace?

"When can I see you again?" she asked.

"You mean when can we scheme to stop this alliance?" he

asked with a grin. A timid smile graced her lips. *Killing. They were talking about killing.* But what other choice was there, when these people had dedicated each of their breaths to darkness? Elias's face softened. "It is for the good of the kingdom, My Lady."

"Cove," she corrected him. "Please call me Cove."

The corner of his mouth twitched upward. "Things often get dark before the Light shines through. We know that from the Scrolls."

The Light Scrolls. "Do you have access to the Scrolls?" she blurted, then glanced around again, checking for eavesdroppers. His presence was causing her to become reckless.

"I do. They are with my parents in the north fishing village. I'll take you sometime, when I have another free day."

"Your parents are Embers?" she asked in a whisper.

Elias nodded. There were two more Embers on this island that she could meet, and they possessed Light Scrolls. She wondered if Elias's mother being a healer to the late queen had meant she was an Ember with the gift of healing, or if she was just a normal healer.

"I—I would love that," Cove said. "I have not seen the scriptures since I was young, when. . ."

She stopped herself. *When my father was killed for being an Ember. And then my mother shortly after.* Her eyes dropped to the ground at the memory, and she regretted bringing it up. She felt his eyes on her as he waited for the rest of her sentence to spill from her lips, but she did not finish it, and he did not ask any more forbidden questions.

They approached the massive bath house, and as always, Cove marveled at the pure art of the architecture. The building of smooth marble sat on the edge of the ocean, and a river of sea water entered beneath the wall where it would flow inside to fill the pool with a constant stream of clean water. The pillars and columns that lined the seaside were decadent with vines and golden depictions of the creatures from legends. Lush gardens decorated either side of the massive archway that opened before them, and Elias held out a hand as he led Cove up the wide steps. He paused at the door.

"I would offer for you to join us," she said, "but I am afraid that would be improper."

He chuckled. "A male servant in the bathhouse with a lady and the princess? I would imagine the king would have my head." She rubbed the back of her neck.

"I should be going," he said. "I am off again four days from now if you would like to accompany me to my parents' home."

She blushed, and her mind immediately went to the Light Scrolls. "Of course I would." He handed her the bag, his warm fingers grazing hers.

"Meet me just outside the north gate. There is a tree there that is incredibly thick. There's a face in the bark," he said, with a little laughter in his voice. "You'll know it when you see it. Or when it *sees you*." She giggled and could feel her cheeks turning red.

"Cove?" Cove jumped, backing away from Elias before he even realized they had company. The princess stood beneath the archway with her arms crossed. Her brown eyes surveyed Elias, and he dipped his head in reverence the moment he noticed her.

"Elias walked me here. A true gentleman," Cove explained. "He carried my bag."

Mina raised her chin and her brows and looked to Cove.

"Well, I am glad you are here, Elias. I seem to have ordered all my servants away and have forgotten the towels." *He is not working today,* Cove wanted to say.

But Elias nodded and said, "I am happy to, Your Highness. I'll return soon."

"Just have them here in an hour or so," Mina said. "Take your time."

Elias dipped his chin and turned, eyes catching Cove's for a moment before he descended the steps with a smile.

"Well, what was that about?" Mina asked.

"It is a long walk, and I desired some company," Cove said nonchalantly, shrugging.

Mina hummed. "I think you should be careful, conversing with servants. Your father expects you to marry into wealth, not lack thereof," the princess remarked as she watched Elias walk the path back to the palace.

"I am not courting him, Mina. It was a simple conversation." *A simple conversation that involved rebellion and a plot to destroy an entire fleet of Edmarian ships and their men, changing the fate of an entire kingdom.*

"Whatever. Let's just swim already. I have been waiting for twenty minutes, and I am roasting out here," she complained, fanning her dewy face with her hand. Cove could tell the princess had refused her servants this morning because her hair had been pulled from her neck in a simple sweeping braid, and her ivory gown was made of a lightweight fabric with golden threads and a beaded tie that had been secured around her waist. Mina's bangled arm raised to the stone plate on the door.

She flipped it to reveal the sign of the crown, which notified others that the bathhouse was in use by the princess and she was not to be disturbed.

Mina had her own private bathing chambers in the palace, as did Cove, but the bathing pool inside the bathhouse was large, and when the two of them had become friends, Mina ensured Cove would have it as a place to practice her gifts. They could not come too often, but Cove enjoyed every minute she could bask in those waters freely. And after seeing the way Elias could control his gifts, she was eager for the afternoon of solitude.

Cove lifted her skirts and trailed the princess inside. The expanse of the room opened before them, and the floor dipped down into a pool of water that stretched across the entire room. The ceiling was held up by pillars and vines crept across them and over the marble ceiling that had been meticulously carved to depict a legendary flood that had once swallowed the lands of Arresia.

Cove stepped out of her gown. She remained in her ivory slip and left her gown and a robe draped over a stone divider. She kept her jewelry on to save time. The seascape view to the east was like a painting, and she breathed a sigh of relief as she sank into the cool water.

Cove floated on her back, feeling the water move between her fingers and around the flowing fabric of her shin-length slip. "So, how was your morning stroll with the prince?" She swept a hand through the water and then struggled to guide it upward. She willed it to spiral in her hand as Elias had, but she failed, and the water splashed around her.

"Surprisingly, not terrible," Mina muttered over her shoulder as she stepped out of her dress.

Cove perked up. "What do you mean?" The princess set her clothing beside Cove's and dipped a toe in the water. Her slip was golden and fell just above the knees, whereas Cove's was longer and white and stitched of much cheaper fabric.

"I mean, it wasn't unbearable. We shared a conversation. He can be quite charming when you get to know him."

"Well, what did you talk about? What did he say?" Cove pried, her voice heightening in concern.

"We talked about a lot of things. His family, his life in Edmaria, his plans for the Dawn Islands. . ." Mina looked at Cove. "Don't worry. This does not mean I want to marry him. It was simply a conversation," she said with a tease in her voice.

Cove huffed and leaned back in the water, twisting the pearls in her bracelet.

"Look, I just don't see a way out of this marriage, so I figure I should try to make the best of it. Maybe I can seduce him," she said jokingly, twirling a piece of her hair. Cove rolled her eyes, sweeping a hand into the air and sending a bit of water colliding with the ceiling above the princess. The water fell, drenching her where she stood. Mina wiped the water from her face and they both giggled.

"I don't think you can change him," Cove muttered as she failed to mold some water into the shape of a bird. "Only the Father of Lights could do that."

"Change me? The Father of Lights?" Mina and Cove both went rigid at the voice and the chuckle that followed, and Cove sent the unrecognizable shape of water plummeting into the pool as she turned away to hide her lightmark.

"Prince Andreas, you cannot be in here," Mina blurted. Cove kept her back to the prince, hoping he hadn't seen anything—hoping Mina could make up a clever excuse for the conversation he had overheard. "We have no escort, and you cannot be alone with me. Especially not in a bath house."

"Lady Cove is here; does she not count as an escort?" he questioned.

Cove could feel his voice getting closer.

"Prince, what are you doing?" Mina asked, her voice growing in worry. Cove breathed deeply from where she faced the wall, silently praying that it was not his steps that she heard wading into the pool behind her.

"I am indecent, Your Highness," Cove said, standing stiffly in the midst of the waters in her underclothes. "Please allow us some privacy to dress, and then we will come out to meet you. I will escort you and the princess wherever you would like to go."

Cove's heart was pounding, and the water rippled around her with each beat.

"Prince," Mina said warily. Cove braced herself as a hand gripped her shoulder and spun her around in the water. She sent some splashing into his eyes, temporarily obscuring his vision. He blinked it out and his eyes immediately fell to her collarbone, where her lightmark glowed through the fabric of her slip, condemning her.

He laughed, and his sapphire eyes seemed to pierce through her. "I thought so," he said. Cove could not breathe. "I wonder what your life would be worth in the trade—or should I take it myself when I visit Oro in the summer?" Cove stared blankly at him. *My life is over.* "The power I took at the last trades," Andreas said, admiring the marks on his hand, "turned out to be quite the disappointment. I hardly notice a difference in my strength." Andreas's grip tightened on Cove's arm until she felt her skin bruising. "One of my other gifts, though, is a sort of intuition. I knew there was something about you that I needed to learn."

"I'll scream," Mina warned. Cove shook her head at the princess. *Do not scream.* "I will tell my father of your threats," she said behind him. "He will have your head." The princess's voice was authoritative, but Cove recognized the shake that was not typically there.

Andreas ignored his betrothed, and instead smirked at Cove. "He does not know, does he? Are you not like family to him? What kind of betrayal would this be? I cannot imagine your punishment."

Cove was silent, but her mind was reeling. "My father is not a cruel man," Mina said sternly, advancing toward Andreas.

"Maybe not, but I am," he sneered.

He is not going to stop. He is going to tell my secret. He is going to kill me. He is going to kill so many Embers. He is going to make Mina miserable. He is going to bring the islands to ruin. He is going to deliver Arresia further into the hands of darkness.

The surface of the water began to vibrate around her. Cove struggled against the firm grip Andreas had on her shoulders, and she looked beyond him to where Mina was approaching. Mina's eyes pleaded with Cove for a plan, and then without warning, the princess leapt onto Andreas's back, attempting to pull him away from Cove. He released Cove and shook Mina off, throwing her to the water below. The back of his shadowmarked hand found Mina's cheek before she could even stand up to catch her breath.

He has to die. For the good of the Kingdom.

Andreas turned toward Cove, and as his hand reached for her in an attempt to drag her out of the water and to her demise, he was pushed to the side in a tidal wave of uncontrollable rage. Cove barely managed to create a current to safely deliver Mina to the top of the steps. Once the princess was on dry ground, Cove gave in, and brought the entirety of her anger down on the Prince of Edmaria, allowing her rage to take over. He struggled to rise to his feet, and his fits of coughing tangled with the sounds of the crashing sea. The water levels continued rising, and Cove let her emotion take over as she rolled him beneath the surface in a torpedo of chaos. She had no control as he slammed into the columns again and again, until bubbles no longer fled from his mouth and his body had gone limp.

CHAPTER 8
A NEW SECRET
COVE

The water receded and Cove breathed heavily, holding her body up on one of the columns amid the pool. She watched in silence as Prince Andreas of Edmaria floated face down in the water.

Mina was the first to speak. "Is he dead?"

Cove braced her quaking body against the column. *What have I done?* Her vision was spotty, and she could not answer Mina's question. She was going to vomit.

Footsteps shuffled quickly from the area where Mina stood, and words of panic were shouted into the bath house. "What happened?" Cove knew that voice. She adored that voice and the strange comfort it brought her as it skittered across the tall ceilings. Just as Cove did not answer Mina's question, Mina did not answer Elias's. Because Andreas *was* dead. And neither wanted to admit it.

I am a killer.

Cove's vision cleared enough for her to see Elias walking toward her in the water, passing by Andreas's body. His eyes darted from the corpse—the man she had killed—to her lightmark, and understanding washed over his face. When he reached her, his hands did not hesitate. They found her wrists, and her eyes looked to his—to the storm she saw there. He cupped her hands against his chest, and she felt his heart beating beneath his shirt.

"Cove," he said.

Their hearts seemed to harmonize, sending an even pattern of waves out from where they stood in the pool as the princess watched from afar.

"Cove," he said again. "Come with me out of the water."

She did not move. Her feet were planted, and her eyes were fixed on the prince. *I drowned him.*

"Cove," Mina said softly. "Listen to him. Come out. We cannot stay here."

I am a killer. Cove blinked, eyes dropping to the hands that held hers.

Those same hands led her out of the water.

Cove stood, drenched in the water that had drowned the prince.

She watched the body floating in the water from where she now stood at the edge of the pool. Mina draped a robe over her shoulders, and Elias tilted Cove's face up to meet his gaze.

"Give it to me. Let me handle it," he said in a low, sure voice. He tied her robe in the front, assuring that her lightmark was covered. He brushed the hair from her face and tucked it behind her ears, letting his fingers hover there at the base of her jaw, while he did his best to hold her attention through the shock. "Go," he insisted. "Go far from here. You decided to go swimming at the west shore today, not here," he said. "Let me handle this." His face was only inches from hers. He looked at the princess, and she nodded. She took Cove by the elbow, stuffed their belongings into Cove's bag, and dragged her from the scene.

At the archway near the exit of the bath house, Cove halted. "I cannot leave him to clean up my mess," she realized. She started back toward the pool, but Mina caught her arm.

"You can, and you will. That is his job. He is a servant."

"No, no, no, I—"

Mina took her by the shoulders. "Cove, I am assuming that he is lightmarked too, since he saw yours and did not even *flinch*," she whispered. Her brown eyes bore into Cove's. "You need to let him do this and then you need to never speak to him again. He is going to get you killed."

Cove shook her head, trying to rid her mind of the thoughts spiraling through at the speed of light. Mina flipped the stone plate at the door, covering the fact that they were ever there.

"Let's go," Mina said, pulling her down the steps and toward the palace.

"Shouldn't we be going to the beach? We must go to the beach. We are supposed to have been there today, we need to make it believable," Cove rambled.

"We'll be seen, and you look like you're going to vomit. There is no way you can be out in public right now. People will suspect something has happened the minute they see your face."

Cove gulped, pausing to heave in the gardens.

"Not here, keep going," Mina said, continuing to tug on

her arm until they reached the safety of the princess's chambers.

She had been plotting a shipwreck. *Multiple shipwrecks.* The wrecking of a fleet in a massive sea storm—one that would kill hundreds. Yet, she had killed only one, and she could not handle it.

Mina handed her a clay pot, chucking the flowers that were in it to the side. Cove vomited as Mina paced the room.

Cove had watched the life drain from his body and had kept going in all her rage.

"He saw your lightmark, he never would have stopped," Mina said, trying to justify it.

Cove rubbed her temples. The ball started in five hours, and Elias was somewhere fixing her mistakes—staging an accident or hiding a body.

"I have to get cleaned up. I have to perform," she said, ripping her arms from her robe.

"The ball," Mina realized. She pulled the wet hair from her neck, holding it against the back of her head as she spun in a slow circle. "We are supposed to announce our engagement in front of the kingdom tonight."

Cove gathered her wits and turned to face her best friend. Her *sister.* "Okay, Mina. You have to act like you're still expecting him at the ball. You'll be surprised when he doesn't show up. You'll be humiliated. You'll be upset, and most of all, worried."

Mina nodded, and Cove's eyes fell to the purpling bruise at Mina's cheek. *What are we going to do?*

The sound of a dozen screams echoed into the princess's chambers, and they both ran to the balcony, peering out at the sea waters receding from the eastern beach. *When water recedes like that. . .*Cove's eyes widened at the massive wave that was headed to the shore.

"*Elias*," she breathed. The two of them watched as he staged the scene. An entire village was flooded, and the water poured into the bath house, making an accidental drowning believable. The waters rose a few feet high into the streets beyond the bathhouse, pulling carts and people's belongings out to sea. Cove winced as mothers' clung to their children, barely outrunning the waters, and as a fishing boat was delivered onto the stone path across from Cove's favorite bakery.

Thankfully, the homes in the village were far enough back that they suffered little damage, and though it was just an unbridled wave to other onlookers, Cove knew it had been meticulously woven to appear disastrous without taking lives. She took a breath of relief, but the worry over what she had done came rushing right back.

She watched silently as the water calmed, pulling itself back out to sea as quickly as it came. She gripped the balcony rail until her knuckles turned white.

Mina gestured to the aftermath of the wave. "This is perfect. So many witnesses saw that this was just an act of nature. No one will ever know."

Cove did not answer. *What have I done? How am I supposed to pretend this never happened?*

"Cove," Mina said, taking her hand. "You can do this."

"I cannot perform—not after this. I cannot be the center of attention this evening."

"No one will suspect a thing," Mina reassured her. "Do not worry about your father or Andreas or me. We are in this together," she promised with a squeeze of her hand. Cove had nearly forgotten that Marinos would be in attendance, and she would be expected to impress all the wealthy contenders in the audience.

Cove walked mindlessly into the chambers from the balcony and sank to the ground near the vanity. She tugged her knees to her chest and Mina kneeled before her. "Don't worry, Cove," Mina said again.

Cove's brows scrunched in the middle as she saw Mina's bruised cheek, and she reached for the handheld mirror on the table above her and handed it to the princess.

"It's just a bruise," Mina shrugged. "It's okay."

"A bruise on the face of the princess, who is to be seen by hundreds tonight, after the suspicious death of her betrothed," Cove said. Mina swallowed then, admiring her cheek in the mirror, running her index finger over it softly. She did not wince.

"That is what makeup is for," Mina said warily, sighing and putting the mirror face down on the floor beside them. "People will be watching us both. We just need to have a plan."

Cove nodded and propped her chin on her knees as they discussed the story they would tell and the truths they would bend to fit their narrative.

"Do not stray from the script," Mina said. "You're going to put on the performance of your life."

A performance it would be.

CHAPTER 9
NO CELEBRATION
MINA

Mina stood at the dais beside her father's throne, the long train of her gown spilling down the steps in a puddle of pink silk. She avoided looking in Elias's direction, who stood tall and proper on the other side of the king. Instead, she peered into the crowd of people, blinking slowly with a pleasant smile as she had been taught to do by her mother many years ago. That was one of the lessons that had been ingrained into her mind.

No matter what has happened, you remain collected. Your people will be watching you. Do not give them reason to worry.

Sometimes, Mina despised her royal duties and wished she could be a commoner. An average woman of her age, with her entire life ahead of her. One where she was able to determine her own future, to choose her own husband, to be loved and not just sought after for the title she had never asked for.

Mina closed her eyes and breathed deeply, grabbing another glass of white wine from the female servant who had been assigned to her for the evening. Her eyes trailed Cove as she wove in and out of the people, no doubt trying to avoid her father, Marinos, who was entering through the ballroom doors now, sporting an untucked shirt, a bottle of rum, and a drunken smile. Mina avoided the urge to roll her eyes. *Late, as always.*

But not as late as Andreas.

"Where is the prince?" her father asked from his throne, looking to the clock on the wall behind the dessert table. "He was supposed to be here already." Mina kept her chin high. *Act naturally. What would I say on any other day?*

"Retrieve me when he arrives, will you?" she said, joining the crowd and pretending not to care. Into her ears flowed the gossip of the commoners, lords, and ladies, as they all discussed the massive wave that had intruded on the eastern shore earlier in the day.

"The wave gave no warning. A few more feet and it could have taken every home on that stretch of the east shore. Thankfully, there have been no reported casualties." Mina's servant followed her, collecting her train from the floor and ushering her to the dessert table toward Cove, only to be cut off by Celeste and Lord Yarris.

"Your Highness, where is Andreas? Is he not late?" Celeste said in an unusual, chirpy tone.

Mina pursed her lips. "He is. But he was also late for our stroll this morning, so I assume that is in his typical fashion?"

She looked at Yarris, and he laughed dryly. "He avoids a hurry when he can. I am sure he is on his way."

"Were you not with him today?" Mina asked. "After our morning stroll, he told me he would be headed back to the ship for a cool bath to prepare for the ball," she lied too easily.

"He did tell me yesterday that he planned to spend the day

at the ship, but I have been with this beautiful woman since last night," he said, gesturing to Celeste. "We spent our day in her chambers and on the balcony, overlooking the beauty of the kingdom." Mina raised her brows, and Celeste gave her a smug look, her green eyes flashing in satisfaction as she tucked a black curl behind her jeweled ear.

"Ah," Mina said. "Well, Lady Cove and I were at the west beach near the docks this afternoon and did not see him there. We must have just missed him."

"Must have," Yarris said. Celeste's eyes flicked to Mina, traveling from her hair, to her bodice, and then back to her very blushed cheek, and narrowed. Mina looked down, hiding her face and pretending to adjust her gown.

Mina fought the urge to touch her cheek and check the tenderness, but instead, she wished them well. "I suppose I shall go wait for my betrothed and prepare for our big announcement. Enjoy your evening, you two."

Celeste pursed her lips. "You too, Your Highness."

Mina walked toward Cove, careful to keep a steady pace, but her mind begged her to retreat faster.

Cove did her best to act natural, and perhaps she did a better job than Mina—but Mina knew Cove suffered from panic attacks, and while her friend seemed collected now, one was likely brewing behind her tired eyes.

"Elias is here," Mina said under her breath, reaching for a dessert from the table.

"You think I didn't notice? I have been trying not to stare all night," Cove muttered, keeping her eyes down.

Mina fanned herself, and if the room hadn't been so hot, she knew Cove would have given her a look of warning. At least it was believable that she could be growing faint from the heat.

"Do not speak to him, Cove. Yarris is going to be a problem."

"Is he suspicious of the prince's whereabouts?" Cove asked hurriedly.

"He is satisfied for now," Mina muttered, plopping a bitesize, powdered pastry into her mouth. Her eyes darted to the left and then she added quietly beneath the hand that covered her mouth as she chewed, "But Arlo is coming to speak to you, so fix your face."

CHAPTER 10
SAFETY
COVE

Cove stood in the midst of a crowded ballroom, each person's emotions knocking at the door of her mind. She was exhausted, and she felt like she could sleep for days, but the power within her was fueled by each swell of emotion, begging to be freed from the confines of her body. It was stirring inside her, twisting out of her control. Anger, jealousy, greed, rage—emotions of the people in darkness around her flooded in, and she was unable to build a dam that was sufficient against them. This was her curse, to feel so deeply with no knowledge on how to protect herself.

"Lady Cove," Arlo said with a dip of his head. She blinked, fidgeting with the bangles around her wrist.

Cove let her gaze sweep across the room as he kissed the back of her hand, and she caught a quick glimpse of Elias. A peace rushed through her, and she breathed deeply, savoring it. He stood beside King Sebastian, watching him intently, but for a moment, as if he felt Cove's attention, he turned his face to her. He was wearing a rather exquisite suit, one that made him almost unrecognizable as a servant. He nodded. *It is done.*

Then he watched where Lord Arlo's lips met the skin of her knuckles.

Jealousy came from somewhere in the room. *From him.* Cove shook the feeling and raised her chin, acknowledging the man before her, trying to focus on anything else. "Good evening, my lord."

Arlo smiled, and behind him, Marinos stood watching, holding up a bottle of rum as if making a toast.

Good choice, Marinos seemed to say. Cove gritted her teeth and felt like she was swaying with the intense pounding of her heart against her chest.

"What is it, my lady?" Cove blinked, remembering where she was.

"Oh, nothing, my lord. It is just that I am to perform this evening and I prefer smaller crowds. That is all."

"Oh, do not pretend for a second that singing makes you nervous. It is in your blood," Celeste said as she approached behind her. Cove turned in an instant. "You're a natural," she said.

"You sing?" Arlo asked, intrigued.

Cove nodded, her eyes falling to the new ring on Celeste's finger.

Arlo noted where her attention had gone and reached for her hand. "Dance with me before your debut, then?" He flashed his yellow teeth. Cove bit her cheek, accepting his offer only because her father was watching. As the harp played a beautiful melody, and their feet moved to the music, his hands found her waist. She already wanted to scrub herself clean of the murder she had committed, but now, also of his touch.

"The princess looks quite bored," he noted. Cove stole a glance at Mina standing back on the dais beside Elias and the king, who were conversing.

"Yes, well your prince is late, and she does not appreciate tardiness," Cove retorted, attempting to cover any chance of doubt with masked curiosity of Andreas's whereabouts. "Where is he, anyway?" she asked.

Dead. He is dead.

"How am I to know? Andreas is his own man. He has always appreciated his privacy, as do many princes and princesses. I am sure he will come." He sent her into a twirl and then pulled her tightly against his body. Her breaths were tight as she attempted to back away. Marinos was still watching, silently instructing her from the corner. Cove's attention darted around the room. Were the walls truly closing in on her?

Arlo worked for her attention, lowering his face so it was eye-level with hers for a moment. She was startled as he began speaking again. "When Andreas is married and calls the Dawn Islands home for a time, will you remain here?"

"Why wouldn't I?" Cove asked carefully. "This is home, and Mina is to be my queen." *And I made a promise to the king to stay by her side.*

"Even if a lord from another kingdom were to ask for your hand? Would you refuse land and an estate elsewhere?"

Cove coughed and twisted away from him in a twirl, hoping for time to mask her concern. He was going to ask for her hand. Right as she began to twirl back into him, hands— the hands that led her out of the water—found her waist and pulled her to safety. It was the part of the dance where everyone switched partners, and Cove breathed a sigh of relief as she watched Arlo seethe with a woman from Tabrana in his arms.

"His Majesty suggested I dance with you. I think I was staring a little too intently," Elias said.

"The king. . .he suggested we dance?" *A lady and a servant?*

"He is a matchmaker, what can I say?" Elias teased, and Cove would have smiled if the joke had not reminded her of the other match the king had recently made, and how one half of it was likely still floating face down in the water. "He is upset with the Edmarians right now, since their prince has not yet shown his face and is making a fool of him. Why should one of them get to dance with you, when I am the king's favored servant and have done him no wrong?" Cove had noticed that Elias was highly favored by the king. Sebastian seemed to care for Elias almost in the same way he did for Cove. Like a child, but not quite.

Cove swayed, wondering if he was as exhausted as she was after the expelling of his power this afternoon. The unusual dullness of his eyes and the paleness of his skin would confirm that forming a tidal wave that large had taken a toll on him.

He was the only servant on the floor, but he was almost unrecognizable in his fine suit. He noticed her attention to his clothing. "The king provided it for me. He wanted everyone to look their best this evening, for the announcement," he explained in a low voice, watching the room around them. Cove led him through the dance, noting every beat and every strum of the harp. He was honorable in the way he held her, but her skin burned beneath his touch.

"You look very handsome," she said, throat bobbing. He did not answer. A mixture of worry and jealousy surrounded the air around him, and his eyes were not on her, but on Arlo, who was trying and failing to make his way across the floor to them so he could pick up the conversation where he left off. Cove gently tapped her finger on Elias's shoulder, and his attention shot to her lips. Her eyes fell to the floor until the blood had stopped rushing to her cheeks.

"What exactly did you do with—"

"Don't worry about that, Cove. Do not even mention it." Cove stepped to the music, her feet tracing the four corners of a square. "Never again," he said sternly, but beneath his tired eyes, a soft smile followed.

"Thank you," she said, and as he pulled her against his body, she had to physically restrain herself from resting her cheek on his chest. She glanced at Arlo where he reluctantly danced circles with another woman. *Elias had saved her twice now.*

He did not even know her, yet here they were on the dance floor, accomplices in a crime that would get them both killed. Bearers of the Light in a kingdom of darkness—both hiding from the world, yet both had been exposed to each other. She was guilty of more than he, yet he had met her in that water and kept her from chains.

"I will keep you safe," he whispered into her hair. A chill ran down her neck and into her shoulder.

Why? She wanted to say. But she knew why. Because they were one and the same. Their souls had been stitched of the same brilliant, golden threads of Light.

A tear trailed down her face, and she felt the brush of his power against her cheek, echoing through that tiny drop of sadness and sweeping it away. "In the deepest waters, I will bring you to dry land. And when your love of the land has been exhausted, I will be your calming sea. You can trust me."

I do trust you.

He did not pull away from her to see if she offered a response. He allowed her to just *be*. He held her closely in a crowded room of people, tugging her to the outskirts of the dance floor, freeing her from the dread of having to finish the dance with Arlo. Arlo stood at the wine table with a grimace as he watched them from across the room. The same room where *her father* stood, closely monitoring.

She pulled away, suppressing that dangerous feeling that seemed to coax her in, begging for her to never leave Elias's side. Concern flooded his face, and she shook her head. She turned her back to Marinos, who was marching toward where they stood on the dance floor, his walk unsteady. She mouthed the words, *my father.*

Elias raised his chin in acknowledgment, and she turned to stand at his side as her father approached.

"Father," she said carefully. "This is Elias."

Marinos looked him up and down, as if trying to place his face. Cove prayed that he would not recognize him in his new attire as the servant from dinner. "That is a fine suit you've got, boy," Marinos said, his words slurring so badly that even Cove could hardly understand them. She translated for Elias, mouthing her father's words over his shoulder.

"Thank you, sir. I am Elias, a friend of Cove's." Elias was gentle and noble and reached out a hand to greet Marinos. As Marinos shook it, his eyes narrowed.

"Your hands are calloused." Cove dipped her head in embarrassment.

"His hands are calloused, Father, just like yours. Perhaps he has hobbies that warrant hard work." Elias was watching Marinos carefully, struggling to decipher his slurred speech.

"How much wealth do you have? Any land?" Marinos

asked. Cove looked to the ceiling, took a deep breath and tried to contain the shake in her hands as she exhaled. *He is drunk, and he is going to get angry. My time is running out.*

"No, sir. No land, and I bear no title, but—"

Marinos cut him off and looked to Cove. "You waste your time with a man that has no title?"

Cove made eye contact with the princess, pleading for salvation. Mina's eyes flashed in irritation as she realized Cove was with Elias, but without hesitation, Mina began making her way toward them. The crowd parted for her, and each man and woman turned to watch her move, as if they were waiting for the big announcement at any time.

"Marinos, how lovely it is that you could make it," she said gracefully. "Have you tried the wine? It is spectacular. We have brought it out special, just for this evening." *Soon, this celebration will turn to mourning.* Cove tapped her fingers nervously on her arm, and Elias covered them with his hand.

Marinos narrowed his eyes on Cove one last time and tapped his watch, then nodded toward Lord Arlo. A man with a title. His grin revealed crooked teeth, and he looked at the princess. "Show me the way, Your Highness." He waved a near empty bottle of rum in the air and nodded his farewell to Elias as the princess pointed him in the direction of the wine table. He did not even look at Cove. Breath rushed out of her lungs.

Once Marinos was out of sight, Mina hurried back to Cove. "You'll sing in twenty minutes," Mina said in a hushed voice. "Are you sure you can do this?" Mina played her part well. A princess, sure of herself, collected amid chaos. Cove was quite the opposite. Internally, she was panicking, thoughts jumping from Marinos, to Arlo, to Elias, to Prince Andreas, and now to her performance. She did not know if she could do it, but she had no choice.

Cove nodded, and Elias squeezed her hand. "Of course she can. I only wish I could hear it for myself."

Cove blushed as her body was racked with guilt. She was thankful he could not. Her feelings for him were quickly blossoming into something uncontrollable. She would not be able to think straight if she knew he was listening.

Cove faked a shy smile, but thoughts were flooding her mind, and she could barely keep her head above water. Mina turned to join her father once more, leaving the two of them alone, but not before she shot Cove a warning glare. *Do not get involved with him.*

Mina is right. I should not be feeling this way for a servant. I am to marry into wealth, and I should not be getting involved with other Embers. It is far too dangerous.

"Cove," Elias said, running a gentle hand down the flowing sleeve on her arm, drawing her attention back to reality. His hand paused at her elbow. They were only inches apart. "If this goes wrong, let us flee together." Cove's forehead creased as she peered up at him.

"Flee?" she whispered, checking her surroundings. Everyone around them was dancing gleefully and talking loudly over the music. She glanced across the ballroom at Mina, then remembered her promise to the king. Cove knew she could not leave, but she let the thought take her captive anyway. "Flee where?" she asked, barely mouthing the words.

Elias glanced around the room, and then uttered beneath his breath, leaning in close until his words were hot on her ear. "To Adullam."

Her heart thundered through her veins.

"Adullam still exists? Where the Lumes hid those many years ago?" she asked breathlessly. Cove's biological father had often read aloud from the Light Scrolls, and she remembered that word. Adullam was a cave found about thirty miles north of the Hollow Coves, where a thousand followers of Light had found refuge during the witch wars and raised an army. That was when the witches were destroying the Temples of Light, and the followers of the Father were not yet in-dwelt with his Light and power.

He nodded and kept his voice at a low whisper. "We could go. We could be a part of something more. We could find a community there, Cove. You would no longer be alone."

Do not get involved.

Yes, get involved.

The battle between instinct and heart unfolded in her mind.

"Mina needs me here, and I cannot flee from my father. He'll sell me out. I'll be hunted." Cove said. She looked at the large clock that ticked on the wall, reminding her that she was running out of time. That was Marinos's threat to her. Find a husband and keep money in Marinos's pockets, or he would reveal the truth that would get her killed.

"If this goes wrong," Elias said gently, "you'll be hunted anyway. And I think Mina would rather you be safe than dead at her side."

Cove's breath shook. All of this was far too much to handle. "I better be going," she said, watching Mina join the king back on the dais. "I have not practiced in a long while. I'll need to warm up."

Elias nodded with concern, and as she turned to leave, he caught her hand.

"What?" she said, shaking off his touch, as if she did not adore the feeling of his hand in hers.

"You look beautiful tonight, Cove." He paused, looking down to the hands that she had separated. "I just had to tell you. You'll be amazing up there." His words were soft and sure, and with each one, she felt the anxiety leaving her body. Her jaw set in uncertainty, and she chewed on her lip.

"Thank you, Elias." Though she deserved none of his kindness and had done nothing to earn it, she left her worries there with him once again as she slipped beyond the veil behind the throne.

CHAPTER 11
THE WATCHFUL EYE
CELESTE

Celeste watched curiously as Cove walked from her dance partner and slipped behind the thin, white veil. He watched after her longingly, and if he were anything like Yarris—who Celeste had succeeded in seducing—it was probably just a look of desire. The girl always wore beautiful—but strange—gowns, and her style was more reflective of the draping gowns of Tabrana than of Oriana, which seemed to fit loosely across the shoulders and chest and flow to the floor. This evening, Cove's gown was a muted mauve, which did little for her complexion. Her earrings matched the hues of the shiny pearl bangles at her wrists. The neckline of her dress was high and the cut was strangely simple. The thick fabric hid her curves, and her long sleeves caught the air and draped to the floor. As she walked, she had to lift the skirts, as if the dress had been made for someone a little taller.

Celeste's attention switched to Mina. The princess stood in pink silk, appearing to nervously await her betrothed's arrival.

Beside her, the king griped about his tardiness, and Mina grew paler by the second. Celeste fidgeted with her thumb ring.

"Is something the matter?" Yarris asked, his hand finding her waist as he pressed his body to her back. She leaned into him and continued watching the princess as his cheek nuzzled into her temple.

"Nothing, sweetheart. Her Highness is only growing weary of waiting, I presume." Celeste's arms were crossed, and she tapped a finger on the back of her elbow. "Is it not strange that the prince is not yet here, when this party is to celebrate him?"

Yarris pondered for a moment. "I suppose I should find him, ensure the alliance is still happening. I would not want anything to jeopardize what we have," he said. Celeste shifted onto her toes and turned to place a kiss on his cheek. *Me either.* She thought. *I need your land.* She twirled the engagement ring on her finger.

The man who had been dancing with Cove made his way toward the king, and Celeste noted a precarious look exchanged between him and the princess as he passed her by, taking up his position at the king's side as his *servant*. Celeste raised a brow and smirked. That was where she recognized him from. Cove had been conversing—*dancing*—with a servant. *Strange.*

As Yarris turned to exit and hunt down the prince, Celeste grabbed hold of his hand. "Allow me to accompany you," she said, following him out the doors of the ballroom and into the quiet night.

CHAPTER 12

THE CURE FOR GREED

ELIAS

Elias was generally skilled at keeping his power subdued—especially after exhausting himself hours before. Now, standing in service next to the king once more, he struggled to imagine peaceful waves caressing his skin as he watched Cove's father across the room. He was unsteady on his feet, and he did not know if it was from his rage or the fatigue. Elias thought he could convince Cove to part from the princess, at least for a time, to spare her own life, but Marinos was another story. If Cove would not flee him, she would die. And if she did flee him, she would still die, because Marinos would have her hunted. Elias gritted his teeth.

He knew where Cove would have a chance at life, but she would not go willingly. Not with Marinos breathing threats down her back. She was stuck here in Oriana, chained to his every demand. She existed to fill his pockets, and he would have her marry into wealth, even when it was sure to end in her demise, as long as he received his bride price.

Elias shifted his attention to Lord Arlo, who now stared

after Cove with his arms crossed. *What if there was a way for Marinos to get everything he wanted? A bride price and payments that never stopped coming because the marriage would not end with Cove's death? Would he allow her to walk free then? Was greed truly the only motivator here, or was there something Elias did not know? Was there something more Marinos sought?*

As Marinos stumbled toward Lord Arlo, Elias knew what he had to do. He saw that the king was well and hastily collected a tray from the wine table, then made his way to offer Marinos a deal before Arlo could beat him to it.

CHAPTER 13
THE PERFORMANCE
COVE

In the cottage by the sea as a young girl, Cove had often been woken by the early morning whispers of her mother's melody creeping through the walls of her room. Her mother would stand at the window, overlooking the pebbled beach that invited the foamy waves to rest upon the shore. Cove would roll out of bed, her hair a mess, and join her mother in the kitchen while they waited for the shape of her father's small boat to form on the horizon—while they waited to welcome him back home. It was a song that had stayed with her all these years—one of devotion and longing for someone just out of reach. It spoke of a certain type of indescribable bond between Embers that Cove wondered if she was starting to understand.

When sorrows roll across the sea
When your hands reach, but don't find me
A tether between souls, and a quiet plea
Will guide me home, back to thee

My land, my sea, my refuge in the storm
You are my calm, my calm, my calm

Cove's voice was pure melody, strong and sweet, as if she had never taken a hiatus. She watched Elias closely as she sang the words, leaving all her anxieties behind her. He did not have to hear the song to feel the truth it conveyed. The feelings she felt for him were the reason she had chosen this tune—a song of connection. She knew he felt it too: the way their gifts sang to one another and wished to merge. This was the bond she had not allowed herself to dream of. This was what she wanted.

He was completely still beside the empty throne as he watched the confessions roll from her tongue.

Do not get involved, her mind warned her heart. *You cannot be with him. You are to marry into wealth. Marinos will reveal you to the world if he catches you entertaining thoughts of a man with no title.*

But the pull between them was magnetic and impossible to ignore, as if it were fate—as if the Father of Lights had placed her here in this kingdom for exactly this. For Elias. For the rebellion. For his kingdom.

Everyone stared in awe of her voice but stood oblivious to the message she was sending to the man she was afraid she was falling for. She kept her eyes on Elias so she would not have to look at her father or at any of the men who might get the idea to ask for her hand as she stood on the stage before them.

Her mark seemed to burn at her chest as she called out to him, and the room started shrinking. Suddenly, she felt how exposed she was, and her worries began to return. There was nowhere to hide. The stage was an island, and she stood vulnerable as a sea of eyes stared at her. The only thing separating them from knowing the truth about her was a thin piece of fabric.

What if it glows right through my dress? She had checked it a dozen times before she left Mina's chambers, in every dark corner she could find. The fabric was thick enough. *Unless it were to somehow get wet. Then the mark might glow through.*

Cove was spiraling.

What if my secrets are uncovered? What if Arlo seeks me out after my performance?

What if, what if, what if.

She inhaled deeply, filling her lungs with a poor remedy for the fear that crippled her.

This is the last song to get through, and then I can crumble.

Elias's arms looked inviting, like she could fall apart in them and they would hold her together. His lips looked like they would keep her every secret. She winced, remembering the deal with her father. She should not be dreaming about the embrace of a poor man. It would not end well for her—or him. Death would meet their acquaintance.

She sang boldly, letting the words rattle down her own spine, letting them make room for more oxygen.

Hold it together.

My calm, my calm, my calm.

Celeste walked in the doors, Yarris behind her, his face blanche—as if he *knew.*

Do not look guilty, she reminded herself. *My calm, my calm, my calm.*

Her eyes found Elias. *You're okay,* he mouthed, but the wine in his hand was shaking as he noticed her unraveling.

He can tell. Everyone can tell I am hiding. They all know.

Prematurely, Cove let the last note fade into the massive

room, and she smiled at the audience, waving slowly as she disappeared too quickly beyond the veil.

Elias was there in a second. "Cove, breathe," he said. They were alone, and she was in his arms. All the *what ifs* seemed to dissipate.

My calm, my calm, my calm.

At the unnecessarily loud clicking of Mina's heels approaching, Cove pulled herself together as best she could without Elias's arms to stop each piece from falling. He quickly maneuvered himself toward the wall, where he held his tray of wine and cheese. His hands were steady now. Arlo was the first to burst through the veil, Mina close behind him.

"Absolutely marvelous, Lady Cove," he said, arms wide. "Your father told me you could sing, but he did not do your talents justice."

"You spoke to my father?" Cove asked. She was going to vomit. Too much was happening. *Too much.*

"Well, your father spoke to me. He was so drunk I could hardly understand him. Surely, he has passed out by now." *Unlikely,* she thought. He still had another bottle or two to go until the liquor stole his consciousness. *When would he come searching for her? Would his lips loosen in his drunkenness? Would he tell?*

"He is eager for you to marry," Arlo added.

Mina watched from the edge of the room, twisting her hands in front of her skirt. Cove bit her cheek until she tasted blood. She smelled the sweet aroma of florals wafting through the room with the sound of the harp, and she kept her gaze fixed on the golden bangle at her wrist, running her finger over the smooth metal. "Yes, well, I have many contenders, and I will not make the decision lightly," Cove said. *My bangle is missing a pearl.*

"Who am I up against?" He laughed. "Surely not the king's servant who had his hands all over you on the dance floor." *So, people had noticed.*

Through the veil, Cove noted that the king was still not on his throne. Then, he slipped into the small room, silver coins in his hand, and eyes on Arlo. Mina and Elias both hurried to his side to stabilize him in his feebleness. *He looks sicker every day.*

"It was under my command that Elias danced with Lady Cove. It was no dishonor. There is nothing romantic between the two of them." *Nothing romantic. There could not be.* "She looked uncomfortable with you, and I thought I would assist." Beside her father, Mina's jaw dropped. Elias's gaze found Cove's, and her cheeks heated thoroughly. *Has he lost his mind? What of his own daughter's comfort in her engagement to Andreas?*

"You'll have to excuse him, My Lord, he is not feeling well," Mina said quickly, tucking some hair behind her ear.

Cove blinked, still speechless, and slowly turned back to Arlo, the room seeming to spin around him. He, too, was taken aback by the king's comment, and Cove had a feeling that shock was only about to increase as Celeste and Yarris entered the small room.

They know. Elias shifted on his feet, turning his attention to Cove.

The king took Cove's shaking hand and dropped her payment of silver into it. He held onto her hand for a moment, narrowing his eyes on her as she trembled. "You sang beautifully, dear," he said. Cove forced a smile.

He continued speaking toward Arlo. "I am not out of my

mind as you may think. I am unhappy because your prince has not yet shown up to announce his engagement to my daughter. Why should you get to dance with her lady while she stands here alone?" He gestured to Mina on his left. "Where is Andreas? Where is his honor?"

Cove leaned against a pillar and braced for the news as Yarris stepped forward.

"Dead, Your Majesty. The prince is dead."

CHAPTER 14
STAKING CLAIM
CELESTE

"Dead? What do you mean Andreas is dead?" Arlo asked, moving toward Yarris.

"Drowned," Yarris choked.

"He can swim. This is a joke. You are playing me for a fool," Arlo spat. Anger did not suit him.

King Sebastian moved forward, yanking his arm from his daughter's grasp. Mina's eyebrows creased in confusion, but her reddened cheek told another story.

Celeste's sights fell to Cove's wrist, where a stack of bangles laid.

"Your Majesty. We found him—his body in the bath house. He was wounded. He must have slipped and hit his head."

"Unlikely. This was a murder!" Arlo yelled. Cove winced at the height of his voice, and Mina looked through the veil to ensure he had not drawn any attention. The crowd happily danced to the music, unaware.

"Before you come to any foolish conclusions that could

cost the islands this alliance, show me," the king said through gritted teeth.

Mina was quick to speak. "Father, you have not left the palace in months, and the bath house is quite the walk. There are so many steps."

"It is not that far," Celeste said matter-of-factly. "I have quite the view from my balcony." Mina's eyes shot up to hers, and Celeste gave her a sly smile. "We can avoid the steps if we take him to the east side of the palace and use the ramps." The king gave her a curt nod.

"Fetch the wheeled chair," he said to his servant. But his servant's eyes were on Cove, and he did not hear the command. Celeste watched them carefully.

"Elias!" The king nudged the servant's arm, gaining his attention. "The wheeled chair. Get it, now! And bring it to the corridor near the exit. Have the servants clear the route. I do not wish to be seen as crippled by my people."

Elias bowed his head and left in a hurry. Celeste watched the silent exchange between Mina and Cove and then turned to Yarris, rubbing her hand up his muscled arm in comfort. He cupped his hand over hers before leaving her side to be with Arlo. They whispered in the corner, low enough that she could not hear them.

"Mina, you'll come with us," the king said quietly. "Cove, can I trust you to keep my guests entertained until we return with a plan?" Cove nodded dreadfully. "This information does not leave this room. The islands need this alliance—and marriage is not the only way to get it. Though perhaps the youngest Edmarian Prince could be a match for Mina." Mina and Cove both went rigid, exchanging a glance. "But we have to be careful about how and what information is delivered to

King Idris, or he will call it off completely, and there will be marriage to neither of his sons." Celeste nodded her agreement, and Mina looked as if she may try to argue against her father's will.

Celeste would protect this alliance. There *would* be an alliance between the Dawn Islands and Edmaria, with or without Andreas. Because in order for Celeste to stake her claim on Edmarian land, she would have to marry an Edmarian lord. And to be granted the king's permission to marry Yarris, there had to be some sort of standing alliance. If Celeste wanted to preserve that alliance, she needed to make it known that Princess Mina was not involved, even if she had been. She would make sure it all fell into place.

"Let us hope this was not a murder," the king grumbled. Celeste only pursed her lips, rolling the small pearl between her fingers—the one she had found in the bath house beneath the water.

CHAPTER 15
FOR HER

ELIAS

As the king and the two Edmarian lords made their way toward the corridor, flanked by the princess and her lady, Elias's eyes only searched for Cove. They always did. To her, he felt some sort of connection that he had never experienced before, a draw that made it almost painful not to look her way. In all his years in this palace, he had walked the halls as a lone Ember. His own Light had been the only spark for him to see by. He knew of the rebellion and occasionally provided them with information, but he was not truly a part of it. He was separated from it by the walls of this palace. Day by day, as he watched this palace and its king slip further into shadow, Elias's hope of belonging was slipping away with it. The day things started to feel brighter was the day Cove had arrived.

There was a familiarity about her, as if they shared the same spirit—the same kind of soul. Souls that had been touched by the Light—souls that would be hunted. To see another Ember was to know them, and Elias knew Cove the moment he laid eyes on her. That was the moment everything changed. He stopped worrying about his own safety and started obsessing over hers.

He was overwhelmed by it—the purpose that sank deep into the marrow of his bones as he first took her in his sights. His life became a vow to her years before they ever spoke. She was a lady, and he, a servant. He promised himself he would stay away for her own benefit—until the night he'd watched Marinos threaten her in the gardens.

Elias should have seen it sooner. Her loneliness, the fear, the threat that was hanging over her head. That evening, the vow had become tangible—a vow he would fulfill even if it meant death. For her, he would be nothing less than the very breath in her lungs, keeping her alive.

He caught a glimpse of her through the crack of the ballroom doors. She would not be accompanying them to the bath house but would be extending her performance for the people of Oriana. She hated singing for an audience. If those nerves were not enough, she had *killed* today. Her icy blue eyes darted across the room, and her face was blanching. Her hands trembled at her sides as they grasped at the skirts of her gown. Elias swallowed his anger as he noticed her drunken father watching her closely from the edge of the stage. He was eyeing the pieces of silver she still clenched in her fist, as if she owed him every cent. Cove was spiraling, and Elias felt her power stirring like a tidal wave.

You're okay, he wanted to say. *You're okay.*

But the door shut before Cove glanced his way, and the king's lips started moving.

"You know the route. Take us," he commanded. Elias obeyed, allowing the king to seat himself comfortably before he began wheeling him across the smooth limestone of the palace corridors, all the way to the eastern gate. They took the ramp down to the beach, and Elias prayed that the scene was convincing. He prayed that Cove maintained her strength, and that he could make it back to her soon. He prayed that she would soon find the safety she had never known. He would be her refuge in the storm, as she had said through song only moments ago. The words had formed on her lips, and he had watched, carefully stitching the sentences together, imagining the beauty of her voice was like the call of the ocean—the only other song he knew.

She was like a song. Her gifts called to him, reaching out as the ocean often did, begging for his touch. The Light she held within her was a beacon in the dark. Elias wanted to understand her. He wanted to love her. And so, he would protect her. He had risked everything just for the chance.

The night was dark and misty, and Lord Yarris held a torch to light the way. Elias focused all his efforts on pushing the king's chair through the fluffy sand on the eastern shore. The bath house became visible through the shadows of the night, and the stars reflected on the waves that entered beneath the foundation to fill the pool. Elias steadied his breathing as they entered the humid air of the bath house. The king raised a hand, instructing Elias to halt. He rose from his chair and faced Elias and the others.

"Well, where is he? Light the torches!" the king demanded. Elias did not have to hear his tone of voice to guess that it was not rage but fear and uncertainty that filled the room. Yarris lit the torches on the wall, one by one, and the glow of the fire slowly illuminated the calm waters. Elias took a deep breath.

Cove is going to be okay. The scene is convincing. No one will know it was her.

Mina walked forward in curiosity, her eyes scanning the surface of the water. Elias watched her carefully, waiting for her to notice the prince was floating face down in the shallow waters right before her.

As she noticed, her mouth opened in a scream that sent the others staggering back. *Quite the performance. Why had I been worried about her again?*

As Mina tripped backward over the silk skirts of her gown, Celeste brought a torch forward, sweeping it across the edge of the water, illuminating the scene. Elias's plan had worked flawlessly.

With every passing second, he was growing more confident that this would work. He wanted no man to die and join eternal darkness, but when that man was to destroy a kingdom —to steal the Light from an innocent woman whom Elias had come to care for—he had no issues covering the murder. Andreas had to die because Cove had to live. Elias accepted that the moment he saw her exposed lightmark and the body floating before her in the water.

He had worked quickly. When he could no longer feel Cove's gifts singing to him, drawing him near, when she was safely tucked away—whether on the western shore as he had directed her or in Mina's chambers—the Light within him brought the sea forth in a great wave, causing the waters to rise in the bath house at unmatched speed.

The prince could have easily been wandering the kingdom or searching for a bath.

There were plenty of witnesses on the street to testify of the wave and how it had crashed against the eastern wall of the palace, the salty water rushing through the alleys, dozens of feet above sea level. It had to be believable—and so it was. Elias commanded the seas but only by the power of the Light within him.

Arlo crouched down to Andreas's battered body and slowly turned him over. His lips moved, but Elias could not make out the words in the dim light. Elias joined him near the ground, pretending to examine the body.

"His bones are broken," Arlo said.

"It must have been the wave," Mina noted, looking at Elias. Arlo narrowed his eyes. "The water level rises and falls with the sea. He could have been swept into the rush of water."

"I am so glad you were not here," the king said to his daughter as one of his unsteady hands reached for hers. She took and held it, watching Elias carefully.

"What was he doing in here, anyway?" Arlo asked, and by the way his lip quivered, Elias wondered if his voice was unsteady. Elias looked back to the king, but Mina spoke first.

"I told him on our morning stroll that I would be here, but my plans changed. Perhaps he came looking for me." *Yes, that made sense for the prince's character.*

"Nonsense. Andreas is a man of honor," Yarris spat. He was angry. Celeste stepped forward, gently caressing his back, but he shook her off. Her mouth fell into a frown.

Mina exchanged a look with her father, and Elias tried to keep up with the conversation. "This was an accident. I will hear nothing more of this being a murder," the king said. He wanted to protect the alliance. "Andreas came looking for my daughter in her most vulnerable state, and he happened to be in the wrong place at the wrong time. That wave destroyed the east markets and flooded a small village. You lost your prince. This is a time for community—not accusations."

Arlo and Yarris exchanged a glance, both men's faces reddening with anger. Mina rubbed her father's shoulders as they watched the two lords bend to collect the prince's body. They dragged him from the water, and Elias watched as Yarris's shoulders began to shake uncontrollably.

This was for the Kingdom.

CHAPTER 16
NEW RULES
MINA

"Mina!" Her father's voice called through the corridor as he approached her room. She was surprised that he had made the trek from the dining hall to her chambers, and she quickly rose from the vanity and walked out to greet him. Mina stopped in her tracks. He was being escorted by a guard she recognized from the north gate of the kingdom.

"Father," she said slowly, studying the brown-skinned man beside him. She looked back to her father. "What are you doing here? I—"

"Your servant came to tell me you were unwell. And Cove is unwell. I was alone for breakfast." Mina swallowed. It seemed she and Cove were both avoiding company.

"I am sorry Father, I—"

"No need to explain," he said with a wave of his hand as he propped himself against the door frame. "It has been a difficult week for you, I am sure." His guard stood at attention beside him, brown eyes looking right over Mina's head and into her chambers behind her. She had the urge to pull the door shut.

Mina's eyes flicked back to her father. She could not ignore his shortness of breath, or the way his arms trembled involuntarily at his sides. She blinked the image away. "Is this you apologizing for nearly forcing my hand in marriage?" she dared to ask in front of the unfamiliar guard. The guard did not flinch, but her father did.

"I will not apologize for seeking strength for my daughter's reign. And I will not apologize for making sure you are safe and that reign is long-lasting. An alliance with Edmaria may be uncertain right now, but I am still to ensure your safety." Her father's chestnut eyes mirrored her own, and she recognized a softness in them. He was trying to love her in the ways he knew how. "Mina." He gestured to the guard beside him. "This is Mateo. From now on, he is your personal guard."

Mina gawked at her father and turned to the man beside him for only a moment before shifting back to look the king in the eyes. "Guard? Since when am I to be paraded around like cattle? My every move to be watched? A woman needs her privacy, Father. I will not have this."

Her father took a deep breath. "I was naive to ever allow you free reign of the kingdom without protection, sweetheart. There is the possibility that a prince was murdered here on our island." His voice fell to a whisper at the word *murdered* and Mina wondered how many of his suspicions he had shared with this new guard. "Mateo will escort you wherever you need to go." Mina crossed her arms and looked back to the guard who still did not look at her.

"No, Father, I—"

He raised a hand. "We will have more to discuss later about

how we can continue this alliance with Edmaria. I expect you to be present at dinner."

Before she could argue further, her father's back was to her, and he crept back down the hall without the help of a cane, in fear his people would perceive his illness. Mina stood silently for a moment, watching after him with her jaw set. She stood as tall as possible, doing her best to look her new guard square in the face, but she only came up to his chin. She counted to three in her head as she glared, looking him up and down, and then, she turned to slam the door.

CHAPTER 17

THE SPOILED PRINCESS

MATEO

The kingdom's beloved princess was spoiled, just as he had predicted. *What princess wouldn't be?* Mateo's friends at the gate were quite intrigued to hear that he had been given a new assignment, to protect the heir to the throne with his life. The rumors were true. She was a woman of outspoken opinion, and she talked to the king with little respect, though, he had to admit, he could tell she cared for him by the way her eyes softened as she had noticed the king's rapid breaths.

It had not been officially announced to the kingdom yet that the princess behind this solid oak door would soon become queen—that the king was dying—but anyone with the slightest ability to make observations could tell that the king was unwell. Mateo guessed that this young princess would have much to learn in leading the islands. But, he could care less about whose reign he served under or the alliance with Edmaria, as long as he still had a job. He was only trying to provide for his family.

His three younger sisters, his mother, and his grandmother lived a dozen miles west on the island of Tabrana, and he went to visit them on his days off. But now that the princess was under his constant surveillance, visiting home might become a problem. It looked like he would be sending the coppers by boat in a money sack. At least this job had earned him a raise. He rubbed his tired eyes as he leaned against the limestone wall beside the princess's door.

He could hear her rustling around inside and wondered what she was doing besides pouting about her father's new rules. *What kind of princess walks around unguarded, anyway? A foolish one,* he thought. At least the king was finally gaining some sense on the subject.

At the height of the afternoon, the door opened and the princess locked eyes with him. Her cheeks were hot with anger, and her chocolate brown hair had been let down from the braids she had worn this morning. It fell to her waist now in textured waves.

He adjusted his posture, standing at attention.

"I have never seen a guard *lean* while on duty," she said with her chin held high, attempting to look down her button nose at him.

"My apologies, Your Highness," he said, standing straight as a board. *I have been working without a good night's rest all week,* he wanted to say. Hard work was something he was sure she had not experienced.

"Do you enjoy your job?" she asked beneath a raised brow.

"Yes, Your Highness," he lied. *I have a family to provide for, and this job came easily to a young man of my stature.* "I enjoy serving my kingdom," he added, hoping to convince her that he was worth keeping when she took the throne.

She raised a brow and spun to walk down the corridor.

He followed, and surprisingly, she did not fuss until the sound of his sword swiping against his belt as he walked drove her over the edge. "Can you make that incessant noise stop?" she said flatly as she stopped in her tracks. She spoke without turning to look at him. He closed his eyes and took a deep breath before unhooking the sheath from his hip.

She started walking again, and he trailed her, careful not to step on the train of her gown. The color reminded him of the wisteria his grandmother tended to on the trellis outside of their quaint home on Tabrana. The princess traveled to a corridor Mateo had not yet visited, and he wondered where they were going and how she typically spent her days. He could guess that her servants woke her up and brought her breakfast in bed, unless she had plans with the king. After that, she was probably catered to with a hot bath, and he doubted she ever had to do so much as dress herself. In the handful of times he had seen her before he had come into the palace, her hair was always styled in a way he could not imagine she had done herself. How many gowns did she have in her closet that she had not yet worn? He looked at her wrist. How many of those gold bracelets did she have stowed away in a drawer while his family scavenged for coppers to purchase food?

Last time he had visited home, he had found his eight-year-old sister fishing from the rocks behind their house. Mateo's mother would not admit it, but his income was not enough to keep them all fed. Unfortunately, fishing straight off of the shore was illegal without a permit, and he had snatched the rod from his sister and thrown it to the grass before anyone could see and hand them a fine they could not pay.

Out of nowhere, this job had been given to him upon his

return to the gate, and he supposed he should be thankful for the slight increase in pay. But the future he saw as the princess's guard was not one he had dreamt up for himself.

Princess Mina arrived at a door and raised her knuckles to the wood. Before she knocked, she paused, turning her face to speak over her shoulder. As the sunlight hit her cheek, Mateo could have sworn he saw a faint bruise. His eyes narrowed. "I am going to need some privacy," she said with an undertone of annoyance.

"I have to check the room before you can be left alone," he said, recalling the king's commands.

"Check the room?" she asked incredulously.

"Mina?" A woman called from inside. "Is that you?"

Mateo nodded. *I will be following all of the rules because I cannot lose this job.*

Mina looked between him and the door, growing visibly nervous. She chewed on her lip and rolled her eyes as she spoke into the door. "Yes, Cove. It's me," she set her jaw, "and my new personal guard, Mateo. He wants to come inside."

"Guard?" the woman named Cove asked from the other side of the door. Her voice sounded groggy, even though it was afternoon. "I do not wish to have any visitors," Cove added. Mina looked at Mateo, her lips in a flat line. Her hand raised in annoyance.

"It is just me," Mina said. "I'll make him wait outside."

Mateo stepped forward. *I am not losing this job.* "I am under the orders of King Sebastian, not you." *Not yet. Hopefully she could respect his loyalty.* "I will be going inside, at least to check for threats."

"Oh this is ridiculous. What threats?" she asked, crossing

her arms. He tilted his head, allowing his eyes to flick to the poorly covered bruise at her cheek. She turned her face. "I'll be back later, Cove. We need to talk."

CHAPTER 18
HOPEFUL HUMS
COVE

Talk of the prince's death began flooding the kingdom, and guilt had eaten its way through Cove's mask of calm. She had not seen Elias since the ball—had not seen much of anyone, really. As far as she knew, Mina had been pent up in her chambers until today, probably pretending to be ill, too. Now it seemed the princess had a guard trying to invade their privacy. Cove had been in bed all day and could not remove herself from the crime she had committed. There was no world where she could feel relief after murdering someone—whether he would have fallen a thousand Embers or not.

To know she had taken someone else's breath—after she had been given the breath of life. A monster was what she was.

She hummed, clinging to the calming words she had heard her mother sing years ago in that little stone house by the sea.

She was once like a shadow, now she glows like a moon.
It is his Light within her that carries her through.

She is not worthy, except by his Light.
Darkness cannot hold her, when he's in her sights.

CHAPTER 19
DREAMS AND SCHEMES
CELESTE

Celeste rolled over to face Yarris, who laid asleep in her bed. She wrapped herself in the satin sheet and made her way toward the balcony, nearly stepping on the wax seal that must've fallen to the floor. She placed it in the drawer next to a letter and turned back to admire the snoring lord in her bed. She came to the balcony railing, looked over the palace gardens, and watched as three servants made their way into the bath house where the prince had died four days prior. Rumors had spread, of course, and Celeste had heard nearly every one of them. But not one spoke the truth of what had happened.

Yarris stirred from his slumber, pulled his trousers on, and joined her on the balcony. He noted her attention on the bath house. "I will not accept that this was an accident, and His Majesty will not either. This was an act of war. From an Ember."

"You think an Ember killed your prince?" Celeste asked. She turned to face him, and he rubbed his sleepy eyes.

He took a deep breath. "I don't know. But I do not see King Idris accepting this as an accident, and I am trying to make sense of it all. When he finds out his favorite son is dead. . .his rage will consume him. He will seek vengeance." Celeste watched the sky as seagulls flew in from the west and landed atop the village homes just south of the bath house. "I will not return to him with this news without the murderer in tow. That wave was unnatural—even for this island. Was it not?"

"You think there is an Ember strong enough to shift the tides?" Celeste asked slowly.

He shrugged. "I have attended the trades, darling. I suspect there are Embers that could do far worse."

"Intriguing," she said. "How much gold would it take to purchase one of those?"

"Hard telling. Degare keeps increasing prices. But when we marry, as a wedding gift, I'll purchase whichever Ember you want."

"Oh, sweetheart. I have no interest in becoming a Despiri." The corner of her lip tugged upward, and his eyes flashed with curiosity. She looked back to the bath house.

"Speaking of marriage," she said, examining her nails as they tapped against stone, "when will we be leaving for Edmaria?"

His brow creased, and she turned to face him completely, leaning against the balcony rail on an elbow.

"I hope to marry. But I must first ask permission from my king. Andreas would have allowed it—but I answer solely to the king now. I cannot lose my honor." Celeste breathed tightly, and he took her hands into his. "I will find the murderer, and I will make sure our kingdoms maintain their alliance. The king has a second son, Merrick. Perhaps he and Mina can marry. Only then, can I marry you."

"I realize you would like to keep your honor, and I realize it would be frowned upon for you to marry a lady of a kingdom who is not allied with your own, but—"

"The Dawn Islands may very well be seen as our enemy, if I cannot prove to Idris that it was an Ember who killed Andreas. Arlo suspects it was your princess, and once he has an idea in his mind, he will not rest until the problem is solved. If it was the princess who killed him, I can assure you, there will be no alliance."

Celeste stiffened. "The princess is many things, but she is not a murderer."

"Tell that to Arlo. She just happened not to be in the bath house where she was supposed to be when Andreas arrived? It is quite suspicious if you ask me, considering she never wanted to marry him in the first place. Now, she is free? Seems convenient, is all I am saying." Yarris shrugged, and his mahogany hair blew slightly in the breeze.

"I know the princess. She is not an Ember," Celeste said tightly.

"I did not say she was. I only hope it was an Ember and not your precious princess, or I am afraid we will not be wed."

CHAPTER 20

NO CHOICE

MINA

"Princess, you are going to be late for dinner," Mateo called outside her chamber door. She rolled her eyes, hastily covering her cheek with more blush. She grabbed the chiffon wrap that matched her lilac gown, draped it across her shoulders, and opened the door.

"Why do you care if I am late for dinner?" she snapped before she saw him, once again leaning against the door frame with his powerful arms crossed.

"It's my first day on the job," he replied, pushing himself from the wall. His hair was a dark brown, much like her own. There was a slight tease in his voice, and Mina wondered what new angle he was taking. Was a playful approach one he was using to prove himself as less of a thorn in her side? "Can a man not try to impress his king?"

"With the punctuality of his daughter? As if he cares about such shallow things," she muttered, pulling the door shut behind her. "He cares more about ensuring he can marry me off to a dead man's brother."

Mateo said nothing, but she watched him closely, wondering just how much he knew about the alliance and the death of the Edmarian prince. What rumors had spread among the soldiers of her kingdom? "Come along, then, if you are to follow my every move," she said. She walked down the corridor, focusing on putting one bangled bare foot before the other, all the way to the dreadful meeting she was required to have with her father in the private dining hall. Mateo followed six close feet behind her.

He opened the door upon her arrival and scanned the room to be sure it was her father who awaited her. Celeste sat in Cove's usual seat, and Mina could not help but grimace. *What is she doing here?* Mateo watched and raised a curious brow as she silently seethed, before motioning her inside. Mina walked with confidence and refused to acknowledge Elias's presence as he pulled a chair out for her beside the lady her father had selected to serve as an unwanted counselor. Mina assumed that Celeste was here to take the king's side and to convince Mina to cooperate.

"Mina, I hope you have an appetite," her father said. "We are having your favorite." He motioned to the bright red lobster on the platter in the middle of the table. Mina did not bother to tell him that lobster was Cove's favorite, not hers.

She dipped her head and placed a napkin on her lap. "I can eat."

Celeste was silent beside her, but Mina could tell she and her father had just been speaking about something Mina did not yet know.

"Mina, you know this alliance is important to me," he said. *Here we go.* "I am dying," he said slowly, looking around at the few servants in the room, finally landing his gaze on Mateo.

Mateo curtly nodded, as if they had some unspoken agreement. Mina drew a shaky breath and looked to the side, blinking her tears away before they could fall. She could not ignore the fact any longer. She would soon be without a father. And she would soon have a husband, if all went according to her father's plans.

"You know how I feel about this alliance, Father." She angrily cracked open a lobster claw. "But I suppose the choice is yours. You *are* the king. You get to do what you see fit for your kingdom. That is all you have been doing here, no matter the expense of my happiness."

She felt Elias's eyes on her as he translated the words on her lips. She turned her face and propped a hand on her cheek as her father frowned.

"In the end, I suppose it is my decision," he said. "But you know I have your best interest at heart."

"The kingdom's best interest, Father." *At least he believed he did.* A ruler always had to put their kingdom first, even above their own flesh and blood.

"I believe my proposal will satisfy you. Of course, we will have to send the written proposal back to Edmaria with Lord Arlo and Lord Yarris. They will deliver the news of Andreas's passing to King Idris, but I believe Idris will offer his other son, Prince Merrick." Mina bit her lip.

"Either that, or he will require reimbursement for the supplies of the Black Temple our kingdom can not afford," she said. The king looked down at his plate. *Precisely.* "It seems we do not have much of a choice, then, but to keep the offer of my hand open to Edmaria. Am I correct, Father?"

He nodded shamefully. "You will help me write the proposal. We will ensure you are pleased with it."

Mina worked her jaw and turned to Celeste, whom she could tell was itching to offer her input.

"I believe it is a wonderful idea, Your Highness," Celeste said. She spun the engagement ring on her hand. "We can still benefit from the strength of their armies, and such an alliance will provide safety for your islands. For your kingdom. Continuing with an alliance will ensure they do not turn on us. This is the best move."

As Mina watched her father prepare to shake hands with death, she knew it was time for her to start acting as a queen. To start putting the good of her kingdom first. For once, Mina knew Celeste was right. She bit her cheek and rose from the table without taking a single bite of the lobster. "Fetch me when you are ready to form the written proposal. I will be there." She left the dining hall for her chambers, listening to the unceasing *click click click* of Mateo's boots behind her.

CHAPTER 21
PROVE IT
COVE

Cove hummed mindfully in the privacy of her chambers, trying to recall the many songs her mother had left her with, until there was a knock at her door. She silenced her melody and pulled the covers over her head, groaning. *Is Mina back with her guard again?* Cove did not want to see her. She did not want to talk about anything that had happened. She wanted only to forget.

"My Lady," a servant said as she cracked the door.

"I do not have servants," Cove called out, watching the door carefully. "So, what are you doing here?" she asked, strange irritation coating her tongue. Cove kept the covers pulled up to her neck.

"I—I know you have always requested no servants. I am just delivering a message."

Cove rolled her eyes. "From whom? My father? What does he want this time?" *To tell me my time is running out? To increase my dues, yet again? To inquire of the state of my hand?*

"No, My Lady." The servant stepped into her chambers

sheepishly, looking down at her apron. Cove recognized her as the one who had tended to Mina on the night of the ball. "I am only to tell you that there is a face that searches for you."

"What?" The servant shot Cove a knowing smile, winked, and went on her way.

A face that searches for me?

"Elias," Cove said aloud as she tossed the covers aside and sat up in bed. *Has it been four days already?*

—

On her way to the only good in the kingdom, Cove could not help but feel an eagerness for the day that she had not felt in a long while. Her hands could not stop turning in the skirts of her linen dress as she remembered him. She had laid awake the last few nights with thoughts of Andreas's breathless body holding her captive. Today, she was choosing to focus on the gift before her. She was not alone. Not today.

Sure enough, just outside of the north gate, she found a face in the bark of a thick palm tree, just as Elias had described. She lifted a finger to trace it, the bark rough against her skin.

"I think it saw you first," he said, coming around the trunk with a dimpled grin and curls a mess atop his head. Cove shook a laugh, unable to fully remain in the darkness in his presence. He nudged her. "Where have you been?" Her eyes dropped, and he did not hesitate as he tilted her chin up with his finger. He glanced around to be sure they were concealed in the privacy of the trees.

"I have not been out much," she said quietly, trying to ignore the burning sensation that seemed to flow from his touch and down her neck. *You are not falling for him. Do not get involved. Marry into wealth, or your father will expose you.*

"Well, that is about to change," he said lightly. "I have a big day planned for us."

"You have a day *planned* for us?" His grin spread wider, and he took her hand, pulling her toward the markets and into a sea of people.

She rarely ventured to the north side of the kingdom and had little worry of anyone recognizing her here, but she kept her head down until they were well beyond the palace gate. She had chosen a reserved linen dress that would hide her identity as a lady-in-waiting. With Elias, she just wanted to be herself. Free, and without worry of what her father might reveal about her if he found she was entertaining a servant.

Elias said nothing of Andreas or of the many rumors that had begun spreading across the islands. She was sure those same rumors were on their way across the seas, slipping from the tongues of sailors, and Cove figured the two Edmarian Lords would be leaving soon to deliver the grave news to their king personally before he caught wind of it elsewhere.

Elias's hand was warm in hers as he led her up the cobblestone path and to the eastern shore, where the markets lined the docks. Three dozen stands and carts sat at the edge of the docks, leaving the smell of fish hanging in the air. She knew her father sometimes still sold to these vendors when he would dock in Oriana from a day out fishing, and the thought of him walking these streets somewhere close by made her skin crawl.

A young female vendor—likely a fisherman's daughter— yelled, holding up a fleshy pink fish as they passed by. "Hungry for some salmon?" Cove shook her head kindly, and Elias watched her as if in question.

Cove realized he could not hear the chaos of the market, the shouting of the vendors' pleas to purchase from them, or the crashing of the sea waves against the shoreline.

"You're not hungry, are you?" she asked loudly above the noise, before it registered that she could have just mouthed the words. He raised his chin in realization and waved at the young girl, politely declining the salmon. She must have also found Elias's smile impossible to return, because it reflected upon her face as she waved him on.

"We have plans for lunch, or I would allow you to try all of the fish in the market," he said.

"On a servant's salary?" she teased.

"Hey, the king pays me well enough, and I am frugal with my spending," he said with a grin. His features were soft but brightened with every smile. Freckles sprinkled his nose, and he ran his fingers through his hair that glistened in the sun.

The islanders were hanging banners and setting up more carts than Cove assumed was normal as most of the kingdom prepared for The Darkening, which was to happen in just under six weeks. Cove always dreaded the darkest week of the year, when the moons disappeared and the sun seemed to hide behind a thick layer of fog—when the witches were most powerful, and Shades bowed down in worship. She wondered what the celebration in the palace would look like if the alliance with Edmaria came to pass. If everything went according to the king's plans, the islanders would have a Black Temple to worship in by this time next year. Cove tried to keep her eyes from wandering as she and Elias traveled through the midst of the people who would celebrate her and Elias's deaths if they knew the two of them bore the Light.

They walked through a narrow alley between houses and

ascended up a small hill. When the path grew narrower, he let go of her hand and ushered her up the path with a hand on the small of her back. His touch was gentle, and the Light within her called to the Light in him.

What is this? she wanted to ask him. *Do you feel it too?*

The alley opened to the eastern docks, where her father's sailboat sat *vacant.*

She turned to face him in the lonely alley. "Elias," she said warily.

"Yes?" he asked with the tilt of his head, ushering her forward. She planted her feet.

"Where are we going? I thought we were going north to your parent's home."

"It is best to sail to their home. It is located on the isle. Your father was kind enough to let me borrow his sailboat." His words slowed on the word *kind,* and Cove's body went rigid.

"My father is not kind of his own accord." *No, never.* "What have you done, Elias?"

Elias took her shoulders into his hands and looked into her eyes. It was as if she was peering straight into a storm. One that would uproot everything in its path before it ever brought the calm. He looked at her with a subtle fear, as if the words he was about to say haunted his every thought. "I cannot get it out of my head—the way he treated you in the garden. I cannot stop wishing I could take you far from his reach, where he will never lay another hand on you." Cove shook her head slowly as his words threaded together. "I cannot think straight, knowing that he rules over you as he does. That he is to dictate who you marry—that he demands a marriage that will lead to your death."

"There is nothing you can do, Elias, I—"

"It is already done. The deal has been made."

"What deal?" she said through gritted teeth. There was nothing Elias could do that would free her from her father's chains.

"We cannot stay here forever, Cove. Neither of us are content in waiting for a change." He was avoiding the topic at hand, but he was right. Cove wanted to do something about the darkness in Arresia. She did not want to cower and hide on this island any longer—like Elias, she did not want to sit and trust that Mina was able to undo everything the king had set into motion. Cove did not want to dream any longer. She wanted to take a stand against the shadows—to fight for the Light. But she could not get mixed up with this man—this kind, gentle servant. *What am I doing? What has he done that he believes will free me of Marinos's threats for good?*

Elias spoke again. "I spoke with your father briefly at the ball, and I met with him yesterday. He agreed to let me have your hand," he paused, watching her carefully. She backed away from his pleading eyes, and he stopped himself from catching her arm. *My hand?* "But that is not what this is about," he said gently. "I will only take it if you accept."

She wanted to say, *What is in it for you?* But instead, she asked, "What is in it for him?" He flinched as he interpreted her words. She heard nothing over the pounding of her heart in her ears. "Elias, what have you agreed to on behalf of my freedom?" She stepped forward. *Why would he make a deal with her father? Why would he do anything for her?*

Thump. Thump. Thump. Thump.

"It is money he demands, and *that* I can provide. I've already given him a downpayment."

Cove gawked. "You did not give my father any of the money you've worked so hard to save."

Elias's face softened in confirmation that he had done just that.

"What? Elias!" She spun in a slow circle. "So you've given him a downpayment. What else does he require of you? You cannot possibly pay him what he is asking for my hand."

He inhaled. "I am to work for him for seven years, and you go free. Then, I may join you in Adullam."

"No," Cove said immediately. "I will not allow it. You cannot fix another mess of mine. I do not know why you try, and I will not accept." Heat rushed through every inch of her body, and she was beginning to feel faint.

Elias took her hand, and her heart rate began to slow.

"You do not have to marry me. But please. Let me do this for you. I am to begin working for your father next week." Her brows creased. He truly had already made the deal for her.

"What of your position at the palace? You'd leave?" *Not for her. Nothing for her.*

"I am free to leave whenever I please. The position opened for me as a favor to my mother, and something tells me the king will approve of our union."

"Maybe if he believes it will keep me here for Mina, but that is not your plan," she said cautiously.

"Sadly, Cove, I believe the king only has a few months left, at best. And of course we cannot share the details of this arrangement with him or he would never approve. We can wait until after his death for you to leave, if it is safe to wait that long. You'll have that time with Mina and then you can go."

Cove changed the subject. "You'd stay here to work for my freedom while I flee to Adullam? Why?"

"I saw the way your eyes lit up when I told you there were more Embers—a rebellion. I know you are lonely here. I have seen glimpses of the joy your father has otherwise stolen from you. You do not deserve to live in fear. You do not deserve to have your entire life mapped out for you. If it is money he is after, I'll give it to him." He stepped one step closer. "Let me do this for you."

"You have done enough," she said in confusion. "More than I could ever repay."

He shook his head. "This is not about that. You owe me nothing."

"Then what is it about?" Cove asked. "Why would you do this?"

"You know why I am doing this."

Cove did know, and there was no denying it. Their very souls reached across the space between, longing to be united. It was one of the most tangible things she had ever known. She put a hand on her forehead and spun in a slow circle, sucking in air.

"There is nothing between us. Nothing," she said. There could not be. Cove could not let him get involved in the shadows that clawed at her back no matter how far she tried to run. She had done nothing to deserve his help, and he had done everything to warrant someone better—anyone better—than her. He would always give, and all she had done for him was *take*.

"Prove it," he said. Cove's eyes darted to the longing in his. He stepped forward. "Prove that there is nothing between us." He watched her carefully but made no move to close the remaining distance between them.

"Prove that the power beneath your skin does not sing

when I am near, that you do not feel the gravity collapsing in our midst." *Stop,* she wanted to say, but instead, she inhaled a shaky breath. He looked at her, eyes pleading. "Prove to me that you do not feel it too."

She could not prove anything. Could not prove anything other than the fact that she wanted his arms to be the arms that sheltered her from any storm, wanted his voice to be the one she heard every morning, wanted his calloused hands to lead her out of the water—always. She could not prove anything other than a love she had never felt before.

Elias closed his eyes and breathed in through the faintest hint of a dimpled smile.

"That's what I thought. That is why I am doing this for you." Cove swallowed the knot in her throat, focusing with all her might not to go to him. *Could she allow him to do this? Could it be that Marinos would truly allow her to walk free, into a marriage that would not get her killed?*

She looked between him and the sailboat from where they lingered in the alley. She began to shake her head, and as she turned to head back to the palace, to forget all that he had told her, to forget him and his selflessness—something stopped her from putting any more distance between them. She expected to find his hand on her arm, but he stood there, letting her choose. She was drowning in a sea of ambivalence.

I cannot let him do this, she thought.

Yes, you can.

Her feet remained planted as she watched him, trying to keep her head above the water. His eyes were gentle and inviting, and as he gazed back at her, noting the slight change of emotion behind her eyes, his hand extended slowly to her.

"What of Mina?" *Am I truly considering breaking my*

promise to the King of the Dawn Islands? Would I actually leave my best friend all alone when she needs me? Can I choose Elias and the freedom he is offering me over the princess I have vowed to serve? "I am her lady. I cannot just leave."

"I am not asking you to leave without a goodbye," Elias said gently. "But if she is truly your friend, if she cares for you as you say, she will allow you to go where you can be safe."

What he was saying was true. If Mina truly loved her, she would let her go. But for the first time in the years she had known the princess, Cove questioned the depth of Mina's love for her. Was it a love beneficial or a love sacrificial? If Cove were to approach Mina with this information—with this plan to leave—would Mina see it as abandonment or as the proper means to keep Cove safe? Strangely, Cove was afraid of the answer. She had once been confident in Mina's hopes for this kingdom. But the words Elias had spoken in the garden were coming back to haunt her now.

When things get bad—and they will with this alliance—she will have to choose a side. All or nothing. She cannot remain in the shadows between.

Could Mina be trusted, when it really came down to Cove or the prospering of the islands that she was soon to reign over? How could they stop the alliance, if not even the death of the prince had done so? It was time for Mina to choose a side, and Cove was worried that side would not be hers.

There was only one person in the whole world that she knew would always be on her side. He was already standing between her and the darkness, shielding her, trying to protect her from Marinos in any way he could offer. He did not just speak empty words and offer only hopes and dreams, he carried her burdens and made a way.

"You are too good for me," she said slowly, and Elias was about to stop her, to refute that statement, but she held up a hand. "You are not working for seven years simply for my freedom."

"I—" Elias started, and she cut him off.

"But if this is the only way that we can be together, I will allow you to work seven years for my hand—for our marriage. For us."

A grin spread across his face, and this time, he closed the distance between them. His hands found her shoulders, he peered into her eyes, then wrapped her in a hug that took hold of every broken piece of her.

CHAPTER 22
TOGETHER THEY GO
COVE

Cove homed in on the clicking of his boots as they walked across the docks. Marinos could never discover that Elias was gifted, or they would both be doomed. Cove would not let that happen. Why had her father agreed to such a deal in the first place? Had it always truly been about the money, or was there some hidden factor Cove was not aware of in this deal? How much money could Elias possibly earn her father through labor, that would make it worth it to Marinos to give up her chances of marrying a wealthy lord? Would it be better for the two of them to run now and be hunted by the mercenaries Marinos would send after them to find Cove? Would he sell her directly into the trades, or would his punishment be more creative? Marinos's threats would haunt whichever path she chose. They might as well choose the path in which her father would be pleased.

The clicking of Elias's boots stopped, and Cove looked up. Elias was holding onto the edge of the boat, offering her a hand. The ocean breeze was strong, and if his shirt weren't tucked into his trousers, the wind would have exposed his lightmark by now. Cove had spent two years on this boat, and this was the first time since Marinos pulled her from the water that she was thankful to board.

"Are we really doing this?" Cove asked as he pulled her onto the boat, and she imagined what his mark looked like in its completeness.

"What? Sailing?" he asked. She playfully glared at him.

"Getting married," she said. What would Mina say when she found out she was planning to wed a servant boy—that she would soon be leaving for Adullam in the coming months? How much truth would she share with the princess? To leave her position at the palace. . .to leave Mina, would be hard. Her only friend—her sister. But somehow, to leave Elias for seven years—this man she had only known for a week—would be a dozen times more difficult. Cove's face was wary, but Elias offered her a smile beneath raised brows.

"Say the words and you can go back to your life in hiding," he shrugged as he cast off the lines.

She shook her head, watching him carefully. "I have one condition, and only then will I marry you."

He paused, looking up from the ropes to meet her eyes. "I don't care much for conditions."

"Even after the king's death, I want to stay with you on the islands or on the boat—wherever you are. You work for my father, but I stay with you," she said. She would not leave him alone with Marinos.

"No, Cove," Elias said. "I want you to be safe. You'll find refuge in Adullam, and I'll join you later when my work is done." She shook her head.

"I find refuge with you," she said sternly. "We should not be apart."

He was silent for a minute and stared at the ropes in his hands. "Okay," he finally agreed.

"Okay?"

He shrugged. "I was kind of hoping you'd say that, because I cannot bear the thought of being without you for one more day, let alone seven years."

Together, then. She smiled. They were really doing this.

—

After about a half hour of staring at each other across the boat between the sails, when the islanders at the market were small, like tiny pearls in the sun, Elias's lips began moving. Cove struggled to hear him against the rippling of the wind through the sails, and she thought that maybe it would be beneficial for her to learn the art of lip reading.

"What?" she yelled, though she did not know why she bothered.

He grinned at the sea below and motioned for her to come to him. She rose shyly and walked across the deck, catching her balance on the shrouds against the rocking of the boat. He held a hand out toward her, and when she took it, he guided her to look out over the railing. His body became warm against her back, and he pointed to the dolphins that swam beside them, weaving through the waves. Elias waved a hand over the waters, sending a current sweeping through the sea, coaxing more dolphins and fish to join the group. It had been years since she had seen dolphins this closely, and she could not help the grin that bloomed on her face.

The sun was hot against her skin, and her light blond locks whipped in the ocean air. She turned her face to him, and he was already looking at her, as if his eyes could not be torn from her.

"Your eyes match the sea," he said, brushing the back of his knuckles against her cheek. She leaned into his touch, soaking up every second. He allowed her room between his body and the rail to twist toward him, and when she was facing him completely, she hesitantly placed her hands on either side of his face.

What have I done to deserve his attention? His care?

As if he saw the doubt written in her eyes, his right hand found hers at his cheek and his other wrapped fully around her waist, pulling her into him. His face drew nearer, and his lips hovered only an inch from hers.

"Why?" she asked breathlessly. "Why me?"

Elias was quiet for a moment, and when her eyes wandered down to his lips, he spoke again. "Because from the first day I saw you—on your first day at the palace—I could see the Light within you. You looked so scared there standing in your father's shadow. Your hands were shaking, but your eyes. . .there was a spark behind them that I recognized right away. I never dreamt of finding that Light in another person. I never dreamt I would ever even get the chance to speak to you. But when I finally did. . .It was always you, Cove. Because even in darkness, you are radiant."

Cove said nothing, only stood frozen as his eyes moved to her lips, awaiting her response.

"I want to kiss you," he said, brushing wisps of hair from her face. Her breath caught in her throat. "But not until we are wed. Until then, I will only allow myself longing gazes and the innocent touch of your hands." His words blended with the rushing waves, and she yearned for him to give into that temptation, to kiss her freely and sweetly as they floated in the midst of the Sea of Dawn, but he was a man of honor, and she would not take that from him. His arm tightened around her waist, and he swept her around and set her down.

She peered out at the northern isle in the distance, where small villages were beginning to take form. "My parent's house is on the eastern side. My mother makes a delicious lobster cobbler. . .I am counting on her making that for lunch."

"Oh? Does she even know we are coming?" *Lobster is my favorite.*

"No, I did not want to ruin the surprise. But I think I've mentioned you on just about every trip I've made home." Cove blushed as she watched the isle grow in the distance. He had noticed her all those years ago, when she had first come to the palace. He had been within arms reach all this time—watching her, wishing for her—when she had not even committed his name to memory. She had only ever known him as the king's servant.

"There is a dock there on the eastern shore," Elias pointed out. "Would you do the honors?" He gestured to the waves below. She raised her brows at him. "Go on," he said, tilting his head. His curls caught the wind, swirling at his temples.

She directed her attention toward the waters below, coaxing and begging them to carry the boat north. But with the brush of her power, the waves grew rougher, and the boat started rocking. Elias caught her waist, keeping her upright as she became unsteady.

"I am sorry," she said. "I tend to breed chaos when I use my gifts." It was true. The amount of control Elias had compared to her was incredible. The way his hands guided gentle waves, the way they could bring a tidal wave, yet also meticulously separate one droplet of water to hover at the rim of a glass.

She remembered the way her poor excuse for a water dove had crashed into the pool, before she had ushered Andreas into eternal darkness. "There was no tactic to the way I killed the prince," she said with her eyes cast down. She remembered the way the water kept rising and falling long after he was dead, battering his body against the pillars. She had no control. "I lost my hold on the water. I was lucky enough to be able to move Mina out of the way first, or it could have ended badly for her."

Elias's hand caressed her arm. "You were panicking. Gifts are driven by emotion. Try to home in on one, and use it to keep a hold on the power you release."

She laughed. She had planned on wrecking not only one ship, but an entire fleet of them. Such destruction took little control.

"What?" he asked.

"It is just that emotion is a tricky one for me. I would not really call it a *gift,* as it is more of a curse. . .but I can feel the emotions of people around me. That makes it quite difficult to focus on only one as you are asking of me."

Elias paused. "You can. . .feel my emotions?" His brows met at the bridge of his nose.

She nodded. "And I can sway them, too." His eyes grew wide. "But I haven't. . .swayed them." She hoped his proposal had been genuine. "Like with water manipulation, I am terrible with control, and I prefer not to dabble in that anyway. It is far too dangerous, especially with my inexperience. I would risk exposing myself every time I tried. Though, if I knew how to sway Andreas or Sebastian away from the alliance, or at least away from harming Embers, I would."

His eyes widened in. . .*awe*? "I have never heard of such a gift from the Father of Lights, Cove. The things you could do for the kingdom. . ."

She shook her head, stopping him from continuing. "It is because of this gift that I am troubled with unrelenting anxiety. I prefer not to feel other people's emotions stronger than I must." This was a gift she did not wish to touch.

"That is where your anxieties stem from?"

Cove shrugged. "I simply feel everything all around me, all at once. All the time." Elias's brows furrowed. "But not with you," she added. "With you," she paused, "there is a peace rooted deep within you, Elias. You are like a calm in the storm."

With a twinkle in his eye, he said, "For you, Cove, that is what I always hope to be."

———

With Elias's help, Cove was able to slowly direct the boat to the docks near his parent's home. He assisted her from time to time and helped her to focus on the peace he had within him. It was the most control she had managed over her power since she had been gifted, and it gave her a feeling of confidence.

"Soon, your tactics will be flawless," he said. He took her around the waist and lifted her down from the boat, onto the wooden docks of the northern isle. "You are incredible. I cannot wait to make you my wife."

Cove blushed, and he led her through the streets toward his parent's home, where her future in-laws awaited them. Her sandals smacked the ground as they neared a small home built of light gray stones, the bright afternoon sun beating onto the thatched roof.

Cove tugged on the sleeve of his tunic. His eyes wandered to her mouth. "Can I ask you something?"

"Anything." His eyes remained on her lips.

She swallowed. "You'll be working for my father. Doing what?"

He cracked a smile. "Your father believes me to be a master fisherman. I have proven my skills to him, and he is confident the two of us will profit more money in seven years than he could from a bride price of a wealthy Edmarian Lord. He is quite motivated by his greed." She was well acquainted with Marinos's greed, but could seven years worth of fish truly profit him the amount of gold he searched for?

She remembered the way Elias had coaxed the fish to the surface of the waters and realized he could easily coax them into a net without Marinos being aware of the Light within him. Perhaps Elias could profit him the coin he longed for. Cove was thankful Marinos was not well-versed in the specifics of the power that accompanied her lightmark or there was a chance she would still be on that boat with him, alone in the middle of the sea.

"Seven years is a long time to spend with him, Elias." The two years Cove had spent on his boat before she had moved to the palace had been enough.

"Seven years will feel but a few days for you, Cove. I would work for your hand until there were no more fish left in the sea."

Cove looked down to her hands, which fidgeted in front of her. Her mind circled around Marinos and Ahlia—around that night in the sea those many years ago, when Cove had welcomed the Light into her soul. Around the secret she had never told anyone. It was a story she had never wanted to speak out loud. She did not wish to reopen wounds and stir up the grief she had fought so hard to suppress. Not even Mina knew of her life before—that she did not share Marinos's blood.

But Elias wanted to spend his life with her, and he deserved to know everything.

"If you are certain Elias, then there is only one more thing you must know before we marry."

—

As they walked the isle village through little cottage homes, Cove reveled in the relief she had found after allowing the truth to set her free. Finally, there was someone who knew every piece of her. Someone to share in her burdens, her grief. Cove would do the same for him. Elias could be trusted; she felt it at her core. It was a deeper trust than she even had with Mina, and though that made her slightly nervous, she was ready for a lifetime with him.

At his parent's limestone cottage, it was Elias's mother who opened the door with a look of relief, embracing her son in a tight hug the moment she set eyes on him. "Elias, I have been so worried," she said, and the emotions that bled from her pores were those of complete anguish and desperation. This was not mere happiness to see her child after some time spent apart. Something was terribly wrong. Cove tried to control her breaths.

"Mother, what is wrong?" Her hair was the same golden shade as Elias's—and it fell in long spirals that were tied back with a strip of white linen. She did not answer Elias's question, but instead, her attention turned to Cove. She blinked rapidly, as if clearing her vision.

"Mother, this is Cove, who I have told you about from the palace. She has agreed to be my wife." His mother stared at Cove for a long moment and looked between the two of them again before looking beyond them into the streets, as if she were checking to make sure they were not followed.

"Come in. Quickly," she said, ushering them over the threshold. Cove stepped forward into the tiny home, noting the smell of vanilla bean and citrus. The curtains were pulled, but in the sunlight that streamed from the door, she saw the tiny scroll that Elias touched as he walked through the door frame. He brought his fingers to his lips and kissed them and then closed the door swiftly behind him, leaving them to see only by the soft light of the sun that bled through the curtains.

"Cove, this is my mother, Keila." Keila smiled at Cove, and Elias's eyes narrowed on her trembling hand as it took Cove's in greeting.

"I–I feel like I know you already," Keila said kindly, but her words came out unsteady, as if her mind was elsewhere. "Elias has told us so much about you," she added as she peered past Cove through the sheer curtains. "Marriage, you say?" Keila asked, eyes flicking to Elias, as if she were just now processing what he had told her at the door. She blinked, and Elias stepped forward, placing his hands on her arms, stilling the unknown fear that rippled through them.

"Mother, is something wrong? Where is Father?" Elias asked gently. His dark brows settled closely atop his eyes as he glanced around the cottage.

Just as Keila opened her mouth, a man, who Cove assumed was Elias's father, came through the door. "This should be locked, Kei. I—" the man looked up at Elias, as if he had seen a ghost. "Son—" his father's words were cut off by a fit of sobs.

"How bad, Hansel?" Keila asked as she rushed over to him. Hansel shook his head. "The safe house had already been raided when I arrived. They took them all." Cove's chest tightened, trying to keep his desperation from reaching down and staking its claim inside her.

Elias's eyes were locked on his father's mouth, and he stepped forward. "What are you talking about?"

Hansel's eyes watered, but he blinked the tears away. "The Embers, Elias. They are loading them onto the ships now. They are shipping them to Edmaria."

"I don't understand," Cove said, stepping forward and butting into the conversation. Hansel's attention shifted, as if he had just noticed her. "How did they find them? The king knows nothing of their whereabouts, I—"

"The king has plenty of secrets. I am sure he granted the Edmarian men reign to gather the gifted," Keila said, rubbing her hand on the back of her neck. "He's likely trying to keep the alliance." Cove watched as Hansel wrapped Keila in a hug, and they seemed to communicate wordlessly—within their minds—as Cove's soulbound parents used to do. She realized that they were likely discussing just who she was. Cove stood a little straighter as Hansel studied her over Keila's shoulder. Then, Cove realized that she and Elias would be able to speak within their minds when they were bound, and he would be able to hear her. She tapped a finger on the table.

"There must be a way to stop them." She looked to Elias. "We could wreck them," she said. "We could wreck them and bring them to another safe house until we can find them safe transport to Adullam." She looked at Keila. "Surely there is somewhere here on the isle we could hide them?"

Keila's mind was obviously turning and then she nodded at Hansel, as if he had given her an idea. "There is a small cove on the west end of this isle—a recess in the bay surrounded by rocks and caves. If we could get them into hiding there, we could bring a boat in to transport them later."

"That could work," Cove said hopefully. "We sink the ships, deliver the Embers to you and Hansel in the caves, and wait for a boat that can take them to Adullam."

Elias's arms were crossed at his chest as he chewed on his lip. "It is too risky with the Embers on board. We would have to find a way to get them off the ships first and then sink them."

"You can manipulate the water precisely enough to guide fish into a net. Surely you can do the same with people once we have sunk the ships."

"Fish cannot drown," he said. "I would have to keep their heads above water, and it would be quite the distance. I—"

"I can help you. I was able to do it with Mina in the bath house." *Barely,* she thought. "I can focus better when I am with you," she added, and that was the truth, though she had such little practice she was unsure what she could accomplish in such short notice. "We must try, Elias. We cannot let them be shipped to their deaths in the trades." He thought for a long moment, and she continued trying to convince him. They could not keep hiding forever. The Embers needed to start fighting back. "We can follow the fleet and wait until they are far enough out that it won't draw attention from the islanders. We'll get them as close to the bay as possible, and go from there."

He rubbed the bridge of his nose with his thumb and his forefinger. Finally, he gave her an answer. "We marry first," he said. She blinked. "So we can communicate, and I can be sure you're safe. And so we can merge our gifts." Cove had forgotten that those who were soulbound could not only mindspeak, but share their gifts of Light. The pull between her and Elias seemed to grow stronger by the minute, and she realized that it *was* their gifts all along, begging to merge.

Cove rose to her feet and joined hands with Elias in the center of the tiny home. Starting with her and Elias, one Ember at a time, the Light was going to take back Arresia.

CHAPTER 23
STRIKING GOLD
MARINOS

The king's servant was a fool. Did he truly think that Marinos would not peg him as an Ember the moment he offered his life's savings and seven years of labor for Cove's hand? As Marinos had watched Elias suspiciously pull in net after net full of herring yesterday afternoon, he had made the connection. Elias had proven to Marinos that he could make him much money indeed, and Marinos was not about to let the opportunity pass him by.

Marinos peered at the many temple builders who had come in on the Edmarian ships. They worked meticulously to hammer metal statues and raise the stone walls of the first Black Temple on the islands. He leaned back on the stone steps in the nearby garden, relaxing in the shade and reveling in the deal he had made.

Ahlia had convinced Marinos to make use of Elias's free labor for a few years, and when the time was right, Marinos would turn him and Cove both in together. Marinos still knew little of Cove's power, but he guessed she was not as gifted as the boy. Elias would be the true prize, and Marinos knew it would be easy to find a mercenary willing to pay what he was asking. Though, perhaps Marinos would spare Cove, being that she would not be worth as much money. Maybe he could still sell her hand into a marriage that would end in the death she deserved.

The two of them were currently enjoying a romantic sail on his boat, which was being tracked toward the north fishing village by Marinos's wife. Marinos guessed the boy knew of other Embers in this kingdom if he had gotten involved with Cove, so Marinos and Ahlia would keep a close watch on him in hopes of striking gold. This was yet another investment that would take time, but it was one that would be worth it.

CHAPTER 24

A PACING PRINCESS

MATEO

Mateo had been given a full night's rest, and he was back at the princess's chamber door before she had ever risen from sleep. A scrawny guard had relieved him for the night, escorted by King Sebastian himself. The king was insistent on showing his appreciation for Mateo watching over his daughter, and he came with an early payment in hand, along with the keys to the small servant chambers just down the corridor from Princess Mina's wing of the palace. Mateo had pocketed both silvers and hurried to his new bed, where he fell asleep atop the covers. At the first glint of light through his window that overlooked the villages in the south, he rose to peer across Oriana's western shore and out to the sea, where Tabrana was a small dot on the horizon.

He smoothed his hands through his textured hair, pulled his trousers on, and sheathed his sword at his hip, recalling the irritation its noise had brought to the princess. He smiled. Princess Mina Sanchez could play the part of a rebel princess in disagreement with her father, but Mateo saw right through her act of spoiled entitlement.

She was privileged, but she was not used to getting her way when it came to the things that mattered. Mateo had escorted her to lunch with her father yesterday, and he guessed she had joined her father in writing up the proposal for an alliance with Edmaria with little to no self-advocating at all. She may have bickered and moaned for a bit, but he had seen it in her eyes at the dinner table the night before. She was swayed into the alliance too easily by her father and her green-eyed lady, who acted under the guise of doing what is best for the kingdom. Mateo could care less, but he could see that Mina Sanchez would make a poor leader when her time came in the coming months, if she stood for her kingdom in the same way she was standing up for herself in this matter.

Perhaps she believed sacrificing her own happiness for the good of the kingdom was honorable, and maybe in some ways it was. But to Mateo, a princess should not bow so quickly in the face of conflict.

Mateo splashed some water on his face and grabbed a fruit from the bowl on the bedside table before heading toward his post at the princess's side.

"Uneventful night, I hope?" Mateo called to the guard, whose eyes were bloodshot as he stood at attention outside the princess's door.

"Absolutely nothing to report, sir. Not even a visitor."

"Go get some rest," Mateo said with a nod, dreading his next eighteen hours on duty.

The princess's snores traveled through the corridor, and he took a deep breath, tugging the itchy collar of his new flaxen uniform to the side. He wondered if the princess would be attending breakfast with her father this morning. He could not help but tap his fingers impatiently for the next couple of hours while he waited for any sign of life other than the sound of blocked nasal passages behind the door. Was it out of line for him to stir her from slumber, if only so he did not have to stand sedentary all day? Surely she was finished pouting by now. Mateo turned at the sound of footsteps coming down the corridor.

Finally, he at least had *something* to do. The princess's first, and probably only visitor of the day was on her way. The green-eyed lady-in-waiting from dinner spun her engagement ring as she approached the princess's chambers and then plopped something small and shiny into a pocket in the skirts of her jade-colored gown.

Mateo stepped in front of the door before she could knock. "Excuse me?" she said, looking him up and down with disgust. A hand found her hip, and the billowing sleeve of her dress hung to her knees.

"I do the knocking," he said. "And I do the announcing. What is your name?"

She was taken aback. "Celeste. But that's Lady Celeste, to you," she said snidely, crossing her arms.

Mateo tilted his head and maneuvered his shoulder between her and the door so he could knock. He made sure to pound hard enough to halt her incessant snoring. "Princess, are you taking visitors?"

"I am sleeping," she muttered, almost inaudibly. Mateo looked to the ceiling. "Is it Cove?" the princess asked with a little more cheer.

Mateo looked at Celeste, who was scowling. "No, it's the other one," he said.

Lady Celeste huffed and pushed him aside. "It is me, Celeste. I need to speak with you." There was no answer. "It's important," she added. Mateo watched her closely through narrowed eyes and thought that she might be more entitled than the princess.

"Come in," the princess finally said, and Mateo shot Celeste a look of surprise that only resulted in a glare from her. He opened the door to see the princess sitting up on the side of her massive bed, bare feet dangling over the side. She was in a robe that matched the pink clouds that often hovered over the seas when the sun was low, and her hair was coming out of her braids in every which way. She shot him a look of annoyance as she met his stare. He raised a brow and brushed his cheek to remind her of the bruise she had there and may want to hide. She brought a hand to her face at once, and turned away from Celeste to sit at the vanity, hurriedly grabbing for the awful pink she had been covering her face with.

"Send her in already," the princess said impatiently over her shoulder. Mateo allowed Celeste entry and stepped to the side before shutting the door.

"I'll be right outside," he called to the princess. "Holler if you need me."

Celeste left about an hour later, and there was not one word from Mina. As the door opened, Mateo stepped inside to ensure she was okay, saw that she was still sitting at the vanity, admiring herself as princesses do, and shut the door. Servants delivered lunch for both of them, and while she snubbed her nose at her platter of what looked to be lobster and pasta, Mateo ate his unidentifiable chowder with no complaints. He was starving, and a meal from the palace was like a feast compared to anything he'd get guarding the gates outside.

He could hear Mina on the other side of the door now as the sun was on its way to meet the horizon. From the sounds of it, she was pacing. His ears followed the sound of rustling fabric and the light slap of her feet against the stone floors. "Are you alright, Princess?" he asked monotonously through the thick wood. He was pacing too, but out of boredom. *Does she never leave her chambers? How many of my days will be spent standing in this corridor with no one to speak to?*

"I am fine," she said.

"Are you hungry? Your father is expecting you for dinner." *Please, give me something to do. Somewhere to go.* At least at his post at the north gate he had friends, and there was a constant flow of people to speak to.

"Not hungry. Tell the next servant that goes by to let my father know I will not be at dinner."

"Are you sure? You did not eat your lunch. No breakfast either, that I can recall." *Please, I am begging you to relieve me of this boredom.*

"Quit speaking to me," she said flatly. "I am trying to relax, and the sound of your voice is grating."

Mateo could say the same about her. But he didn't. Instead, he said, "It does not sound like you are relaxing. How many miles have you walked this afternoon, pacing back and forth like that?"

He could almost hear the eye roll through the door, and he crossed his arms as he leaned against it, awaiting her response. The door flew open without warning, and he stumbled backward into her chambers. She stood there with her hands on her hips, lips in a flat line.

"You're still in your robe?" he asked.

"And you're still leaning on the job," she snapped.

He rubbed his jaw. "Do you not want to get out before sundown? Perhaps a walk?" He was truly going stir crazy if he would brave a stroll with the insufferable princess just to get out of this palace.

"You are my guard. Not my advisor. It seems my father already has that position covered with Celeste," she muttered. "Stand guard outside my door as you have been appointed to do, or I will request my father send you back to where you came from." Mateo stiffened and backed into the hall. *I do need this job, and it is really not my place to question how the princess spends her time, unless it endangers her.*

He nodded.

"I am preparing for bed, and I need silence. No more questions," she said, with irritation coating her voice. Mateo looked beyond her out the windows, where another two hours of daylight still lingered. "I need rest."

He rocked on his feet in boredom. *I need the pay,* he thought, remembering his family in Tabrana—his three younger sisters and their big brown eyes, the flesh that clung to their bones too tightly. *With this job, I can provide more than what I have been. This is good. Even if I have to stand here all day.*

"Yes, Princess," he replied, taking his position in the hall. "You will not hear another word from me this evening unless prompted. Get some rest." *How much rest could she possibly need?*

CHAPTER 25

LIKE EMBERS IN THE DEEP

COVE

They stood beneath the mast of her father's boat, fingers interlocked, hands shaking. Cove could not help but peer toward the mainland, where she knew a hundred Embers were being marched onto the Edmarian ships. Maybe she could convince Mina to speak to her father, to convince him otherwise. But Cove knew that was not an option. It would mark the beginnings of war. The Edmarian soldiers would never allow the island's Embers to go free—not when they were worth so much and were such a threat to their cause.

"Cove," Keila said gently from behind her. Elias squeezed Cove's hand and then released it, allowing her to converse privately with his mother. Her smile was kind, and her eyes held a light in them that she recognized. "I am sorry our meeting was so. . .rushed. I hope to get to know you someday. I have always wanted a daughter. To me, that is what you are. I can feel the Light within you, and I know that the Father will use you and my boy for great things." Keila's eyes sparkled in the golden, late-evening sun.

"Elias has quickly become everything to me," Cove said. "He has taken the place of all my worries, and I think I owe that to you. The three of you are already more my family than my adoptive parents ever have been." She had never spoken that truth aloud—but today she had done it twice. Elias had offered such tenderness when she had shared the horrors of her childhood with him, when she had told him that Marinos was not her true father. Not even Mina knew the truth about Marinos. With Elias she did not have to hide anything. He knew it all, and he loved her.

She looked to Hansel and Elias and then back to Keila.

She placed a wrinkled hand against Cove's cheek. "It was my honor to raise him," she said with a tear in her eye.

"It was *our* honor," Hansel said behind them. "He has grown into an honorable man." They both turned, and Hansel stood holding a corked bottle. There was a small scroll inside it. Cove could not help but stare at the rare texts, and he smiled, extending the glass to her.

"A wedding present," he said, tucking it into her hands. Her heart hammered against her chest in anticipation as she took the scrolls into her hands for the first time since she had come to the Light. "I must stay here with Kei. I wish not to be separated from my wife in these times of darkness. We will pack and make our way toward the cove." Elias joined Cove at her side again, and Hansel looked between the two of them. "A marriage is not about the ceremony, but the commitment. Have a private ceremony, just the two of you, before you are to enter this trial. The soulbond that will follow is like nothing you have experienced before." His eyes twinkled as he looked at

Keila. "It is a gift from the Father. A mirror of his love for us. Spend time reading the scrolls, vow to love and take care of each other," Hansel said. Elias wrapped an arm around Cove, and she leaned into him.

"Do not let the darkness separate you," Keila said.

Never.

"Are you ready?" Elias asked beneath a nervous smile.

"I am," Cove said, wrapping her hand around his arm. She tucked the Light Scrolls into her satchel, and they hugged his parents goodbye. They stepped up onto the bow, where they had a view of the vast Sea of Dawn, and joined hands. Hansel untied the boat, and he and Keila held each other on the docks as they watched their son and Cove take toward the mainland of Oriana, where a hundred Embers awaited rescue.

Elias unfurled the sails as his power steadied the boat and pushed it along at a reasonably quick pace, working with the wind to take them across the vast inlet. They planned to marry on the short sail to the mainland, dock in Oriana, and pack their bags in case something went wrong with the plan—which they would be enacting in the next twelve hours. If they were seen meddling with the Ember stock, they would not be returning to her father, but would instead be fleeing to Adullam. Some small part of Cove wished for that outcome— that she and Elias could be joined with their people sooner rather than later. Marinos would be vengeful, and he would spread her secret far and wide, but it would be too late for him to profit from it. She would be hunted, and she'd probably be found, but Marinos would gain nothing. It was Mina who she worried about.

Cove stared across the water, where she could see Tabrana in the distance, barely visible through the ocean fog. She twiddled her fingers in front of her, breathing deeply over and over.

"What are you thinking about?" Elias asked. His tunic billowed in the wind as he clung to the rope while making his way to her.

"I do not think I can tell Mina," she said. There was no time to ask Mina's permission. It would only slow them down or put a halt to the plan entirely, and the Embers would suffer for it. Elias may not have been able to hear, but he was a good listener. He nodded for her to continue. "What you said in the garden. . .you are right about her," she said. "If she did not have me to protect, I do not know if she would care for Embers at all." Cove could not share these plans with the princess. She could not trust Mina with the information she would demand if she knew the plan, and Cove could not risk losing what she had found with Elias. For him, Cove would leave tonight without a goodbye, if she had to. "She is my friend, my sister. But without the Light, I am afraid she will not see why this needs to be done." She swallowed. "Elias. . .I promised the king I would be here for her after his death."

Elias's eyes softened. "And we will do everything in our power to ensure that you can be. If all goes well, we'll be close by for the years I work for Marinos. The two of you will still see each other often. But if this evening's plan goes awry, I will do everything in my power to get you out of this kingdom alive, despite your promise to the king. You are my priority, Cove."

Her brows knit together.

"Are you sure you want to do this?" Elias asked, resting his hand on her elbow. Cove bit her cheek. She thought of Mina, then, of the Embers who needed her help. Her gaze shifted to Elias, who stood before her. She pictured a life with him and then she imagined all the death they were about to bring in the sinking of the Edmarian ships. A breath shuddered out of her.

"I fear we have no choice. I do not wish to kill, but I can feel the Light dwindling in Arresia. Is it not our duty to preserve our people? Our kingdom?" Elias had spoken similar words to her after she had killed the Prince of Edmaria—that Andreas would have taken many lives—*hers*—and that the killing was justified. But that fact alone did not stop the guilt from creeping up her spine and unraveling into darkness.

Elias nodded. "My father said the fleet is scheduled to leave at dawn," he said. "Your father is expecting his boat back this evening. We'll spend the night at the docks together, and in the morning, we will rent a boat and set sail after the fleet. We will keep our distance, but we won't let them out of our sights."

They had run through every possibility, and the only plan that had a chance at working without condemning them, was this one. They could try to free the Embers from their chains in the night, but even if they succeeded, there would be nowhere to hide them quickly enough. Then, they would still have the Edmarian men to deal with. Hansel explained how the Embers were in chains, locked to chainplates on the ship decks. Elias assured her that with his help through the soulbond, she could channel her rage toward the wood around those locks and bust the Embers free so they could separate them in a current away from the ships and to the cove. It would take power like she had not utilized before, to create a current of water that strong.

"We can do this. I know we can," Cove said.

"Whatever happens, Cove, the Father of Lights has a plan. I hope you can find rest in knowing that." Cove nodded silently as the docks of Oriana became a speck on the horizon.

When the main island was in view, and there was only an hour of daylight left, Elias pulled her to her feet before him. "Are you ready?" he asked. Cove looked to Oriana, where her entire life had been dictated by Marinos, where her every move had to be calculated. It was in that palace that she had spent all these years in solitude, even during her friendship with the princess. There were things Mina did not know or understand. But Cove's Light had finally found its match.

"I've been alone here. All alone," she whispered.

"Never again," he said softly as he closed the distance between them.

She had always wanted this, but she had not allowed herself to hope for it. Who would she be to turn down such a gift when it was right in front of her? She would miss Mina, but she would not let herself miss this.

"Yes, Elias. I am ready to be your wife."

He smiled, and through the words of his mouth, he began binding himself to her. His vows were like a song, complete with music and the chill that goes up the spine when it touches one's soul.

"Cove, I promise to be your guiding light, a leader through the depths of the sea, a protector. A shelter in times of trouble. I promise to love you as the Father of Lights loves us. I promise to be a testimony of his love, always, and to be your calm in the storm." And he was, all of those things.

Cove's eyes watered, and he gently brushed a hand against her cheek. The wind carried her hair across her face, and she began, careful not to look past him to the nearing, wretched docks of Oriana.

"Elias, I promise to share every secret, every heartache, and every ounce of joy with you. I promise to nurture your flesh as if it were my own, and to be sure you never know a day without my love. I promise to be a reminder of his radiant Light, even on the darkest night." Elias beamed at her, pulling her into him.

"On this day, let us be sealed together in his Light. What the Father has called together, let no man separate," Elias said with the widest of his abundant smiles. He pulled back from her and cradled her head in his hand. Cove's chin tugged upward as she awaited his touch, and he leaned in, savoring every second, as if they had all the time in the world. Their lips met, and his hands held her tightly, like he was holding her together, and she felt her body relax as the peace within him soaked into every pore.

There was a melody inside of her as they kissed, along with a sort of glistening tether that had snapped into place. A new element gleamed between them in their minds as they gave into each other and became one. His power danced along the tether, begging to merge with hers, and she sent a whisper of Light toward his, watching them swirl together in the middle. Their Light was the same shade of blue, and she laughed at the feeling that consumed her, as it filled in all the pieces she had not known she was missing.

She opened her eyes to watch him, and he stood there in complete awe, his forehead resting against hers. "Incredible," he breathed. The feeling spread across her body, and it was like they were of one body, one mind. "You hold more Light than you know."

She smiled. "I love you, Elias." His lips parted, and he leaned back to view her face.

"Say it again."

She studied him, and then spoke once more. "I love you."

His face crumpled. "Beautiful," he choked, and a tear fell from his eye. "I can hear you. I can hear you through my mind. I–I can hear you."

"You can hear me?" She marveled at him—at the miracle of it all.

He grabbed her face in his hands, laughing. "I can hear you!"

She did not know whether to laugh or cry. His joy was immense, cracking through her chest, and the feeling was euphoric. She hugged him tighter, and he lifted her up. "At the sound of your voice, that tether between us shines like gold."

He set her back down and pulled back, leading her into a twirl and looking her up and down. "You are beautiful. Every part of you," he said as he pulled her back into his chest, swaying back and forth with the gentle rocking of the boat.

Beautiful. Cove blinked back her own tears.

They neared the docks, and Elias kept her in an embrace, allowing power to go out from them both to slow the boat. She felt the power move through and out from her, and she began to understand the control he had spoken of earlier. She examined her hands, noting the feeling of invisible Light going out from them. Elias still stood behind her. He leaned forward, and his lips brushed her ear, then traveled across her jaw.

"Go to your chambers, pack a bag, and meet me back at the docks as quickly as you can. I'll trade the dockworkers a few coppers for a day with another boat, and I'll prepare the cabin. The darkness will not take our wedding night." A chill ran down Cove's spine, and she turned to kiss him, freely and without restraint. He smiled against her lips and then muttered, "Hurry back," as she forced herself away. She gripped the satchel at her hip tightly, assuring the Light Scrolls were tucked close.

One of the dockworkers began tethering her father's boat, and Cove traced her lips with her fingers as Elias began rolling the sails. She gathered her skirts and took the dockworker's hand as she stepped down. But as her feet hit the docks, fear seeped into the air around her, and she felt it hanging there, warning her. Contempt followed, then anger, as if they were darts targeted at her head. Cove searched the docks and boats around them, looking for any telltale sign that something was wrong. That was when Cove spotted a person on the docks, standing dormant as they watched Elias tie the sails.

Cove turned toward her husband, who was oblivious to the warnings in the air. She squinted against the foggy dusk skies, trying to make out the silhouette that stood watching. Her first thought was Marinos, but it was not him.

"Mina?" Cove yelled, stepping forward. Elias turned toward her at the sound of her voice through his mind and glanced toward Mina, where Celeste now joined her in the blue hues of the approaching night. Celeste's silver ring flashed in the moonlight, and she rolled something small and round between her fingers as she watched Cove with a sly smile. *A pearl.* Cove's attention dropped to the bangle at her own wrist.

No.

Mina's face looked horrified, and Cove realized that it was her from whom the fear came. Celeste was the embodiment of contempt, and it was Yarris—and Arlo—who now stormed the docks in pure anger, with six Edmarian soldiers behind them.

Her husband's name rolled from her tongue slowly. "Elias," Cove warned beneath her breath, backing toward the boat.

"You're okay," he said gently through the bond, words of peace and calm. He jumped down from the bow, landing in front of her, taking in their surroundings. He was a shield to her as the Edmarian men's boots thumped across the wooden deck of the boat. But as they grew nearer, their eyes locked on Elias, Cove realized it was him they were after. Not a soul was looking at her. Not one. Except Mina.

Cove shook her head, pulling on Elias's hand, but his feet remained planted between her and the oncoming darkness. *We need to flee, get on the boat. . .jump in the water. . .something. Anything. Elias, they think it was you,* she said into his mind. Her own mind was reeling, searching for any possible escape.

But only two words came back down the new tether that bound them: *Let them.*

"No, Elias!" A fit of sobs burst out of her throat. *What had she done? Why had she ever allowed him to get involved?* Cove tried to step in front of Elias, to block him from Yarris's unrelenting grip, from the chains that locked onto his wrists, but Elias sidestepped, keeping her behind him, accepting his fate. His death in place of hers. His wife.

She screamed, and she could have sworn that someone returned it from across the sea.

Yarris and the soldiers began to walk him off the docks, tearing his body from her arms. It was as if they had not even seen her there, clawing at them to release the other half of her. Celeste still watched from her place on the docks and gave Cove a *wink* as she tossed that little pearl into the air and caught it.

Why him when she knows it was me?

The waves began to rise, and water began to pour over the docks. The anchored ships began to sway, and the storm that had been three miles out to sea began rolling in quickly, covering the skies in navy clouds of rain. Mina's eyes were wide as she watched Cove lose hold on every ounce of power running through her veins.

Cove. She let the power take her. She did not care if she utterly destroyed these docks and everything in them. She would not allow them to take Elias.

Cove. Again, that voice inside her mind. The voice of reason. *I need you to hold onto peace. I need you to let them take me. You are going to give yourself away, and they will take you too.*

Cove did not care. She would not let him be punished for something she had done. She could not lose him—could not be left alone again after knowing him.

She readied to open her mouth, to tell the truth of what happened in the bath house that day—but suddenly, there was water in her throat, and she was thrown into a fit of coughing.

Cove. That voice again. *Do not speak.* Cove watched after him—the vessel in which that strangely stern voice came from. He was being walked onto the ship where all the Embers awaited their doom in spelled chains. He was unable to utilize his gifts on his own, but he had channeled it through her to preserve her innocence.

She coughed against the power within her until her throat cleared, and then Mina was standing over her where she knelt on the docks amid the pouring rain.

"What have you done?" Cove spat.

Mina's eyes were wide, pleading. "It was you or him," Mina

whispered. "Celeste saw us from her balcony. She knew the three of us were present. I was protecting you."

"He is my husband!" Cove yelled, her voice cracking in two at the word she had not yet spoken aloud. *Husband.* Arlo's jaw set from where he watched on the docks beside Celeste. Celeste—the lady who had never particularly cared for Cove and her closeness to the princess—was smirking. The second Elias had been torn from her grip, Cove knew she would not stay here. She would follow that ship to the ends of the earth. But now, she knew she had no choice. If Cove knew anything by the look on Celeste's face, it was that she knew the truth about her, and that she would use it against her when it became convenient.

"Your husband?" Mina asked breathlessly in the rain. Lightning struck the skies amid the brewing storm behind her, and Cove turned her back to the princess, taking toward the ships. She kicked her sandals off, and one after the other, her bare feet smacked against the wet wood as she advanced toward the ship that was now disembarking with her husband on board. Yarris stood tall, waving proudly from the bow.

She could sink the ship. She could do it. She had access to Elias's power now, too. She did not know how she would get the Embers to safety this far from the north isle, but she had to try. He would not die in place of her.

Someone caught her arm and yanked her backward, stopping her from advancing toward her husband. "He is a murderer, don't make a fool of yourself," Arlo said into her wet hair. She fought as he held her against him. Rain and tears streamed down her face.

Elias heard what was happening through the bond, and his voice, even within her mind, was heartbroken. *I love you, Cove. Do not come after me.*

"I do not care if he murdered your prince. Quite frankly, I did not care for your prince at all," Cove said to Arlo.

He gripped her arms and turned her to face him. He shook her violently. "You do not get to speak that way about Prince Andreas." Cove spat in his face and tried to tear herself from his grips.

Mina caught up to them, eyes still pleading with Cove for forgiveness. Arlo kept his hold on her. "Let me go!" she screamed, her satchel smacking against her hip as she bucked against him. Arlo did no such thing, and Mina shook her head, instructing him to continue restraining her.

"Mina. He is my *husband*," Cove begged. Her voice broke into a million pieces.

Mina's brows sank in the middle, and Arlo kept his arms around her. "He is not your husband. The marriage has not yet been consummated, has it?"

Cove tried to wriggle free, staring after the fleet that was beginning to make its way north, toward Edmaria. Mina came into view in front of her, her eyes still pleading, dancing between Arlo and Cove and the harsh grip he had on her. "You did not consummate? You can still marry an Edmarian Lord." Mina looked at Arlo for a second, and then back to Cove, eyes pleading. She spoke quickly. "The alliance with Edmaria is likely still happening, if King Idris accepts my proposal to Prince Merrick, which is making its way north on one of those ships as we speak." *They would continue chasing an alliance, even after the murder of Andreas?* Mina's eyes darted left to right, and for once, Cove could not tell what she was thinking. "You must marry into wealth, Cove. You do not want this. Elias has tricked you. He has taken advantage. I told you not to get involved with him." Cove balked at the princess and finally broke free of Arlo's grasp.

"You know nothing," Cove shouted, and the rain continued pouring down upon her. Arlo and Mina's sights fell to Cove's chest, where her lightmark had broken through the darkness. The rain had soaked her dress, and against the night sky, it glowed like a star, revealing her guilt.

Arlo grabbed for her, but she stepped backward. He looked at Mina. "It was her," he said, pointing a finger. The princess's head began to shake in denial. "You lied to protect an Ember. You are a traitor!"

Mina was a traitor in more ways than one. The princess looked between Cove and Arlo, and suddenly, Celeste was behind the Edmarian lord. Cove watched in confusion as the glint of a knife flashed in Celeste's hand and slid into Arlo's back before she could register what was happening. Cove gaped at Celeste as the Edmarian lord staggered forward, and she reflexively moved to the side as his body fell.

Mina stood in silent shock as Lord Arlo joined his prince in death. Blood pooled around the hem of her dress.

"Why?" Cove whispered, gawking at Celeste.

"We cannot have an alliance with Edmaria if he believes our princess to be a traitor. Leave this kingdom and do not return," Celeste warned through gritted teeth. "Because if anyone asks me, I will say it was you who killed him." Cove looked between her two old friends, crumpled face lingering on Mina for only a second before she darted for the seas that separated her from her soulbound husband.

—

Cove leapt into the sea without hesitation. Her dress and the satchel at her side weighed her down. The waters surrounded her, and she used all her might to push through the dark depths toward Elias. Toward her calm in the storm. Thunder raged, and she continued swimming north after the fleet of darkness.

Don't. Elias's voice echoed down the bond as she grew nearer and her power brewed a storm. He held tightly to his portion of their shared Light, refusing to release it to her. Why wasn't he helping?

Help me, Elias. Release your power to me. We can still sink the ships.

It is too late, Cove. We have been discovered. There is not one place on this island where we could hide these Embers and get away with it. Save yourself, Cove, and forget about me.

I will not. She sent her unyielding words down the bond, in refusal to leave him alone.

Get away from these ships, before they see your lightmark glowing in the water.

No, she said again, swimming faster, desperately, in anguish like never before. This time, all the emotions she felt were her own, and they raged in the waters around her, taking hold of her power.

Cove. He warned her, but she did not listen. She was gaining on the fleet, and they were nearing the northern isle. She began channeling that anger toward the ships, allowing the water to rise against the sides of the boats in tidal waves of destruction.

She reached deep down inside the well within her, readying to pull up more and more power, but suddenly, there was nothing. The well had gone dry and there was nothing at all.

Every bit of her power rose involuntarily to the surface of the waters around her as he used her as a channel to bypass the spelled shackles on his wrists.

A current swept her to the west, and the distance between her and the fleet increased.

No. Elias, stop.

She fought against his power, the power that was supposed to be shared, but that he had taken all for himself. He wrapped her in it, and sent her out to sea, away from him. Away from any danger that threatened her.

I promised to keep you safe, and that is what I am doing. In the midst of the vast sea, even there his hand shall lead you. Remember that, Cove. Until we meet at Dawn. I love you.

And then, the bond went silent.

Elias.

There was no response.

Elias.

Elias.

"Elias!" She screamed it aloud, and her voice carried the plea across the waves.

His name spilled from her mouth with every ounce of water she pushed from her lungs. Alone. He had left her alone. She had been here before, seven years ago.

She turned her face to the sky. "I gave my life to you, and this is what you do with it? Was this your plan?" She yelled, raged, at the Light that carried her away from her husband. She treaded the water for hours, fighting the current until she could no longer move her legs, until the darkness had swallowed up the fleet, and it was only her and the stars, floating embers in the middle of the deep.

CHAPTER 26

THE FRUITS OF HIS LABOR
MARINOS

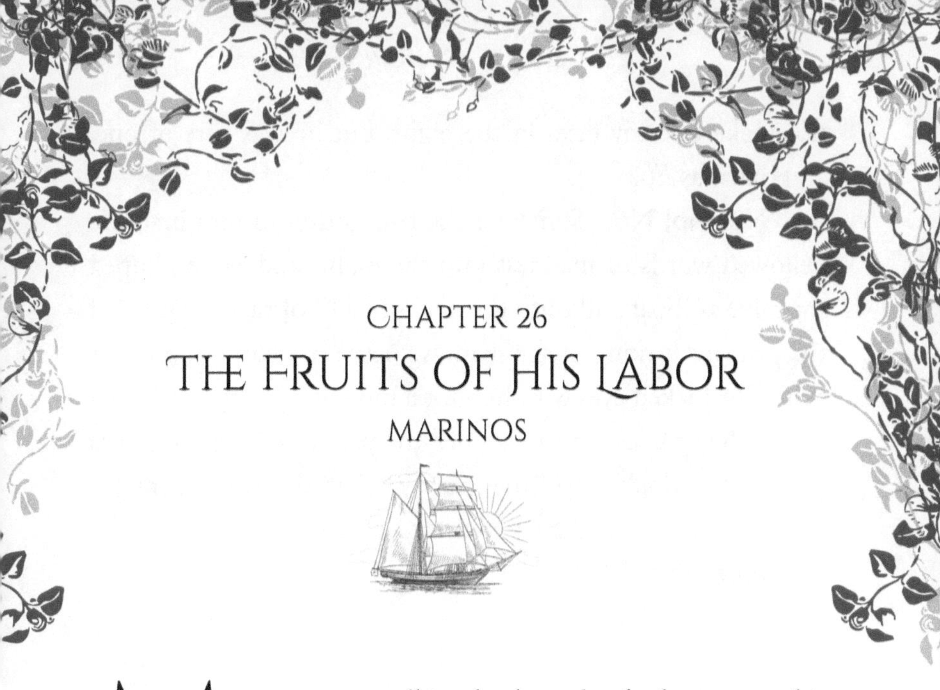

Marinos was walking back to the docks to meet his daughter and new son-in-law when the storm blew in. Heavy rain and winds that could tear sails tore through the islands, and he rushed toward where his boat rocked at the docks. The sails were already damaged, and he cursed under his breath.

He searched the boat for any sign of Elias and Cove. They had to be here somewhere. He needed to know if Cove had accepted the proposal or if he would need to go another route to get his coin. He squinted against the night, shielding his eyes against the sideways rain.

There in the sea, being tossed in the waves, was the Edmarian ship that was made to hold Embers. He struggled to make out any of the faces aboard and quickly collected his monocular from the cabin in his sailboat. His footsteps were heavy across the deck. He tracked the ship with the glass, examining the Embers that were chained to the deck. He could not make out any faces in the night, but he was sure of one, and that was *Elias*.

"No! No! No!" Someone else had gotten to him first. He bellowed words of madness into the night, and as he jumped from his sailboat and onto the docks in a fit of rage, he noticed the princess lurking in the shadows between boats, wiping her tears. She locked eyes with him for a moment, her gaze swelling in fear. She turned to run toward the palace, and Marinos was left on the docks, realizing exactly what the tears from his daughter's best friend must mean.

Someone had stolen the fruits of his labor.

CHAPTER 27
OUR LITTLE SECRET
MATEO

Mateo had been standing guard for two hours in utter silence. Not a sound came from beyond the door, not even a snore. He tapped his foot. He had not been on this job long, but the princess was supposed to be sleeping, and he had never, in his years of barracks living with a hundred other men, encountered someone who snored as loud as she did. Perhaps she was lying awake, her mind wandering through all of her princess problems.

He took a deep breath and looked to the darkening night outside, where a relentless storm was rolling in. Rain was starting to blow into the corridor, and Mateo backed against the door to keep his feet dry as it pattered around him.

The wind howled as it traveled through the corridor, bringing a cold sheet of rain across his face. He wiped it with the back of his hand and sighed, checking his pocket watch. He would be relieved of duty at midnight. Hopefully the storm would not last the entirety of the next four hours, but at least things were switching up a bit. He observed the silhouettes of the palm trees swaying in the rainstorm and watched as one came crashing into the outer wall of the princess's chambers.

He swung the door open in an instant. The room was dark as he searched through the hues of deep blue and black for any sign of her shadow. "Princess?" he called. He noticed the leafy top of the tree was still nestling itself against the foot of her bed and jolted forward, hands searching through the empty covers.

"Princess Mina?"

There was no snide comment, no response at all. He scanned the room, eyes catching the billowing curtains at the balcony and the heels that had seemingly been kicked off right before a descent. "Mina Sanchez, this better be a joke," he muttered, before searching her chambers one more time.

He looked out to the stormy kingdom below, searching for patience as he threw himself over the railing and shimmied down the trellis. *I cannot lose this job. I cannot fail. My family is counting on me.* He had not one clue which direction she would have traveled in—he knew little to nothing about her.

Perhaps she was more rebellious than he thought. Maybe it was not all an act. Maybe this was her showing Mateo and her father that she should have a say in her own life. It was obvious she did not want a guard following her every move. She valued privacy, but why did she require it? What was she hiding?

Mateo ran a hand through his wet hair. They were on an island. If she truly wanted to go anywhere—to run, per se—she would go to the docks, where there were boats that could take her anywhere she wanted to go. *Where the Edmarian ships were currently disembarking from.* Mateo took toward the eastern docks.

He did not know what she was doing at the docks, but he

was almost certain he would find her there. He had not predicted such a move from the princess, that she would leave her chambers without a guard despite the king's orders. Perhaps she would make a decent leader after all.

The rain was not letting up, and the ocean was battering the shoreline. Mateo continued forward, shielding his face against the rain. The vines in the gardens were rustling with the storm, and the trees were dropping fruit to the slick cobblestone paths around him. Lightning was lighting up the kingdom every few seconds, and he caught a glimpse of a silhouette of a woman moving quickly toward the palace. He intercepted her, stopping her in her tracks.

"What are you doing?" he demanded through gritted teeth. In the flashing of the storm, he could see she had been crying, though her tears blended with the rain, her face was swollen. The old bruise on her cheek was fading but visible. He surveyed her wet clothing, eyes halting at the red stained hand that held the bloodsoaked hem of her dress. "Is that yours?" he asked, grabbing her hand. She withdrew, backing up a few steps. She was breathing heavily, as if she had been running for a while.

"It is none of your concern," she said, dropping her skirt to the ground and trying to speak with the dignity of a princess. He set his jaw and searched behind her for any sign of what, or *who*, she had been running from.

"If you die, I'm out of a job, and I really need the money, princess," he said flatly.

"Listen, Maxwell," she said, followed by an exhale.

"Mateo," he corrected her.

"Whatever. I won't say a word about your failures tonight

if you don't say a word about the state in which you found me."

Mateo grimaced, looking at the blood that stained her clothes. *What trouble had she gotten into?* His eye twitched, and he worked his jaw for a moment, thinking long and hard.

"Deal," he finally said. "It can be our little secret."

PART TWO
THE REBEL

CHAPTER 28
CHIEF OF COLLECTING
LEITH

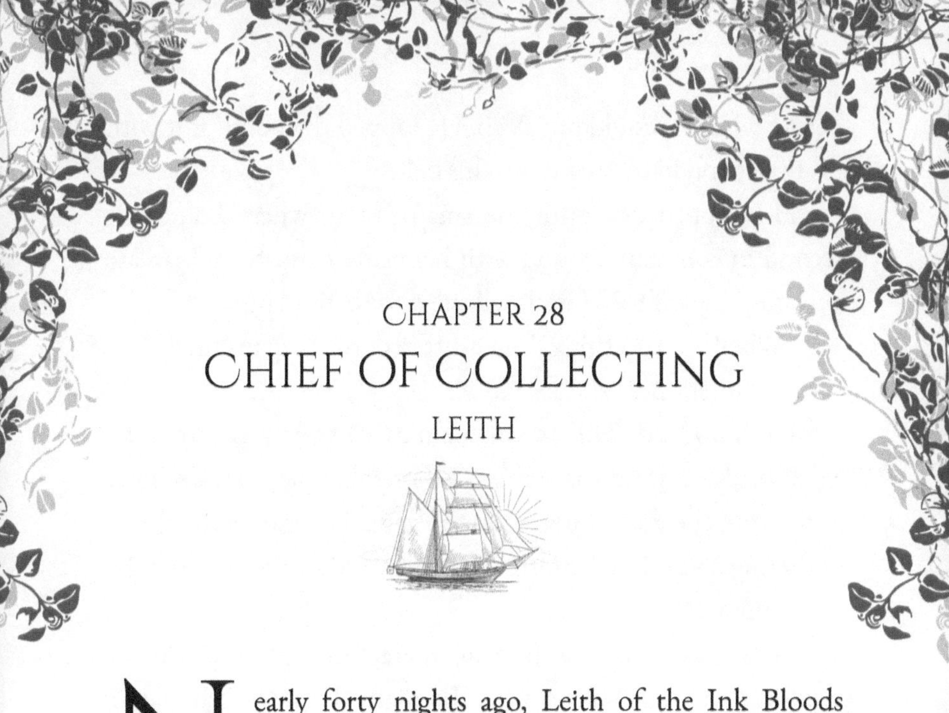

Nearly forty nights ago, Leith of the Ink Bloods heard a scream, and something strange had awakened inside of him. The mountains around Ink Valley quaked with the scream that seemed to echo through the valleys and across the seas. He had told himself it had only been a nightmare. But he had not been the same since.

His nights consisted of tossing and turning and thinking up ways in which he could ensure Ink Valley's success against Oro. No idea he had found in the corners of his mind would suffice. His thoughts could focus on one thing only: the woman with fiery red hair and a temper to match.

Leith gathered his weapons, unsure of his plans for the evening. All he knew was that something awaited him in the cave in the midst of witch territory, and he would need protection. He selected a dagger from his wall, careful to choose one he had spent an hour sharpening the evening before when he could not sleep. He tapped the point of it with his finger and harnessed it into his belt.

He stepped out onto the small porch, where Edme, his second in command, stood with her arms crossed. "Where are you sneaking off to?" He closed the door behind him.

"Where do you think?" he muttered, rubbing his tired eyes.

"Another one?" she asked.

Leith nodded. The two of them made their way across the small bridge toward the stables. All of Ink Valley was sleeping, aside from the guards posted at the gate. The moon above was withering away, and tomorrow night would be the start of The Darkening.

Leith passed by his favorite mare, opting for the black stallion that would blend with the night. Edme did the same, choosing a young charcoal mare to travel by. As Leith mounted the horse, he tried to hide the wince that came as he put pressure on his leg.

He did not hide it well enough, though, and Edme rolled her eyes.

"What?" he asked, positioning himself on his horse and rubbing his calf.

"Oh nothing. It is just the constant reminder you have of why that girl is a bad idea, and yet you are still stuck on her." Edme lit the torch as they neared the gate. "I am telling you, she is your worst idea yet, Leith. Leave her be."

"Everything okay, chief?" One of the guards yelled down from the watchtower.

Leith nodded. "Just fine. Keep a good eye on things. I'll be back by dawn." Leith looked at Edme. "Mind your own business, you have a lot of it."

Her lips formed a pout, and she tried to ride ahead of him, but he cut her off.

They wove in and out of the trees on horseback, watching closely for any sign of danger. Heading into witch territory in the night was not ideal, but Leith was collecting an army, and he had been signaled that yet another unsuspecting soldier awaited him.

He and the witches had similar interests in their quest against Degare, but Leith would be a fool to ally with them. With the army he was creating, he did not need their help. And so, as he and the Volcanian woman made their way through the Witch Lands, they stayed vigilant.

"Just another mile south," Leith said to Edme. "I find them here all the time."

Edme nodded, her brown skin glowing beneath the light of the torch.

Sure enough, as they neared the cave, Leith saw the silhouette of a body, washed up on the shore between jagged rocks. He stayed silent, dismounting his horse and motioning for Edme to halt and stand guard. Leith quietly approached the body, watching closely for any sign of life. The wet fabric of her dress stuck tightly to her pruned skin. Blonde, almost white hair cascaded from her head and laid across the rocks.

She was breathing but unconscious. Leith knelt and turned her over.

A glint of blue light pierced the darkness.

Leith smirked. "She's gifted."

CHAPTER 29
SHADOW'S VALLEY
COVE

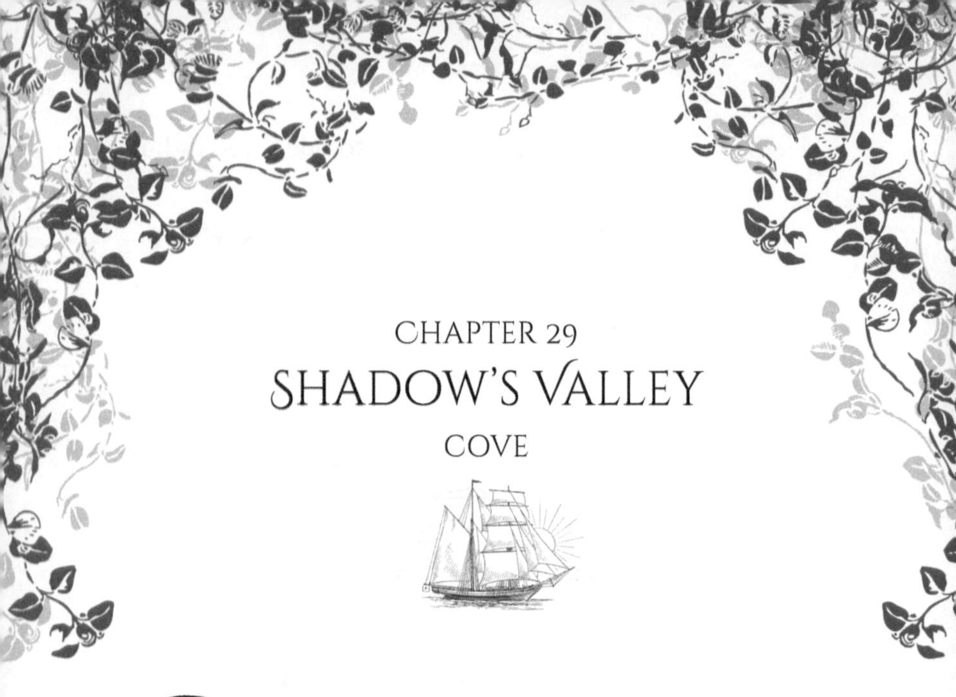

Cove awoke in a strange bed. The covers were warm, and there was a fire in the hearth, but she was still cold down to her bones. *Why was she so cold?* The structure around her was unfamiliar. Unlike anything she had ever seen in the Dawn Islands. If she had to compare it to something, she would compare it to Elias's parents' home, but this one was made of wood and. . .*mud?*

Elias.

A piece of her was missing. She sat up, grasping her chest.

"Good morning." A strange man sat at a desk before her, his hazel eyes widening as he angled his head in curiosity. His feet were up on the desk, and his fingers were locked behind his head. There was a wall of daggers behind him, and his hair was dark like Mina's. Cove swallowed. There was a soreness in her throat and a dryness to her mouth, as if she had not had a drink in days.

"Where am I?" She was shaking with chills, and he gestured

for her to have a seat by the fire. Two feathers hung from a leather strip on his arm.

"You're in Ink Valley," he said as Cove rose from the bed, slowly making her way to the chair on wobbly legs. She had to brace herself on the wall to move steadily across the floor. She tried to get a read on his emotions, but the air around him seemed guarded somehow.

"And where is Ink Valley?" she asked slowly, looking around and trying to peek out the window. She had never heard of it.

"About twenty miles north of where you washed up. Found you between here and the Hollow Coves." *The Hollow Coves? Had Elias delivered me to Adullam?* A distant horn sounded outside, and Cove's eyes darted to the window. She was in a village, and the horn had signaled something to the people outside. Some began rushing into their homes and some stayed outside, positioning themselves toward the direction in which the siren sounded. The man was watching her with some level of intrigue.

He continued. "What were you doing in the water?" The events of that evening all came rushing back to her, and she tried to keep her composure. She was in Ozanna. In *Oro.* She did not feel particularly threatened by him, but something was not right. Did he know she was an Ember? *Who is this man?*

"Tell me who you are first," she demanded.

"My name is Leith. I am the leader of the Ink Bloods. They call me the Shadow." Cove's eyes fell to the exposed shadowmarks on his neck that barely peeked out above his collar. Her throat bobbed as she swallowed her nausea.

Not the leader of Adullam. What had happened to the rebellion Elias had told her about? Where were all the Embers?

She spoke carefully, trying not to show her fear. "And you found me in a cave, near the Hollow Coves?" He nodded. "And you brought me to your home in Ink Valley." She swallowed again against the dryness in her throat. "Why?"

"Because I have a proposal for you." He raised a brow.

"You do not know me," she said warily.

"Maybe not, but I have seen the mark on your skin, and I know what that means for you." He clicked his tongue.

Cove breathed deeply, trying to remain in an outward state of calm. One of Elias's many gifts to her.

"You're running from something, are you not?" Leith asked, and Cove's mind darted to all of the people who she now hid from. *Marinos. Celeste. Even Mina.* "I believe we can help each other."

Cove remained silent. Had she escaped her father's grasp, only to be entangled in another net of extortion? She narrowed her eyes on him. Leith chuckled.

"I suspect that as an Ember, you want to put an end to the trades, do you not?"

Cove nodded, slowly beginning to put the pieces together. *Not every rebellion is made up of Embers. Some only want to end the trades because they fear the power the Despiri are gaining,* Elias had said.

Leith continued. "I do not want Degare gaining anymore power. Will you join my cause or not?"

She was silent for a long moment, and Leith began to whistle while he awaited a response from her. It was a common tune she had once hummed on her balcony. A beautiful melody—one that reminded her of home. Her eyes narrowed on him, and he watched her carefully, tauntingly.

There was a knock at the door, and a voice to follow. "There is a Vestelian woman here to see you."

Leith stopped whistling. He looked to Cove for only a moment before he buttoned his top button and tugged his collar upward, concealing his shadowmarks. "Come in," he said in a guttural voice, but his tone suggested he was intrigued. Cove directed her attention to the door as a red-haired woman was ushered into the hut by two guards. The Vestelian woman appeared to be a warrior, though she carried no visible weapons. Her eyes were wild, of two different colors, and they surveyed Cove for only a passing glance before they darted to Leith, who still sat behind the desk. His eyes followed her across the room with intensity.

He waved a hand at Cove, dismissing her, and she stayed concealed beneath the blanket, swaying as she met the guards at the door.

"To what do I owe the pleasure, beautiful Ravenna of the Valley?" Leith said to the woman behind her. Cove stole one last glance before she joined the guards outside, in the depths of the Shadow's valley.

CHAPTER 30
DEAD RIVALS
LEITH

"What troubles you?" Leith asked as he stepped through the doorway to his hut, making his way toward his wall of daggers.

Edme circled around the room, tension rolling from her shoulders, as always. She was an intense woman, always aware of what could go wrong. Always cautious, never relaxed.

"Prince Andreas of Edmaria was found dead."

Leith stopped by the corner of his desk, tapping a finger on the wood and slowly turning around to face the Volcanian. "And where did you get this information, princess?" Her lips fell flat, and he watched her dark eyes flash with her next words.

"Like you, I have men posted in every kingdom." She set her jaw.

"You do not trust me?" Leith asked. Leith's contacts had notified him of the death of the Edmarian prince weeks ago— likely before even King Idris had been given the grave news of his eldest son's passing, but those were things he had not yet shared with Edme.

"I trust only myself," Edme said bluntly. Leith nodded, understanding fully. He took Ravenna's dagger from the wall and examined the blood red stone in the hilt. His mind jumped to the necklace she had worn around her suspiciously bruised neck.

He'd first noticed her slight limp when she had tried to waltz into his hut with false confidence, and as she had tilted her chin up to put on the act of said confidence, Leith had seen the whisper of a bruise peeking out from beneath her collar. He chuckled to himself as he realized both of them were hiding truths beneath their clothing, and Edme shot him an inquisitive glare.

Ravenna—new shield-maiden of Vestele—did not trust him, but he needed the alliance, and concealing the truth about his valley until the deal was done seemed to be the right move. He did not know how desperate Ravenna was for an alliance, but Leith did not think anything could have stopped him from making that deal. Not even the threat of the witch guardians. He had recognized the pattern of the bruises, but he had needed a closer look to confirm, and as she had unbuttoned her collar, he had found what he was truly searching for: the necklace he had seen on Ashreya Ozanne when he had come to Vestele four years before. He suspected it was a relic of utmost importance, and the fact that Ravenna was now wearing it would make things much simpler for him.

He now wished he would have kept the necklace instead of the dagger, but he was afraid such a request would have turned her away from the alliance. He needed her to trust him. Witch guardians or not, the benefits of an alliance with the Dove of

Ozanna outweighed the risks, and he would stand by that decision.

Edme was still glaring at him, arms crossed over her full figure. "Your men are quick," he said. "I suppose the death of Prince Andreas means Edmaria's alliance with the Dawn Islands is off the table?" *Does she know about Princess Mina's proposal to the youngest prince, and that Idris has accepted?*

Edme shrugged. "There is no word other than that which I have told you." Leith watched her closely for a moment, wondering if she was hiding things from him out of spite because of the recent choices he had made. Choices she did not agree with.

"Shame," he finally said. "Alliances make the world go round." Edme scoffed as she watched him twist Ravenna's dagger over in his hands, red ruby glinting in the hilt.

"Maybe alliances between kingdoms, Leith. But your little alliance with the Vestelians will not accomplish much," Edme said. "It has already done more damage than good." Leith sat down and let his head hang over the back of the chair.

"Oh, Edme. You always have such a positive outlook on things."

"I do not think you realize how serious the curse of the witch guardians is. I can feel the curse inside me. They will never stop coming for me." Leith knew exactly how serious the curse was. It was why Ravenna had come to him in the first place. He would guess the guardians had come to claim her witch mother's body, and Ravenna had stopped them from completing their task. When one kills a guardian, they are hunted for life. "Not only am I cursed because I protected her for you," Edme said impatiently, "but your soon-to-be bride carries that curse on her shoulders like a flame in the night.

They flock to her. Ink Valley will fall victim to that curse, just as her people have. You *will* regret this."

Leith shook his head. "This is the only way, Edme. I am sorry you are cursed, but it is nothing you—with the help of Ink Valley—cannot handle." Edme scoffed at him.

"I should have let her die," she spat.

"Now Edme, that is not very nice," Leith said.

"I mean it. When she returns in five days and this alliance is sealed, those guardians will track her here, just as they are now tracking me. When your soldiers start killing them to protect the valley, that curse will just keep growing. It only goes down from here, Leith. You've done it to yourself," Edme said, and then she left him in the silence of his hut.

CHAPTER 31
PRIVY
COVE

Cove had been given a hut of her own. There were no windows, and the door was always locked. The walls were crafted of a charcoal-colored clay, and the floors were made up of a few uneven stone slabs. She could hear the sound of a river outside, and occasionally she noticed distant voices of a stern tone that reminded her of the soldiers in Oriana. She spent the night lying awake, listening to the rushing water, wondering if she could manipulate it without laying sight on it. If so, perhaps she could use her gifts to escape, but she had no clue what laid beyond the walls, and she did not like the idea of attacking blind.

She was in solitude most of the day. She was used to the figurative solitude of being the only Ember in the palace. But that was before she met Elias. Before they had become one. Now that he had been torn away from her—now that the darkness had separated them—well, her bones ached. She should have never had to know solitude like this again.

Her hut was dark, but by the glow of her lightmark and the tiny oil lamp by her uncomfortable cot, she had all the time in the world to read through the Light Scrolls that had been safely tucked away in the corked bottle in her satchel. Thoughts of Elias had her hands shaking from sunup to sundown, and the rhythm of her heart felt as though it were missing beats. Guards brought her meals and water twice a day, and she had been given a new set of gray linen clothes to wear. It seemed they were being careful not to supply her with too much water despite her dehydration, and she wondered if and how they knew what her gifts were.

When she wasn't reading or trying to lose herself in the rushing river, she was trying to reach Elias through the bond that had gone silent. His absence was the entire weight of the ocean, pushing down on her chest. She could not bear it. She would do anything to get him back, and she was finally considering an escape from Ink Valley when the doorknob turned.

She sat up on the cot. "Good evening," she said timidly.

Leith gave her a funny look as he quickly shut the door behind him, dagger strapped on his hip. "It's the middle of the day," he said. She had seen no sunlight pouring in through the crack of the door—outside had looked almost like the blue hour after sunset.

She creased her brows. "The Darkening?" He nodded, and his dark hair shifted atop his head.

It was the darkest week of the year already? "How long have I been here?" she asked.

"Four days, if you believe you are privy to such information." His hazel eyes flashed.

Cove did the math in her head. That would mean she had

been in the sea for *forty* days. *No, that cannot be. How am I still alive?*

Forty days at sea should have been impossible to survive.

She blinked, trying to recall her days in the water, but aside from those first grueling hours after Elias had been taken captive beyond the night horizon, she remembered nothing but the deep and peculiar sleep that had come upon her when Elias must have used up all the Light within them both to carry her to Adullam, where he thought she would be safe. She rubbed her eyes. *Has the Father of Lights spared my life yet again? For what purpose?*

She remembered Elias's last words to her and the faith they conveyed in the Father's protection over her. *In the midst of the vast sea, even there his hand shall lead you.* She had been led here and kept alive—the Father's Light from within Elias forming an ark around her—but Adullam was no longer there in those caves. There had been no one there to help her, and the Shadow, as he called himself, had found her first.

"It has occurred to me that I never asked your name," Leith said dryly.

Cove pondered for a moment and decided there was no harm in giving him her true name. Not in this territory, a sea away from any of her known enemies.

"Cove," she said tightly. "Am I a prisoner?"

"What do you think?" he asked as he pulled a wooden chair out from the corner. *Why was he always so passive, always answering her questions with another question?*

She shifted to put her bare feet on the floor. "I think you are keeping me here for one of two reasons. One, you have secrets. Or two, you are afraid I'll run away."

"Right on the mark," he said with a finger in the air.

"Are you going to share any of your secrets with me?" she questioned, growing bold enough to keep the shake from her voice. *Why did he care to bring her here in the first place?*

"You first," he said.

She narrowed her eyes at him. He was good at hiding his emotions, and they did not seem to project as strongly as the average person's. It made him quite difficult to read. If she was still alive, and he had not really threatened her yet, but had saved her life in bringing her here out of witch territory, perhaps she could trust him—to an extent. But trust no longer came easily. Not when even her best friend had turned on her.

"I come from the Dawn Islands," Cove finally said. Leith sat on the chair, leaning forward with his elbows on his knees. He clasped his hands and nodded for her to go on. "I was a lady to the princess. She knew my secret and kept it for years. But. . ." Cove paused, wondering just how much information she should give him.

"But you killed the Prince of Edmaria." Cove went rigid, and Leith smiled. "No need to deny it, I never cared much for him." *How did he know? Was her entire life to be built on secrets? Would they follow her wherever she fled?*

Cove was silent for a moment. She nervously traced a thumb over the back of her hand, speaking slowly. "You. . .were not in support of an alliance between Edmaria and the Dawn Islands?"

Leith moved his head from side to side, weighing his words. "Alliances can be dangerous when they are in support of keeping the poor weak and making the rich richer—both in money and power. I don't quite like the idea of Edmaria taking Oro's place as a world power is all."

'What makes you think Edmaria will not prevail against

Oro?' Andreas had challenged. *Had there been a reason for his arrogance? Had he known something she did not? How could any kingdom in Arresia rise against Oro—against the king who turned light to darkness?*

"You think Edmaria could be successful in rising above the King of Oro?" Cove asked.

"Perhaps," Leith said with a shrug. "But I have plans for Ink Valley to rise above them *all*."

Cove swallowed. She did not dare ask about his plans; he shared them willingly. She had learned from her years in the palace that such information was valuable, even if she was not to be involved. But she had a feeling he was only sharing these things with her to render her involvement, most likely against her will.

"I am building an army, Cove." Cove nodded slowly, recalling his comments about her lightmark.

"An army of Embers," she said, throat bobbing.

He nodded. "An army of Embers against Degare. I was hoping you would be willing to fight for my cause." She said nothing, just focused on breathing deeply.

"I am engaged," he added. Cove sat up a little straighter. "To be wed in four nights."

"Congratulations," Cove said too quickly, not allowing her eyes to move from the dagger he now held in his hand.

Leith chuckled. "She is to be very powerful, but she does not know it yet."

"She is an Ember?"

"Not exactly," Leith said with a smile. "But she is the Dove." *The Dove?* A pit formed in Cove's stomach. She knew the prophecy he was referring to—every Ember knew that prophecy, that hope.

"How do *you* know of the Dove?" she asked cautiously.

"Thanks to my mother, I know the scrolls like the back of my hand," Leith answered. "I know the power the Dove holds."

So the Shadow was after the Dove. The Dove was said to be one to usher in eternal Light to Arresia—to bring the dawn with the rise of the old kingdom of Ozanna. *So why did Leith want her? Was he trying to stop the prophecy, just as Edmaria had been in dissolving the Dawn Island's status as a kingdom?*

"With her on our side, I suspect we will bring down Degare and his trades within the year," Leith said. "The end of the trades would make your life a whole lot easier." He watched her closely. "Are you with me, or not?"

Of course she wanted to stop the trades and end Degare's reign. What Ember wouldn't? But Elias was likely headed to the trades right now. She did not have a year to wait, and she was not foolish enough to think she could escape this valley and get to Edmaria to save her husband from a foreign kingdom on her own. She needed help, and in exchange for Elias's safety, she thought maybe she would strike a deal with Degare himself, even if it meant risking the end of all hope for the return of Ozanna.

She tapped her finger. "I have one condition."

"I love conditions," he said with a smirk.

"You asked me when I arrived here what brought me to Oro." Leith tilted his head. "It started with the prince's death, but it was my husband who sent me." Her voice nearly broke at the word *husband.* "I did not have a choice in the matter." She chose to leave out the part about how he thought he was sending her to Adullam, because this man, she still did not trust. Leith raised his brows. "It is not as you think. He was saving my life."

"Go on," Leith said curiously.

"He took the punishment for a crime I committed. Now, I need to save him. And I believe you can help me." Cove's boldness had everything to do with saving Elias's life.

"How so?"

"The Edmarians took him on a ship with a hundred other Embers, bound for Oro. I need to get to Edmaria before he does. Before they take him to the trades to kill him. If you gather your armies to help me, you can provide a safe place for the Embers on that ship and enlist them in your rebellion. I am sure they would happily join for a chance at revenge."

"And just how long do you think it takes for a ship to get from the Dawn Islands to Edmaria? By the time we make it there, they will have already left for Oro. It is likely that this shipment is meant for the Summer Trade." The Summer Trade would not be happening for seven weeks. She had some time. Cove breathed a sigh of relief.

"Don't get too comfortable," Leith added, examining his nails. "Once they bring him to Oro, they'll have him in the prison there. He will not be treated well."

"At least I know where he'll be," she said, trying not to imagine the worst. "Can you get me to Oro, or not?"

Leith studied her and rose from his chair. "I can get you into Oro."

CHAPTER 32
SALT IN THE WOUND
LEITH

L eith stood waiting at the gate, searching for the red hair of his betrothed emerging from the Dead Wood, waiting for her to make her appearance in the final hours of The Darkening. His plans to bring Degare's reign to an end were all falling into place. Soon, he would have the alliance that secured it. She was to come with three Vestelian witnesses, and tonight, they were to be wed at the third moon's rising. He tapped his fingers impatiently as the glow of a violet crescent began to peek through the trees.

Edme watched him from a few hundred feet away with her arms crossed and a smug look on her face. It was dusk, and he had expected Ravenna by now. "See any sign of her?" Leith called to his head guard who hardly left the tower.

"No, Chief. Nothing for miles." Leith nodded, his jaw tightly set. He could feel Edme's stare burning into the back of his head. The fluttering of bat wings sounded overhead, and the chirping of crickets echoed through the forest, blending with the song of the river. There was a faint smell of smoke in the air, and Leith cleared his throat against the strangely bitter smell before turning to the guards that stood before him.

"At the first sign of her, come and get me. I want to be here when she arrives." They nodded as he turned toward his hut, but Edme was standing directly behind him, blocking his path.

"I do not think she is coming," she said pompously.

He gritted his teeth, trying to cage his anger. "Give her til' morning, then you can rub salt in my wounds all you want. But this alliance is imperative, and you know it."

The following afternoon when Leith was still without an alliance, Edme marched into his hut. He sighed, twisting the tarnished gold ring on his pinky.

"I told you not to trust her," Edme said from where she frowned at him across the room, arms crossed over her chest. Despite the chill in the air, she wore a sleeveless, tawny, chiffon gown that flowed to her ankles. Her fierce gaze was forever unwavering beneath her unruly, black curls as she awaited his apology for not taking her advice, and for not allowing her to kill Ravenna when she had the chance. "I told you she would bring nothing but sin upon the world, yet you agreed to marry her."

Edme's accusations were mostly true. He had agreed to marry Ravenna without a second thought, and he had trusted the young shield-maiden, foolishly. She had not caused him any grievances aside from the witch guardians that now wreaked most of their havoc on the angry Volcanian woman who sat across from him.

He had trusted Ravenna of the Valley and she had betrayed

him. The red-haired maiden had come unexpectedly on the day of the Gauntlet, like a storm. When she had thrown that dagger into his leg and looked upon his face with those vibrant eyes, a new plan had begun weaving itself together in his mind. Then, weeks later, as if it were fate, she strutted into his valley and laid it all out before him. She had set a trap, and he had walked right into it, unaware. It was too good to be true, that she had delivered to him exactly what he was searching for on a silver platter. At least he had still had his wits about him and was not so foolish to assume there was not some catch to her promise.

After noting the marks on Ravenna's neck made from beasts that he was far too familiar with, he and Edme had followed her back to Vestele under the cover of darkness. He had given Edme strict orders not to harm her, and though Edme had a mind of her own and was accustomed to the role of queen, she had reluctantly obeyed.

Just as Leith had suspected when he had followed the shield-maiden into the Dead Wood, the catch to their marriage alliance was that the pretty little dove was being tracked by the witch guardians. She had only been searching for a way out from under the claws of the curse, and in sealing an alliance with him, she would have gained his unwavering protection. It was not a problem, he had thought. He and Edme had returned unscathed, aside from the new marks that Edme bore on her soul for killing dozens of guardians with her wildfire. The Ink Blood Clan was strong enough to take down the entire race of guardians if they had to, and he would have made sure Ravenna was protected, if it meant she upheld her end of the deal: marriage. It truly was that simple.

Ravenna had been honorable in her dedication to

protecting her village with an alliance, and a part of him admired her for it. What he did not expect was that she would stand him up on the night they were to be married. Perhaps she had found another way out of her mess, or perhaps the guardians had already succeeded in killing her. He bristled at the latter thought, though he knew Edme had obliterated so many guardians that evening weeks ago, that the vengeful species would have likely forgotten about Ravenna for the time being, as they yearned for revenge on the woman of wildfire across from him.

He had been so close to all the answers he sought, and they had been torn away right before they met his grasp. He should have demanded the pendant from around Ravenna's neck that day as a ledger. Surely, she would have returned if he had kept not only the dagger with the red gemmed hilt, but both remnants she had of her late mother. Then, all his problems would be well on their way to being solved. He ran the shield-maiden's valuable blade between his fingers, admiring the pure stone.

He turned to Edme. "I do not think you understand what is at stake, princess." Her face hardened as she fought the urge to correct him. He knew things she was unaware that he knew about her recent endeavors. He knew exactly what had led her here to his valley, to aid him in *his* endeavors.

"I understand fully. And because you refused to end her when you had the chance, the King of Oro now holds her in his grasp," she spat. At those words, Leith leaned forward in his chair.

"What do you speak of?" he asked.

Edme's dark brown skin seemed to burn with rage as she prepared to speak. He placed his hands on the edge of the table and rose, awaiting the response that rolled from her sharp tongue.

"When Ravenna had not arrived by yesterday at dusk, I sent a dove to Vestele."

Leith studied her carefully.

"The bird returned with nothing but a piece of rastweed in its talons. Its feathers were stained black with ash."

Leith looked at Edme under lowered brows. The royal kept her chin up, awaiting his reaction. Degare's signature destruction was with rastweed smoke and fires that engulfed whole villages. Leith was certain the king had come for Ravenna, and for the same reasons that he had wanted her first. It was for those reasons that Leith knew Degare would not kill her. Not yet.

Leith envisioned her in the wretched, colorless kingdom, her vibrant beauty standing out like a red rose in a thicket. When he remembered her wit, he smiled softly to himself. Ravenna would give Degare a run for his money. Though she had come to Leith's valley and tried to appear submissive and desirable, she was obviously persistent in getting what she wanted; just as the Volcanian Queen was that stood before him. Ravenna was strong and capable. He had seen proof of that in the Brunts and in the way she had sought to betray him to protect her own.

She was fearless, but in the grip of the shadows, he doubted she could see her way out. Perhaps she could still use an alliance. Perhaps he could still get what he needed from her. In the process of retrieving it, he would make sure the King of Darkness regretted stealing his betrothed. He would make all of Oro pay for it.

Leith's jaw clenched harder, and it was all he could do to

remain collected as his mind twisted around her name and combed through all the ways he could reclaim her from Oro.

Ravenna.

That name held the solution to all his problems. Ravenna was his.

"I sent some of my men to Vestele this morning at dawn," Edme continued. Her voice was rough and wild like untamed fire. Behind it was the promise of retribution on Degare for what he had done to the mostly innocent people of Vestele, and the room seemed to heat around them. "They sent word back."

"Any survivors?" Leith asked.

"Yes."

CHAPTER 33
EMPTY VESSEL
COVE

Cove's body felt like an empty vessel. She strummed the tether within her mind frequently, keeping it at a constant vibration, hoping for a sound, or a word—anything that could mean he was okay, but there was never an answer. Her body shook with the tether that bound them, and she wondered if he felt the separation, too. He had chosen this. He had chosen to leave her. He had chosen her life over his.

Why did I let him get involved? She remembered the peace she had felt with him. Being with him was like getting a full breath of fresh air when she had been taking labored breaths her entire life. Elias's presence was not draining to her, and his emotions brought joy, not sorrow. She had been living in a sea of sorrows her entire life, trying to catch a breath above the pain and suffering of those around her that threatened to drag her under. Those people had no hope—no Light. Cove longed to be surrounded by Light, by those whose minds had been transformed. By those who did not fear—by those who did not bleed night. She had let him love her because she did not think she would survive another day without it.

She held the scrolls in her hands, careful not to crumple them with the agony that was coursing through her body. The agony was all her own, but suddenly Leith entered her hut, and his agony followed, magnifying it. Today, his emotions lacked their usual concealment.

"What's wrong?" she asked as the door slammed behind him. She could feel the anger that trailed him through the door and scooted her body back into the wall behind her cot. She pulled her knees to her chest, watching him carefully.

"I have a plan to get you into Oro," Leith said, cutting straight to the chase before he had even laid eyes on her.

"But?" He looked at her with bloodshot eyes that revealed his lack of sleep.

"There is more for you to do than just save your husband. When you work for me, it is not only about you and your needs anymore. Do you understand that?" He spoke hastily, and with a new sternness. He was fearful of something.

Cove nodded. She needed his help, and he needed hers. "What do you need me to do?"

"As you can see, I am still unwed," he held up a ringless finger. "My betrothed did not show up last night as she promised."

Cove raised her brows. "She betrayed you."

"Not exactly," Leith said, pacing slowly across the room. "The King of Oro took her."

Cove's heart thundered in her chest. "Degare has her?" *As he would soon have Elias.*

He nodded. "And I need you to go ahead of me while I prepare my armies. You have reason to be extra diligent. I trust you because I know your husband's life depends on your success. Now, so does Ravenna's." He rubbed his palm down his face and blinked his tired eyes. "You know how important she is to me. I'll get you into the castle as a servant. You'll be able to spy, look through inventory sheets, make note of anything that can help us—and report back to me while I prepare my men."

Cove watched him closely, noting the redness of his eyes and the nervous tapping of his fingers. Was she better off finding her own way into Oro? Was she better off not getting involved in his mess? Would he even allow her to leave, knowing the Light she bore within—that power he obviously sought for his armies?

As if he read her mind, he continued with the reminder she needed that she should trust no one. "I know the secrets you bear," he said slowly, "that you are the Ember who killed the King of Edmaria's favorite son. Surely you would not want that information to be released." Cove chewed on the inside of her cheek.

"Deal," she finally said.

He sighed loudly, and Cove thought the relief that traveled through the room was strange. "Happy to have you with us," he said, "but Cove, if you find your husband before my armies make it, you cannot abandon your post. I need you inside the castle. You are the eyes and ears of this operation. You are to help me get my Dove back." Cove swallowed. *Would I truly deliver the Dove into his hands to save my husband?* "Help me get my Dove," he reiterated, "and I will help you find your husband."

She nodded. Anything for Elias—and she could not save him alone.

CHAPTER 34
SHADOW'S SPY
COVE

Leith left her hut and was back within the hour. She was packing up her Light Scrolls when he returned. "You're leaving those with me," he said, nodding to the parchment in her hand as he shut the door. He was carrying a sack and what appeared to be a linen dress.

She opened her mouth to argue. She was keeping the Light Scrolls. "It is bad enough that you are going into Oro with a lightmark on your skin. You are not taking the Scrolls too. At least you'll be able to hide your mark easily beneath a servant's uniform. They will provide one when you arrive. You will be in the servant chambers with other women, though. You'll have to be careful," he said, gesturing to her mark. He tossed the clothing onto the cot beside her. "They are expecting you. For now, put this on. I'll wait outside." He stepped out the door as she held the dress up before her. It was similar to the one she was wearing on her last day with Elias. She undressed, pulled it over her head, and combed her fingers through her tangled hair as best she could.

Leith was standing outside her hut on the edge of the village when she emerged. She took a quick glance around, taking in all the fruit trees and buildings that lined both sides of the river. There were arched wooden bridges connecting the lively side of the valley to the inky side of black stone. A few dozen people walked amid the village, carrying buckets of water on their heads, skinning fish, scrubbing linens on washboards, and hanging clothes to dry. She saw none of the lightmarked Embers Leith had told her he was gathering, and she did not know if she was relieved or disappointed.

Was he lying or are they here, imprisoned behind doors as I have been?

One of the stablemasters made his way over, leading a black horse by the reins. Suddenly, Cove's stomach began to turn. "I have never ridden before," she admitted sheepishly.

"You have never ridden a horse?" Leith asked dumbfoundedly. He scratched his chin and turned to the horse then back to her. "It's really not that difficult." He turned to the stablemaster and ordered him, "Go get a saddle."

She eyed the massive animal that towered before her. One swift kick could kill her; she bristled at the thought. *For Elias,* she reminded herself. When the stablemaster returned with a saddle in hand, Leith spoke again. "Be thankful you don't have to ride bareback. She's quick, but she listens well." Leith studied her, and she could tell he was beginning to doubt if she was capable of this mission. She stepped forward, ready to learn. "Okay," he said slowly as the stablemaster finished securing the saddle. "Just pull yourself up on the saddlehorn," he pointed to the knob at the top of the saddle. "You can use the mane, too, if you need. Step here," he pointed to a loop of leather that hung low by the horse's side.

"That's the stirrup," he said. "Put your foot in it and throw your other leg over."

Cove raised a brow. Because of the books she'd read in the palace, she knew enough about horses to know that ladies rode sideways. "Straddle it?" she asked.

He took an impatient breath. "Yes, it will be far easier than riding sidesaddle. Trust me."

She didn't, but she listened to what he said and hoisted herself up onto the horse's back. When she was successful, a smile spread across her face. "Great. Now use cues to coax her forward. You can use the reins or your legs to steer. Pull back to slow or stop her." Cove nodded, giving it a try. The horse took a few steps forward, and she fought to maintain her balance atop it.

Leith handed her a satchel and she secured it across her body. "There's food in there and a map. You can read a map, can't you?" Cove nodded. She had spent two years at sea with Marinos and Ahlia—she could read a map quite well. "Good. The terrain between here and Oro is rocky. The mountains will slow you down if you get off the route I've drawn for you. Try not to stop more than you have to. There is a shadow valley you'll have to cross through, but with that lightmark, I have no doubt you'll be fine."

"The Valley of the Shadow?" she blurted, suddenly remembering Celeste and Yarris's conversation in Oriana.

"Too scary for you?" he asked, crossing his arms.

"No," she lied. *I can do this. For Elias.*

"Good. You should be there in a matter of days. The stablemaster in Oro will take your horse and point you to the steward. From there, they will give you the rundown of your duties as a servant. But do not forget your duties to me."

Cove's throat bobbed. The leader of one of the rebellions Elias had spoken of was standing before her, and she was taking orders from him. They were seemingly united in their quest against Oro, but only because of the secrets he held over her head. Cove suspected that their plans after Oro fell were quite different. "Lastly," Leith added, "if there comes any information that can be beneficial to my operation against Oro, you are to go to the beach at the edge of the kingdom. There will be a flock of ravens there. I keep them fed, and they are trained to travel back and forth from that beach to Ink Valley. Take your messages to the ravens, and I will receive them."

Cove nodded warily, unsure of the alliance she had made.

"Are you ready?" he asked.

Yes, ready to find my husband.

"I am," she said aloud. And with that, Leith smacked the rear of the horse, and Cove was off to find the Shadow's bride.

Cove was surprised that she was not having more difficulty in her travels. The horse was a gentle giant and led Cove north without a fuss. The sound of insects quieted the further north she traveled, and the terrain was becoming more rocky now as they wove in and out of the trees of the creepy Dead Wood. They were nearing the mountainous territory that separated Oro from the rest of the continent. The towering mountains seemed to serve as a sort of natural gate that spanned hundreds of miles from the west to the east, and Cove knew that Elias was the only person for which she would willingly enter into the jaws of Oro.

The three moons hung in the sky above her, taunting her

with their light. She sat on the bank while her mare drank from the stream beside her, the moons' silver glow like a sheen on the water. Cove looked around and then held up a palm. She pulled some water toward her, testing her control as she formed a water dove. Since she had felt Elias channel his power through her, she had gained some understanding of how to master her own. This time, she smiled as the water obeyed her, its shape actually resembling the bird of hope with its fluttering wings splayed out. *What would become of the Dove in Leith's hands? There nestled in that valley of rebels, would her wings become black as ink?* Cove took a shuddering breath and let the water crash to the ground at her feet.

She dug around in her satchel, searching for the food Leith claimed was there. She found a bit of jerky wrapped in a sheet of wax and a jar of some type of nut. Most of the weight of her satchel came from a dagger and the pile of red fruits at the bottom. She grabbed one of the fruits, but before she could take a bite, her horse turned its head toward her, watching her intently. She smiled softly. "I suppose you deserve a bite," she said, extending the fruit toward her. The mare's lips tickled Cove's palm as she took the fruit. Cove jumped back, wiping the spit from her hand on her dress. "Quite ill-mannered, but you're sweet," she said as she took another fruit from her satchel. Beneath it, something shiny glowed in the moonlight. She reached for the tiny flash of silver to find a small ring with a note tied to it.

"A ring to remember your husband by, until you meet again. When you find him and help me get the Dove, you will both have a home here, in Ink Valley."

Cove's brows lowered as she twisted the ring in her fingers, examining it. *Was this some type of bribery, masked as a gift? Or was this a way for him to trick her into trusting him? Perhaps it was a debt she would be expected to repay.* Cove knew these games, but she placed the ring on her finger anyway. She and Elias had not traded rings with their vows, but she quite liked having one to mark their union. Ring or no ring, after she found him, they would not be returning to Ink Valley. This alliance she had made with Leith served one purpose, and that was to find entry into Oro to get Elias back. She would not be foolish enough to trust him. Soon, he would just be another face to run from.

Cove laid down in the grass, listening to the water sing. She let the tips of her fingers glide over the water as she admired the new ring on her hand, humming until she had lulled herself into a dream. A dream where Elias still held her tightly on the bow of that sailboat in the sea.

A tether between souls and a quiet plea, will guide me home, back to thee.

The tether that pulled her to Oro was still silent, but she let her words travel down it as she rode north anyway. The Valley of the Shadow was becoming visible in the distance, and Cove's nerves were beginning to jitter. She felt the horse's fear thickening with each step forward, and that only made her own uneasiness grow.

Elias, I am coming for you, she spoke down the thick thread that stretched between them.

You'll never believe the week I have had.

Why did you have to take the fall for me?

I love you.

We will be together soon, she promised—hoped.

You know those rebellions you told me about? The ones that aren't of the Light but fight to overthrow Oro? Well, you sent me right into the heart of one, and now I am wrapped up in the middle.

Have you ever heard of the Valley of the Shadow? I am about to go in. Now would be a wonderful time to say your final goodbyes. She sent those last remarks with a bit of sarcasm.

The Valley of the Shadow was hugged by tall rocks on either side, leaving only a narrow crevice for Cove and her horse to enter. She took a deep breath, touching the lightmark at her chest. "You saved me from death before, I suppose you can do it again," she said aloud to the Father of Lights. "Perhaps this is all some plan to get me where you need me to be. . .I did vow my life to you. But Oro? Really? Where they would have me dead? I have to admit, I do question your methods."

Elias had felt like such a gift from the Light but had so quickly been torn from her. She would follow him anywhere, and she supposed she should follow the Father of Lights anywhere, too. Wherever that may be. She looked into the lightless valley where the sun did not reach. He did not seem to be here, but his Light was within her, and she trusted that.

She nudged her horse forward. Once they entered, there would be no going back. She tugged her collar to the side, allowing her mark to dimly guide the way. There was a crunching of rocks, or maybe bones, beneath her mare's feet, and Cove shivered.

Anxiety threatened to overtake her, but she focused on the

Light as she twisted her ring over and over again. The sound of a thousand bats squeaked overhead as they all flapped toward the sky, bursting from the valley around her. She stiffened and closed her eyes, urging her mare to go faster. The horse did, becoming clumsy with distress, and Cove tried to calm her with a gentle but shaking touch to her mane.

"Shh. Easy. Easy," she whispered and wished she could convince herself of those words. The black valley stretched as far as the eye could see, and it took about twenty grueling minutes before Cove could see the light on the other side through the seam between the steep mountains. She held her breath, praying for the legendary shadows to stay in their slumber, and when the daylight finally hit her face again, she wept with both fear and relief.

Oro was near.

The books Cove had read in the palace in the Dawn Islands did not lie about The Kingdom of Oro. It was just as she had imagined it. It was a kingdom the sun did not shine upon, and one where vegetation was scarce. The air was heavy with sorrow, and the rocky black soil stretched from her toes at the edge of the beach to all the land set before her. The Black Sea called to her at her back, but it was a song she did not wish to hear. The sea and the lands here were cursed with the very darkness that had once had a hold on her heart, and her hands began to shake.

You walk in the Light now, she thought to herself. *Do not be afraid.*

The castle in the mountain towered above, casting its

shadow over all the kingdom. She coaxed her hesitant mare into the looming darkness. The kingdom was silent aside from the pounding of her heart in her ears and the clicking of hooves on the stone. She tried to focus on the latter.

She kept her chin high as she approached the iron gates, where several guards stood with solemnity painted on their pale faces. They said nothing as she halted before them. She gulped down the knot in her throat and removed her hood, letting it drape behind her quaking shoulders. She begged her body to still, but in its fight to keep the darkness from knocking on the walls of her mind, it found no rest.

The darkness cannot touch you.

The lightmark that was hidden at her chest throbbed, and she inhaled deeply before stating her business in the heart of darkness.

"I'm here to serve in the castle," she said too timidly.

"Yes, we have been expecting you," one of the guards grunted. His red cloak was the color of blood, a raven's crest at his back between his shoulderblades. The gate creaked as another guard swung it open just wide enough for her to pass through with her horse. One of the guards pointed her in the direction of the stables to her left, and she nodded her thanks.

That was easy, she thought.

Inside the gates and up the steps, the kingdom's people traveled with a sort of emptiness behind their eyes. A worn banner hung over the square, and Cove was reminded that celebrations of The Darkening had just ended. She fought the urge to grasp at her mark as she continued through the square to the stables. When the stablemaster had collected her horse and the steward came out to greet her, she maintained her composure by focusing on the only thing that could offer her an ounce of peace.

Elias, whether you are listening or not, I am here to save you.

CHAPTER 35

WHERE ALLEGIANCES LIE
COVE

The first two days in the castle of Oro went smoothly, though she was still impatiently waiting for the shipment of Embers to arrive from Edmaria. There was not anything to report, as she had not yet met the Dove Leith spoke of—the red-haired woman to whom he was engaged—but Cove was finding her way around and heard many whispers about her.

The kitchen was crawling with gossip now about every topic imaginable. "I hear Prince Merrick is to marry the Princess of the Dawn Islands. Princess Mina, I think, is her name," a servant said. Cove chewed on her lip nervously. The proposal Mina had sent to Edmaria the night Cove had left had already made its way to the King of Edmaria, and he had accepted. When would Mina receive the news? How long would it take word of Merrick's acceptance to travel back across the sea? Who would she confide in? Would she even care? The night everything had happened, Mina acted as though she had changed her mind about Edmaria—as though she suddenly approved of an alliance.

The servants continued whispering, their hot air filling the kitchen around her. "Rumor is that the eldest prince was murdered," one started. Cove shifted uncomfortably beneath the words that were not directed at her but felt like accusations. She kept her eyes on the dirty floors. "Despite it, King Idris still seeks an alliance. I think he is just working to secure such a deal so he has more Embers to sell to Oro. I hear his kingdom brings in most of Degare's stock for the trades."

Cove expected such things from King Sebastian, but from Mina, who had called the proposal, *my proposal*, Cove felt a sense of betrayal she had never seen coming. Cove's mind was cloudy regarding the events of that night, but she knew one thing: because of the woman she had once called *sister,* her husband was being marched to his death within the walls of this kingdom.

Nausea worked its way up Cove's throat as she listened to the rest of the gossip around her. Nothing had surfaced about Sebastian's illness or Mina's quickly approaching coronation. *How much longer does the King of the Dawn Islands have left? A month or two at best,* Cove guessed, being that she had been away from the islands for seven weeks now.

The servants now whispered about the red-haired girl and what exactly the King of Oro wanted with her. If Cove had to guess, it was for the same reasons Leith wanted her: power. No one here knew her as the Dove mentioned in the Light Scrolls, born to the once-barren queen, but Cove would bet that Degare did. The question was: *Where is her power? Does she bear it, or has it yet to be given?*

"She's up in the tower. Her poor, sweet guard has been run

ragged," one of the older ladies was saying. "He's a very sweet young man. He has not been getting much sleep. I wonder what the girl has done that she warrants constant supervision, even from a cell."

"She must be important to Degare, is all I can say," another servant said with a shrug as she scrubbed a dish in a bucket of soapy water.

"I think she is an Ember," someone chimed in.

"If she was an Ember, the king would have killed her by now." Cove tensed, rubbing the back of her neck beneath her thick braids. She eavesdropped while sweeping the broom into every little crevice of the kitchen. A thick layer of dust plumed into the air. *Whose job had this been before me?*

"Speaking of the girl, I am taking her guard breakfast now. I am meeting him at the bottom of the tower before he begins duty. When I get back, I need this space tidy," she gestured to the wooden table in the middle of the kitchen. "I am beginning to feel a bit ragged too. There is so much to do that I cannot keep up." Cove perked up and turned to face her.

"Miss, I would be happy to deliver his breakfast for you."

She paused and looked Cove up and down. "New and eager I see," she said, as if noticing her for the first time. She handed her the plate. She looked around at the other servants bustling about the room and gestured to Cove. "We have more help, ladies! Finally, the need is being met." Cove smiled and dipped her head, hustling out into the hallway with the platter in hand.

She had learned the halls of the castle quite quickly, but in comparison to the palace in Oriana, it was much more difficult to navigate. The corridors were cold, dark tunnels that had been carved through the castle in the mountain. It reminded her of a maze. The kingdom itself was just as dark as all of the stories told. She had come well prepared, though, imagining the worst as she always did.

Thankfully, she had not yet seen the king or his witch. She hoped she could gather some useful information from Ravenna's guard. As she found her way to the bottom of the tower, where Leith's Dove was caged, she felt a strangely familiar pull. She stopped in her tracks, searching the dimly lit hall for any sign of that Light that called to her in the same way Elias's had in the palace.

"Is that my breakfast, I hope?" a voice called out from the shadows. Cove whipped her head around. A man Elias's age rose from where he had been sitting at the tower steps, and his gentle, but tired, gray eyes were the first thing she noticed. He scratched his head, ruffling his brown hair.

She surveyed him carefully with a tilt of her head, wondering if the Light that was almost palpable in some way, was coming from him. He stepped toward her, and she kept her feet planted. "I'm Zephaniah. I haven't seen you around here before," he said, introducing himself. His voice was kind, and he spoke with patience. She extended the plate toward him, saying nothing.

He took it into his hands and offered her the hint of a smile. "Thank you," he said. She could tell he was curious about her stunned silence, but he said nothing else before he turned to ascend the steps of the tower.

"Wait," she called after him. He halted and shifted to the side, waiting for her to speak.

"I also brought this for you," she said, pulling a red fruit from her apron. She examined it for a moment, flipping it in her hand and placed it into his palm. He wrapped his fingers around it and left her with a smile.

Cove did not return to the kitchen right away.

She lost track of time as she collected herself, practicing her breaths and allowing herself to think. When she finally returned to the busy kitchen, she found a frantic servant by the name of Mirren. "Jara has sent for two servants—myself and one other. Beatrice is nowhere to be found. I need an extra set of hands, or Jara is going to be livid."

Cove stopped in the doorway, looking around at the busy kitchen servants. Everyone was moving with haste. The woman Cove had spoken to earlier made eye contact with her across the room in a way that seemed to say, *What took you so long?*

"Oh Mirren, stop your whining," she grumbled. "We have our hands quite full here, but take the new girl." She nodded to Cove, who stood at the threshold of the kitchen behind Mirren. Mirren turned around, shocked to see her there, and Cove's cheeks reddened. "She'll help you. We can get by. Just go," the lady added with an eye roll.

"Well, let's get going then," Mirren said with a sigh. *I am going to meet the witch.* Mirren was middle-aged and built stoutly, with brunette hair that was tucked neatly into a bun. She scurried like a mouse all the way to the witch's chambers, and they moved so quickly that Cove barely had enough time to grow anxious.

Cove knew castle etiquette and had spent years watching Mina's servants tend to her. Now she was to tend to the king's witch. This would be the perfect placement for her, if she could keep her identity hidden. What kind of information could she gather from watching the king's closest confidant? Maybe she could find information on Elias and the ship he was on. She could only pray.

"We'll stop by the servant quarters first. We need to grab a new set of clothes for the prisoner Jara is questioning today." Cove straightened. *Prisoner? Could she be talking about Ravenna?* Mirren eyed her. "She's close to your size. Maybe a bit taller. Broader shoulders. Select something accordingly, and make it fast."

Swiftly, Cove went to the small dresser beside her bed and selected an olive linen dress. She chose the thickest one she had, figuring Ravenna was freezing in the tower through the chilly nights. She did not need the dress anyway; she had four others. It was difficult for Cove to change or bathe in front of the other servants, but she had found ways around it that did not raise suspicion.

As she followed Mirren into the witch's chambers, she did her best to remain unseen. She knew the witch dealt closely with the Ember Trades and their stock. Cove quickly scanned the room for any sign of documentation or information that may be useful later. A pile of papers sat atop a dark wooden desk, and on them, Cove could make out a list of names with other information. Her stomach turned as she guessed they were a list of the Ember stock for the trades and made a mental note to come back later. She averted her eyes and followed suit as Mirren curtsied in the presence of the witch.

Cove lifted her chin and tried to make herself small. Her breath caught in her throat as she saw the Dove in the witch's chambers, admiring a tapestry on the wall that depicted a scene of jagged black rocks and pools of black water. Her hair was long and tangled, her dress covered in stains, and Cove noticed dirt beneath her nails as she reached out to touch the tapestry. Jara leaned on the back of a chaise, her body tall and thin, and snapped her head back to Ravenna.

"Do not touch that," she spat, and Cove was shocked to see Ravenna roll her eyes without care. She watched her closely, wondering what it was that had caused the shake in her legs and her other signs of physical distress but had not been powerful enough to quench her fiery spirit. Jara's slender face turned toward Cove, and her strange, orange eyes flashed as she laid eyes on her. "Oh, a new one," she said, before waving a hand in the air toward Ravenna. "Clean her up and get her a clean set of clothes. Make her not reek." Cove dipped her head and followed Mirren as she led Ravenna past the witch's bed and to the bathing chambers.

Quickly, Cove and Mirren dumped buckets of water into the tub while Ravenna stood against the wall and watched. Cove wished she could use her gifts to maneuver the water, but she continued the heavy lifting that she was not used to.

"We must move quickly to appease Jara," Mirren muttered to Cove before turning to Ravenna. "Quick, come here." She motioned Ravenna over, and forced her around with a hand on her shoulder so she could begin undoing the corset of Ravenna's oversized dress. Ravenna kept her eyes on Cove for a moment before obeying Mirren, and Cove wondered if she recognized her from their brief passing in Leith's hut. Cove had been on the edge of death that day: the color drained from her pruned skin, body malnourished, wrapped in a blanket, and hair a tangled mess. She doubted Ravenna would be able to place her face, but Cove dropped her eyes to the floor anyway.

Reluctantly, Cove welcomed the emotions in the room around her and allowed them to swirl into her soul so she could better understand Ravenna. There was sadness and fear, and a sense of yearning there, and Cove wondered if it was a longing to leave. To take a chance at escape. Cove studied her as her legs quivered when Mirren dropped the dress from her shoulders.

Cove collected it from the floor and placed it near the wash basin, unable to ignore the stench rolling from it, much of which likely came from the wound just above Ravenna's knee. *What had this poor woman been through?* Mirren placed a few drops of scented oil into the tub, the floral fragrance reminding Cove of the gardens she'd once walked with Elias. She smiled to herself and looked up at Ravenna, offering her a hand.

Ravenna was careful not to allow her wound to be submerged, and Cove fought a cringe as the water went black around her. Mirren began scrubbing almost immediately, and Cove took the cue. They moved quickly, using pumice stones to cleanse her skin. Ravenna's face was in a constant grimace, and Cove offered Ravenna a smile that she hoped would suffice as an apology. Cove dipped her stone into the warm sudsy water next to the tub and took one of Ravenna's arms into her hand. She scrubbed, but not as harshly as Mirren. With a knock at the door, Ravenna stiffened, and fear bled from her pores. Cove took a shaky breath against the horrors this woman must have endured and placed a gentle hand on her shoulder.

She could offer her no promise that she would be okay. She could offer her no true consolation. Cove was working against Degare, but in doing so, she was only planning to deliver Ravenna into the hands of another enemy. In return for her own husband—her own happiness—she would send this woman to Leith. *What exactly was it that he had planned for her? Was it worse than what Degare had mapped out for her life?*

Four servants came into the bathing chambers, each carrying more water. After she and Mirren had drained and refilled the tub, Mirren attempted to undo a ratty braid from Ravenna's hair, and Ravenna quickly stopped her.

"Leave it," she said tightly as a strange longing for vengeance filled the air. Cove wondered what that braid meant to her, and as they rinsed the remaining grime from Ravenna's skin, she could not help but try to offer Ravenna some kindness.

"My name is Cove," she said as she offered her a towel. The words of kindness felt like a betrayal—a means of manipulation. She had learned such things from Marinos, and it disgusted her.

"I am sure you have been told my name by now," Ravenna replied monotonously. Ravenna took the towel and dried off, wrapping it around her and securing it at her chest. Cove wanted Ravenna to trust her, not just because she needed her trust for this mission to work, but because she felt sorry for her. Cove only wished she was worthy of trust.

Ravenna was uneasy about something, but she turned toward Mirren. To Cove's surprise, Ravenna offered them her name, and even coaxed Mirren's name out of her, despite Mirren's glowering, as if they did not have time to exchange names.

Ravenna sat on a stool now, and Cove stood at Mirren's side to braid her hair. It fell to her back and was the color of terracotta. Cove was working her fingers through, weaving little strands, remembering how she used to style Mina's hair. Cove's throat bobbed, and she stepped back from Ravenna at the burst of annoyance that came through the door from the witch, who stood beyond it now. Cove stood still, awaiting her orders.

"She does not need to look like royalty," the witch hissed as she stomped into the room. Cove and Mirren hastily finished tying the braids, leaving most of her hair cascading down her back. Mirren followed Jara out into the main chambers, and Cove took the opportunity to speak with Ravenna in private. *What information could she possibly provide?* It seemed she knew even less about her own situation than Cove did. Maybe Cove would just be a friendly face.

Cove extended an unworn dress to her. "A new dress," she said with a smile. "Well, it is one of mine. I thought perhaps it would keep you a little warmer in the tower."

She gave Ravenna a knowing wink, and it was met with a whisper of annoyance and a quiet, "Thank you."

Cove swallowed and helped Ravenna into a pair of stockings. Ravenna stared at her intently, as if trying to figure her out. Cove was aware that she did not look like she belonged in these lands. "My family is not from here. We come from the Dawn Islands," she offered as Ravenna stepped into the clean dress.

Ravenna tilted her chin. "Which island?" Cove moved behind her, and Ravenna's eyes trailed her for only a moment.

"Tabrana," Cove answered as she began lacing the corset.

"Why have you come here?" Ravenna asked. It seemed the Dove would be asking most of the questions today.

"To serve," Cove replied. *To serve the Light. I want to serve the Light. Not Leith, not Degare. You are the Dove, Ravenna. Meant to usher in the Light to Arresia with the return of Ozanna.* "Why else?" she asked, hoping Ravenna would ask a different question. Cove began humming a tune then, trying to create any distraction she could. It was the same tune Cove had heard Leith whistle only weeks before. The same tune her mother had once taught her.

Ravenna said nothing else, and Cove wondered if this song could offer her a bit of peace, too. So she continued through the melody, repeating it as many times as she could before the dress was laced and Ravenna was ready for the witch. As Cove followed her out of the bathing chambers, she passed Zephaniah, who waited with shackles in hand. His gray eyes revealed none of his true feelings, but by the emotions that poured from his soul, Cove could guess where his allegiances lay.

They were, at the very least, with Ravenna, but Cove would venture to say he was loyal to the Father of Lights.

Cove gulped, watching Zephaniah stand firm in the agony of it all, and she hurried out the door. The sound of shackles clasping on wrists followed her out.

How can I deliver this innocent woman into the hands of darkness? she thought. *How am I to complete such a mission?*

What am I to do?

CHAPTER 36

REMNANTS OF GRIEF
COVE

The guilt and shame of leaving Ravenna in those chambers with the witch was eating away at Cove's soul, along with the absence of her husband. She now knew where the witch's chambers were, and she knew that within the stack of papers on her desk, there was information that could lead her to Elias. Though she had come here for him, something inside her longed to free the Dove.

She and Mirren split ways without so much as a goodbye, and before Cove returned to the kitchens, she found herself climbing the steps to the tower, where she knew Ravenna would soon return. As she ascended, walking past the many cells that lined the circular stairwell, prisoners reached out of the bars, grabbing toward her. She hugged the wall closely, remaining just out of reach as their fingertips grazed the hem of her skirt. They were out of their minds, and Cove could see that this tower in particular was generally one used for solitary imprisonment. Cells were not shared here, and no guards stood on duty. It would seem that Ravenna was the only prisoner who warranted a soldier's constant guardianship.

Cove had never seen such conditions, and she wondered if there was a place like this in the Dawn Islands that she had been unaware of. She knew there was a prison on the south isle of Tabrana, but she had never wondered who it kept in its cages. Who were these prisoners, whose moans filled the tower around her? She did her best to block out the agony that followed her up the steps and greeted her from above. It was all around, begging to be felt.

Breathe.

She dared to look into a few cells as she searched for a vacancy, noting that none of the prisoners bore visible lightmarks. These men were likely here for crimes like poaching, theft, treason, and murder. She knew that most Embers were held in the Ember Prison outside of the castle while they awaited the trades, and she guessed that was where Elias would be placed when he arrived. How was she going to travel across the kingdom and into the prison to retrieve him? Such a task seemed impossible. Before she made any moves, she would need to be sure he was there. That would be her first step: find her way into the witch's chambers and check the inventory sheets that she hoped she had.

Cove knew when she had made it to Ravenna's cell. It was the only one she found empty, and the closely nibbled core of the red fruit she had given Zephaniah littered the ground, along with blood and dirt and grime. Cove winced as she stepped into the cell. There was nothing but a remnant of grief within the walls. Aside from love, grief was the deepest emotion one could feel. Even when you think you've overcome it, it's there, lurking in the shadows, ready to drag you back down.

She held her breath as she raked the cell, gathered the two buckets of riddled water, and descended the steps, letting her power silently sweep over it so it would not slosh out. When she finally got to the base of the steps, arms burning, she realized she could cradle the water inside the buckets with her power, keeping the weight from her arms. No one was in the hall, and even if there were a crowd around her, no one would notice. Something within her had clicked into place when she and Elias had merged their gifts, and when he had channeled his own Light through her. She understood the way it worked now, and control came much easier.

She breathed a sigh of relief as she used her gifts to lift the water an inch off the bottom of the bucket, carefully keeping it contained inside as she carried them to the cesspit. She quickly made her way to the well and collected two new buckets, then filled them with drinking water for Ravenna. Hauling the buckets up the steps, even with her power keeping the weight of the water off of her, was tiring. The ascent combined with the utilization of her power had drained her of energy. She realized she would need to practice her gifts to learn to prevent exhaustion even after the smallest of tasks. She made one more trip to grab a mop and quickly tidied the cell. She was not sure if she would get in trouble for doing so, but she could not sit back and do nothing.

Right now, this was the only way she knew how to help. A little kindness when you feel like you're drowning can go a long way. Cove recalled the day she and Mina became friends, when she had needed a friend more than anything. Was Cove just as bad as Mina, though? Would she betray Ravenna in the end, just to get what she desired?

Quickly, Cove scribbled a note and left it beside the buckets.

Enjoy the new dress.

Hesitantly, she signed her name.

She told herself that a friend for a while was better than no friend at all.

Cove heard his voice before she saw him. Something about his commanding and churlish tone revealed his title before she laid eyes on his crown and staff. Through Cove's mind flashed the hundreds of lives that had likely been lost at the tip of that bloodstone weapon. She thought of Andreas's hand wrapped tightly around it, as he had boasted about right before she had killed him.

There was a sense of justice there, but she would not allow herself to feel it. She had never wanted to take a life. Not even the life of one who would take hers. Now that Elias was gone, brewing inside her was a storm that brought with it new and unfamiliar rage. She stopped herself from staring as King Degare passed by her in the hall. She had been told what to do in such a situation, so she bowed low and kept her eyes down. He paid her no mind, and as he turned the corner, he began speaking with the guard who escorted him. Cove hurried toward the end of the hall, listening closely.

"Jara thinks Ravenna's gifts may have been hidden within some sort of talisman. Have your men on high alert for such an item, but do not tell them why I search for it." *A talisman?* So that was what Jara was searching for. Cove chewed on her lip. *What sort of power lay inside a witch's talisman?* Cove knew it would not be of the Light, and though this was the first piece of information she felt would be beneficial to Leith, she found herself not wanting him to know.

CHAPTER 37
SHATTERED STONE
COVE

Ten days later, Cove was readying for bed. Her sleep had been broken lately, and she longed for a full night of rest. She'd be up early in the morning, before the sun with the other servants, rushing to the kitchens to get breakfast started. She had seen nothing of Ravenna, the witch, or the king in over a week, and she vowed to herself that tomorrow she would make an effort to find something useful.

Elias.

She whispered his name a hundred times, considering the endless silence as something she deserved. Unspoken words glided down the bond. *I never should have allowed you to help me. I am not worth this trouble, and you are worth too much to be taken from this world. I need you Elias, but I do not deserve you.*

As the other women were dressing for the night, Cove combed her hair and looked out over Oro through teary eyes. A movement in the streets caught her attention, and she homed in on Zephaniah, who quickly strode past the barracks and toward the slums. A strange presence seemed to follow him—

not exactly an emotion, but Cove could feel it nonetheless. It was something dark, pressing at his back, urging him on.

A distant scream echoed out into the kingdom, and Cove recognized it as Ravenna when Zephaniah clutched his stomach. Cove closed her eyes and breathed through the anguish that traveled up into the servant's chambers. When she opened them, Zephaniah had disappeared into the night, and she was left wondering where he'd gone. She wrapped herself in the warm blankets of her bed and the shallow emotions of the servants around her. Their problems were much lighter to bear than Ravenna's.

But as the night passed, Cove found no hiatus from the thoughts that plagued her. Elias was on a ship to Oro, to be sold in the Ember Trades. Ravenna was in the torture chambers being whipped or cut or beaten. Cove was here, unable to do a thing. Not even the sound of a dozen servants snoring around her could drown out the Dove's cries.

Cove cupped her hands over her ears. "What is the purpose of all of this?" she dared to whisper as she stared at the stone ceiling. "What are you doing? Where is your Light in this kingdom of black?" she whispered almost inaudibly.

Cove did not know what she expected, but there was no answer from the Father of Lights. He was silent, and she was tired of waiting.

She began her nightly routine once more, hoping she would slip into sleep sooner rather than later. *Elias. Elias. Elias.* She twisted her ring and repeated his name over and over in her mind, but Cove could not slip into sleep until Ravenna's screams could no longer be heard from the torture chambers.

All of the servants awoke at the deafening sound. Bits of rock tumbled from the ceiling, coating their beds in a layer of dust. Some of the women hid under the covers, but most took shelter beneath their beds as the strange darkness ripped through the kingdom.

Cove shielded her head with her arms and made her way to the window. Rocks broke free from a few buildings below, but despite the shaking, the castle stood tall around her. A pit formed in Cove's stomach, and she gripped her chest against the sudden, overwhelming darkness. It was a darkness she could feel in her bones.

"What is happening?" one of the servants cried.

"It's an earthquake, stay down," said another.

"Not an earthquake," Cove whispered to herself between panicked breaths. This was something far worse. Cove did not know what, but something was terribly wrong.

She turned from the window, slipped into her shoes, and rushed out the door. "Where are you going?" a voice called after her. She continued forward through the halls without responding.

Cove held back a cough as she made her way to the base of the tower, rubbing her eyes against the dust. She could hear the complaints of prisoners and Degare's distant voice as he ascended to the top of the tower with his men.

A few moments later there were screams, and a voice Cove recognized as Zephaniah's shouted above the sound of crumbling rock. "Let her go!" She knew they had Ravenna—the Dove. And she guessed the darkness that had been awakened tonight was the power from the talisman they had sought. Cove paced at the base of the tower. *What can I do? What should I do?* She rubbed her arms nervously as she debated ascending the steps, before she heard the shattering of something like glass and metal.

"No!" Degare's voice rumbled through the corridor. She could not see what was happening, but the king was distraught. "No, no, no!" Cove ran a hand through her hair, letting the cool air touch her forehead. *Is Ravenna alive? Is the Dove okay?* She searched for a place to hide—to stay concealed so she could find out what was happening. She saw a thick curtain that draped over the only window near the tower and slipped behind it.

"We'll fix it. I can fix it, Degare," the witch's smooth, calming voice said. *Has something happened to his bloodstone staff?* Cove could only hope. Then, Elias would be safe.

Cove leaned against the window sill, staying still behind the drapes. When she finally heard the many feet descending the tower, bringing with them a palpable, violent anger, she quieted her quick breaths.

"Take him to the torture chambers," Degare spat. Cove peeked out to see Zephaniah, chained and defeated between two guards. "Jara, gather servants to collect the bloodstone from the tower. I want every last remnant. If you do not have it mended by the Summer Trade—"

"I will, Your Majesty," she assured him. "Do not worry."

Cove swallowed, watching as Zephaniah was dragged over the threshold of the torture chambers. *What can I do? How can I help him? Should I go up the tower and collect the bloodstone to put a stop to the trades?*

How could she? She was sure there were soldiers standing

guard over the precious stone.

Degare grimaced at the Dove, unconscious and bleeding in the arms of a tall soldier. She had been tortured from head to toe, and she now bore shadowmarks across what little skin was left untouched. Cove winced, looking between Ravenna and the torture chambers and toward the tower where the bloodstone lay. *What should I do?* Cove wondered.

"Take her to a room," Degare ordered his soldier. "Order servants or a healer—I do not care. Just keep her alive until I can get that power." *What can I do?*

Tend to her, a voice seemed to say. *Go to her. Be a light.*

Cove breathed deeply. *But what of Elias? What of the staff? I could stop the trades, I—*

I need you to go to Ravenna.

Cove bit her cheek and slumped into the window while she waited for the corridor to empty. Then, reluctantly, she gathered the courage to follow the soldier to Ravenna's new chambers and stood tall behind him before speaking. She was thankful she had slept in her linen dress last night, as she had been unable to gain a minute of privacy to change into her bed clothes.

She cleared her throat. "Do you need assistance?" she asked.

"Open the door," he grunted. Cove nodded and hurried to push the door open for him. He turned to the side to slip through the door and laid Ravenna on the bed. Blood began staining the sheets around her. "Stop the bleeding. Keep her alive until the healer comes," he said. "Can you do that?"

Cove nodded.

"Very well," he said before positioning himself outside the chamber door.

CHAPTER 38
WRESTLING WITH LIGHT
COVE

The healer had come quickly and relieved Cove of the stress of keeping Ravenna alive. She was an elderly woman with long gray hair and dark, wrinkled skin, and by the way she carried herself, Cove knew she had been working in this castle for a long time.

"You did well, child," she said to Cove, not looking up from Ravenna's body. "But we need some clean water. Go fetch some. Quickly." Cove recognized the fear in the healer's voice and guessed it to mean Ravenna was fading.

She glanced around the room and went straight to the bathing chambers, where there was not a drop of water in sight. An empty bucket sat next to the tub, and Cove looked out the window toward the commoners well that was in the street below. She took a moment to feel the power swimming in her veins, and she knew she could do it. While the healer was distracted, she drew water toward the bucket, coaxing it in silently with barely a splash, and carried it to the bedside.

"Found some," Cove said nonchalantly. The healer did not look up, and instead, shoved a jar into Cove's hand.

"Help me apply this salve. Apply generously everywhere the skin is broken. I have a few jars, so don't fret about running out." Cove nodded, taking the salve into her hands and unscrewing the lid. It was thinner than she expected, and it spread easily, filling in every red gash on Ravenna's back. "We need clean, wet cloths to cover these wounds." Cove nodded, gathering some linens from the wardrobe. She used the healer's scissors to cut strips and dipped them into the water before laying them across Ravenna's skin.

When daylight came and Ravenna's body was covered with medicine, the healer deemed it safe for Cove to go get some rest. She sauntered toward the servant chambers. She was thankful the torture chambers were silent for the moment, and she wondered if Zephaniah still lay inside. She had her answer as she came closer, watching as the witch and a brunette healer waited outside the door. Jara was speaking too quietly for Cove to hear, but the emotion that engulfed the healer was pure dread.

Cove watched from afar as she solemnly slipped through the door.

Over the next several days, Cove wrestled with the Light: when she heard Zephaniah—*felt*—his agony echoing from the torture chambers; every day that passed while Ravenna remained unconscious; when she heard the staff had been successfully rebuilt and the trades would continue on...What did the Father of Lights expect her to do with the darkness in this kingdom? *What am I here for?*

The darkness was far too much. She needed Elias. She needed her calm.

In her servitude here, was she working for Leith, or Degare, or the Father of Lights? Or would she serve herself and do whatever she must to find Elias? She did not trust anyone other than her husband and the Father of Lights, but if she was being honest, she was finding it hard to trust either right now. Elias had left her in the dark grip of loneliness, and the Light was seemingly silent as she walked through it.

Cove could trust herself, though, and on her list of priorities, Elias was at the top. She would do whatever it took to get him back, including defying Leith and going against the King of Oro.

They both wanted Ravenna for her power. What was stopping Cove from going after it too? If Cove could somehow offer Ravenna friendship and freedom, would she help Cove get Elias back? If Ravenna was as powerful as they say, nothing could stop her. She was the Dove, meant to bring Ozanna back to power—to usher in the Light to Arresia. Cove could benefit greatly from having someone like that on her side. She released a shuddering breath.

She just needed to think of it as an alliance and not a form of manipulation.

When Ravenna woke up, Cove would be a friendly face. They would come up with a plan, and together, they would overthrow Degare. The trades would end, and when Cove was back in Elias's arms, all would be well again.

It had been eleven days since Ravenna had broken the stone. None of the servants knew Ravenna's true identity, but the rumor in the kitchens was that Jara was figuring out a spell that could transfer the power from Ravenna's body to Degare. The king was wary about using his bloodstone staff on her again so close to the Summer Trades. Cove had no plan yet, but she was thinking one up as she sat in the corner of Ravenna's room, wishing for her to wake.

Fear swept through the room, and as Cove looked up, she saw one of Ravenna's shadowmarked fingers twitch. Cove rose to her feet in haste.

"Good morning," she said, keeping her distance. Ravenna tilted her head toward Cove and scanned the rest of the room.

"Where is my guard?" she asked immediately, fear growing around her.

Cove adjusted her stance, shifting her weight from one leg to the other. "You have guards posted outside," she said coolly, keeping her arms crossed in front of her. She knew the guard Ravenna inquired about, and she did not want to be the bearer of bad news.

"I do not inquire about those guards," Ravenna said. Her eyes darted around the room, as if they were searching for a way out—or for a weapon. Cove was thankful she was still restrained in shackles. Cove walked toward her with her hands raised.

"I am here as your servant until Jara can figure out a spell to remove the vast amount of power from your body." Ravenna studied her for a moment. "Do you remember what happened?" Cove asked gently.

She watched as Ravenna replayed the horrors of her weeks here in her head. "How long has it been?" she finally asked.

"Eleven days. Your body has endured much. . .trauma," Cove spoke in a sympathetic tone. Empathy came naturally to her. Deep down, she truly did wish to help Ravenna and be her friend, but she was also hoping she would get something out of it.

The healer had not been back since yesterday, and Cove had been the one to replace Ravenna's bandages and apply salve. "Some of your wounds were infected," Cove said, gently reaching to pull a piece of gauze from Ravenna's shoulder. Ravenna's freckled face scrunched up in a wince. "The salve I've been using has helped. Only a few more days and you should be able to move around and get out of bed." Cove tried to offer her some hope.

"And go where?"

There was a swelling of despair from Ravenna, and Cove looked at her, realizing how little hope she had. *What had happened here in this kingdom, and in her life, that she knew no hope at all?* This woman was supposed to be the Dove. A symbol of hope, yet she knew none. Being near Ravenna was difficult for Cove. It was the greatest challenge she had found here in Oro. Cove's curse of empathy, even when she did not want to feel it, was overwhelming, and Ravenna's grief tore through her every second she stood here. Cove held her breath, unable to build a mental barricade strong enough to keep such powerful feelings from dragging their talons across her soul.

Cove's vision became blurry through thick tears as she silently fought, and when she blinked them away, she saw

Ravenna was weeping too. Cove's hand was in Ravenna's in an instant, and for a moment, Cove was with Mina again, hands cupped together in a gesture of comfort. But Mina had betrayed her, and Cove served a princess in another kingdom now.

Ravenna's eyes were full of questions, but she did not speak. Cove knew exactly what Ravenna wrestled with. She sighed. "Zephaniah—I haven't seen him," Cove said gently. "I only heard him once. . .in the torture chambers." Cove could not bear to look at Ravenna as she bore the weight of those words, so she shifted her attention back to the many wounds across her shadowmarked skin, trying to blink away images of Andreas's marks that flashed in her mind. "I am sorry," Cove said to Ravenna. When she was silent for a long while, Cove dared to glance back in her direction. Ravenna was staring mindlessly at the ceiling, stuck in the darkest crevices of her mind.

Could this woman truly be the Dove of Ozanna? Even with the shadowmarks that now cover her skin?

The mark on Cove's chest seemed to burn from the inside out. *Be a light.*

Cove stiffened, glancing around the room to be sure they were still alone. "There is still hope," she finally offered. *Are you really doing this?* she asked herself. She had never willingly shared this secret before. There were people who knew, but she had not offered them the information that could get her killed. They had all found out on their own, and by Light's grace, she was still alive.

Ravenna was still staring at the ceiling. Cove took a breath and spoke words aloud that she preferred to hide deep inside. "I am an Ember, Ravenna." Cove nearly choked on the words, but they were masked in confidence. Ravenna's body went rigid, and she shifted her gaze to Cove's. Cove swallowed as she tugged the collar of her dress to the side, exposing her lightmark. She surveyed the chambers once more before hovering a hand over top of the glass at Ravenna's bedside. She separated three drops of water from the glass and watched as they rose and fell back into the glass. She smiled to herself at the memory of Elias revealing himself to her in the same way. "I am on your side. You can trust me," she said. *We are both against Degare. We can work together.*

"What are you doing in this castle?" Ravenna whispered, as if she feared for Cove's safety. "You could be killed. Helping me could get you killed."

Cove chuckled. She knew the risks, and Elias was worth them all. Cove needed Ravenna on her side to get him back, and in order to convince the careful and calculative Ravenna to ally, Cove thought maybe she would need to be as honest as possible.

"I am not only here for you," Cove said slowly. *That is enough information.* She blinked the wetness from her eyes and then spoke words she was not even sure she believed. "There is a grand scheme that is much greater than you, but you *are* a part of it." Cove did believe Ravenna was a part of it. But looking at her now, she could not see Ravenna capable of filling any of the prophecies of the Dove her mother had once read aloud to her in that cottage by the sea. How could a woman so broken, so hopeless, become a beacon of hope? How could this shadowmarked woman, who seemed to know little of the Light, become someone who would usher it into Arresia for time and all eternity? How would she even have a chance if Cove allowed Degare or Leith to claim her power as their own, and if she had no Light to guide her? Cove bit her cheek and pondered on her next words.

Ravenna needed hope. Cove was only one person, but Leith, he had an army.

Cove could feel a whisper of hope beginning to stir in the room as Ravenna processed her words. *A grand scheme.* "Yes," Cove said in response to the puzzlement on Ravenna's face. *It is what you are thinking.* "There is a rebellion of sorts." There were many, and while Cove was not a part of the one she had hoped, she would be as soon as she found it. Ravenna looked at Cove as if she had read her thoughts. "And no, I cannot read minds," she added with a smile. "I can feel emotions, and to a degree, I can influence them." She wished she had more practice in that area. "I try not to be too invasive, but yours are very easy for me to feel," she said, motioning for Ravenna to sit up so she could change the bandages on her back.

Ravenna's emotions of torment were exactly why Cove wished she had not been cursed with such an ability. Experiencing such a wide range of emotions, even when she was not trying to search for them, was exhausting. The only thing she appreciated about this gift, was that she saw its potential to be used for good. She had always been too afraid to practice, in fear she would get caught, but now, with a willing participant. . ."I can help ease the torment in your mind, if you wish," she offered, peeling bandages from Ravenna's back.

"No," Ravenna said quickly, and a wave of Ravenna's guilt gripped Cove in the stomach. It was the kind of guilt that makes one want to scrub their skin clean of the wrongs they had committed. It was the shame and regret of words unsaid and choices made too quickly. It was the familiar type of guilt that followed death. Cove wondered who she had lost, and for what reason she bore the blame.

"Guilt is a tough one," Cove said as she opened a jar of salve. Ravenna shot her a look of frustration at the repeated invasion of her emotions, and Cove bit her lip. *You need her to like you. Or at least, trust you.* She scooped some salve onto her fingers and gently pressed it into each healing wound on Ravenna's skin.

She needed to offer her some information that could persuade an alliance. She needed to reveal the plan. "The witch has been searching nonstop for a new way to take your power, but the darkness has limits," she said. "The bloodstone in the staff was not enough to contain your power for the transfer." *You need to stress the fact that she could die. Show her why she needs you,* Cove thought. "They will stop at nothing, and they do not care if you die in the process."

Cove's eyebrows knit together for a moment as Ravenna's indifference to that fact overtook the air around her. *What now? If she doesn't even care if she lives?* "You may not care," Cove said, "but others are depending on you."

"Who? I have no one left." Cove had wondered earlier who Ravenna had lost, but perhaps the question was, who hadn't she?

Cove swallowed. "I seek a way to shift the power the king already possesses. . .to someone else. *You.*"

Ravenna's body went rigid. "Why me?" she asked.

Make her believe there is hope. Remind her of the rebellion, Cove told herself. *Even if you do not consider yourself a part of it, it makes you more desirable as an ally. King Degare will fall, and it can be by the hands of this Dove, if you give her hope.*

"He is far too powerful with his magic, and we have been

searching for a way to dampen it enough to have a chance against him for years," Cove said, stretching the truth. She did not know exactly what Leith had been up to for the last few years, but she knew he was building an army, with Degare as the target. "I see it fit to jump at the opportunity when I see one," Cove paused, "whether I have had time to discuss it with my leader or not." Leith was not her leader, and she would not be discussing this plan with him either. "If we are successful, you'll possess enough power to bring the entire kingdom and all its Despiri to their knees." Cove knew Ravenna wanted nothing more than vengeance for what had been done to her— for what had been taken. But would she take the offer when she had nothing left to fight for?

"I'll do it." Ravenna said with the confidence Cove wished she had.

Cove tilted her chin and held back a smile, trying not to seem too eager—too naive. "Don't you need to hear the plan first?"

Cove laid out the plan for Ravenna. She offered her every ounce of information she had retrieved over the last few days in Oro, about Degare's plans for her and about the bloodstone staff being recreated with the help of the Delle Witch Clan. In the last week as Ravenna had been asleep, Cove had found the dark corners and crevices of the castle where soldiers liked to exchange valuable information. With the servants, she did not even have to try. They gossiped and spread information like wildfire. It was up to Cove to determine what was the truth and what was a lie. Finally, she had pieced everything together, and she had a solid plan.

Cove was tired of waiting on the Light to guide her. More than anything, she needed to save Elias, and so, she would do it herself.

She would sneak into the witch's chambers and alter the spell that she was to use on Ravenna. Instead of Ravenna's power going to Degare, Degare's power would be transferred to Ravenna. Afterward, Ravenna would hold enough power to destroy Degare, the witch, and all of his Despiri. She could even take the kingdom if she wanted to, and hopefully, she and Cove would remain allies.

With the king gone and the Ember Trades over, Elias would be safe or at least kept alive long enough for Cove to find him. There was no measure too great. Cove would ensure this plan worked, and with Ravenna's help, she was certain it would.

CHAPTER 39
ALONG THE MOONLIT RIVER
LEITH

It had been a month since Leith had sent Cove to Oro, and still, he had not heard a word from her. He was beginning to wonder if she had made it safely or if she had fled. *No,* he had seen the desperation in her face. She was going to Oro for her husband and to keep her secrets concealed. Because of those two truths, Leith knew he could trust her, and he had successfully roped her into joining his cause. Cove's power—though not as strong as Ravenna's—would benefit them greatly. Leith's armies were ready, and he was only waiting for a message from her.

The attack came quickly. None of the guards had seen the witch guardians coming down from the mountain tops and into the valley, where a hundred huts housed Leith's people. The guardians were ruthless, ripping doors from hinges and pulling the inhabitants of the homes out into the streets in their search for Edme.

"Where is Edme?" he yelled to the soldier at his right, who stood with wide eyes as he witnessed the carnage before him. The guardians did not care who stood in their way, even those without the curse were not safe.

"I haven't seen her!" the soldier shouted above the wailing of the Ink Bloods. Leith gritted his teeth, turned in a circle, and took it all in.

Edme, where are you?

She was asleep, like everyone else in the middle of the night.

Leith had not prepared his people for this. He had increased the number of guards on watch at the gates, but he had not foreseen the guardians descending from the steep mountains on either side of the valley.

"Sound the horn!" Leith commanded his men. They scrambled to blow the warning sound that would awaken the Ink Bloods into the horrors of the night. Leith threw his daggers and watched as they met the rotting flesh of the giant monsters' hearts, the curse on his own flesh growing with each of their final breaths. He drew his sword and ran into the fires that now exploded across Ink Valley in a burst of heat.

There she is.

Edme stood amid the flames, defending his valley. She made eye contact with him for a moment, and he felt the blame she placed on him. That blame bore more weight than the curse of the witch guardians that now plagued him. She had warned him, and he had not listened. He had been so caught up in his longing for the alliance with Ravenna, that he had endangered his entire clan.

He swung his blade, ending another witch guardian's life.

The curse that grew upon his soul was unending. Soldiers and guards were awakening from their slumbers, coming out to meet him in the war. The guardians continued pouring from the mountains, tumbling down in complete and utter chaos. Black silhouettes that brought death and destruction.

Ravenna had known the severity of this curse when she had proposed the alliance. Ravenna knew how badly his people would suffer, and he had been a fool. He had wanted her— needed her for his own plan—so badly that he had let her cloud his vision.

An hour passed, and though the beasts were dwindling in numbers, the guardians kept invading the valley. The mountains shook beneath their feet, and Leith fought alongside his men until every guardian had fallen.

"A fool, I tell you!" Edme said, throwing her sword down as she slayed the final beast. "Look what she has done to your people! Your home!"

Leith looked around, breathing hard and fast. Ravenna *had* wrecked his home and taken his pride. He spat into the black blood at his feet and left Edme where she stood. "A fool!" she shouted behind him.

The bodies of his people were scattered across the valley. Men, women, and children slaughtered. His people moaned over the losses—lamented over their loved ones. Beside the river, a mother clung to her son, whom Leith recognized as a new warrior. Through the smoke that burned the witch guardians to nothing but ash and bone, he saw a young wife weeping over her husband's breathless body. He saw two children and their mother, sitting outside of their home that had been leveled by the beasts. He turned to the moonlit river, where he could count at least seven bodies of his beloved warriors strewn about the bank.

One by one, Leith counted the dead. One by one, he witnessed the atrocities that each family in Ink Valley faced because of him. Because of Ravenna's curse.

Leith slammed the door to his hut. He grabbed Ravenna's dagger from behind the desk and chucked it into the door frame. A few moments later, Edme pounded at the entry.

"Come in," he said. She walked in the door, eyeing the dagger that he had just plunged into the wood. She raised her brows and sighed.

"We found another Vestelian," she said flatly. Leith pinched the bridge of his nose and inhaled.

"I'll be right out," he said. They had found eight Vestelians on the edge of death nearly four weeks ago when Edme's men went to retrieve them from Vestele. How another one had survived in the forest all this time after being poisoned, he did not know.

"You'll want to hurry," she urged him.

Leith sighed and trailed her out the door and across the bridge over the river. The entire valley watched his every step as he made his way to the gates where he could see two figures awaiting entry into his home. One was familiar somehow, standing with broad shoulders and dark hair, but Leith did not recognize him as one of his men. The other figure—the Vestelian the man was keeping upright—was small in comparison. Leith narrowed his gaze as he approached them, looking past the Vestelian as he tried to place the other's face. A moment of realization hit him, and his breath hitched as he looked to the side at Edme. She gave him a knowing, dreadful frown and continued forward. It had been years since Leith had seen that face, and that he was here, could only mean one thing.

CHAPTER 40

A TIME TO MOVE

COVE

The kitchens were dark and surprisingly quiet, lacking the chatter of two dozen servants who had not arrived yet. Cove was here because she could not sleep, but she decided this was the solitude she had been craving. Cove lit a candle and began her duties, scrubbing the dirt off of potatoes for about an hour while she hummed. She wondered which village these potatoes were taken from and if its people were starving while being forced to provide crops to Oro.

A few servants began trickling into the kitchen, each taking up their own tasks. Cove did not lift her eyes, but felt one settle in beside her at the table.

"Oh, it's you," she said with a chipper tone as Cove cut potatoes with a dull knife. Cove glanced up, immediately recognizing Mirren. "Thanks for your help a couple weeks back. Jara scares me, but she trusts me enough to keep me as her primary servant. That has to count for something, I suppose." *If Jara trusts her, how much does she allow her to know?* Cove wiped her forehead with the back of her hand and smiled shyly.

"Happy to help," she said. *Now is your chance. Ask questions. Find anything useful.* "How has Jara been these last few days?" Cove asked, collecting the potatoes from the table and plopping them into a bowl. "I hear she's been working on the big spell. Now that the girl is awake, I am sure the king is pressing for her to make haste," Cove said nonchalantly as she began to cut another batch.

Mirren nodded. "Jara finished up the spell late last night. She is resting for the first time in days. That is why I am here in the kitchens—until she rises to prepare for her meeting with the king this afternoon."

Cove raised her brows. The spell was finished and Jara would be leaving her chambers unoccupied soon? *Perfect.*

"Oh, what are they meeting about?" Cove asked, quickly regretting her obvious interest in their whereabouts. She had no right to ask such things, but Mirren did not even bat an eye.

"Something about the stock for the Summer Trades," Mirren said with a shrug. Cove gulped. *Elias is included in that stock.* Mirren kept talking as Cove tried to hang onto her wits. "You're new here, but I'm sure you've heard about the sheer size of the festivities. This is only the fourth trade, but I am sure it is going to be larger than the last. His Majesty is promising something even greater in Autumn."

There was a long pause before Cove responded. "I wonder what he has planned," is all she could manage. Because today, she realized, was the day she needed to begin moving. The silent spying, the gathering of information, the piecing together of the puzzle. . .it had all led up to this.

Cove took breakfast to Ravenna before the sun had risen and updated her on all things she had learned in the kitchen. Cove helped Ravenna to her feet beside the bed, and she was able to stand longer today than yesterday. The power that ruled over her body, and the still-healing wounds, had leeched the strength right from her, but when Cove left for the morning, she was beginning to see the hope behind her eyes.

Cove started her detour to Jara's chambers, where she hoped to find the spell. Her heart was pounding in her throat, reminding her of the life she had been given. The life she had promised to the Light. She bit her cheek and moved forward into the shadows, body being tugged as if she was tied to a stone that was sinking toward the blackness of the seafloor.

The meeting Jara had with Degare turned out to be a meeting to choose the stock for the Summer Trade, which was happening in a matter of weeks. Cove's throat bobbed as she envisioned the stack of papers on Jara's desk. She only hoped they remained there, where she could search through and learn of his whereabouts. *Has he arrived in Oro yet? Are we once again in the same kingdom, no longer separated by an ocean? Is he finally within arms reach?*

Cove took a breath and then spoke down the still-silent bond. *Elias, you cannot stop me. I will find you. Whether you want me to or not.*

Cove paced back and forth outside of the witch's chambers for a few moments before knocking. She had brought clean linens and a bucket of water. It was the perfect excuse to go inside when the witch was not present. She waited for half a minute after the first knock and knocked again.

Thankfully, there was no answer. The witch was gone, and Cove was free to alter the spell and look through the inventory sheets. She entered the room with hope, making a beeline for the desk. Atop it sat a stack of parchment as thick as her thumb was long. Only the top few pages were of any importance, and she separated them from the rest as she scanned the list of Ember descriptions. As she went down the list of all different ages, she wondered how many of the adults had children who had also been taken for the trades. Many families found the Light together. When Cove had first come to the Light, it was after her parents had both been killed for their allegiance to it. Cove knew it was something worth dying for, and she had put her full trust in it—in the Father. But now, here she was, taking matters into her own hands. Utilizing darkness to save her husband.

She swallowed and blinked away the thought, continuing through the papers.

#764, Male, Age 40s, Black Hair, Brown Eyes, From Matuk, Location of Mark: Neck,

Gift: Fire, Power: Strong, Starting Bid: 43 Gold Ravens

#587, Male, Age 30s, Brunette Hair, Blue Eyes, From Usholk, Location of Mark: Ankle, Gift: Strength, Power: Moderate, Starting Bid: 28 Gold Ravens

#428, Female, Age 19, Red Hair, Brown Eyes, From Toremon, Location of Mark: Wrist, Gift: Healing, Power: Weak, Starting Bid: 11 Gold Ravens

#834, Female, Age 62, Silver Hair, Green Eyes, From Verring, Location of Mark: Shoulder, Gift: Cloaking, Power: Very Strong, Starting Bid: 52 Gold Ravens

She looked through every description, searching for any who could match Elias's description. *Male, Age 20s, Golden Hair, Blue Eyes—or maybe they would categorize them as gray— From Oriana, Location of Mark: Back, Gift: Water Manipulation.* She searched the lists twice, to no avail.

Elias, just say something. Anything. Please. Tell me you are alive.

Like always, there was no answer. Could he hear her, or was he ignoring her every plea, in hopes of keeping her safe? Were her words even reaching him? Could it be possible that he had met his end already? He had to be alive. She would feel it— she would know in the threads of her soul if his heart were no longer beating, right?

Cove wiped her eyes and looked to the table, where Jara's spellbook lay open. *You can still find him. This will get you one step closer.* She hurried over to it and struggled to decipher the strange language. Her exploratory studies of ancient languages in Oriana had not proven very beneficial. Some of the words on the pages were familiar, but she had not seen them in ages. She focused on those ones, trying to piece the rest of the spell together around them. She studied it for over ten minutes, referencing a book Jara had open at her bedside. It was a book about the ancient witch language, that she assumed Jara had to use to write the spell. An hour later, when Cove had it translated, she smiled to herself.

She knew exactly where to alter it to gain the outcome she desired—Ravenna, her ally, with all the power and Degare with none.

CHAPTER 41
TOO FAR GONE
COVE

"It's finished," Cove said tightly as she walked into Ravenna's chambers. Ravenna sat up, her red hair hanging in a mess of frayed braids. Cove shut the door gently behind her, taking pride in the relief she felt from Ravenna. Cove was making a difference after all.

Perhaps the two of them *could* bring about Degare's demise. Cove was beginning to believe it herself, that she would have Elias back in her arms soon.

She handed Ravenna a dagger she found in the bag she kept stashed beneath her bed in the servant chambers. Ravenna would soon use it on Degare, after the spell was over. Leith had packed the satchel when she left Ink Valley, and inside, along with food and the ring she now wore, was this singular weapon. Cove felt a fleeting pang of guilt as she examined the silver band on her finger. She would not be sending word to Leith, and she would not be delivering the Dove into his hands. This was her plan now. Her mission to save Elias.

When you work for me, it is not only about you and your needs anymore. Do you understand that? Leith had asked.

Cove swallowed. She was a bargain breaker. But who better could she trust than herself to get Elias back?

Cove saw Ravenna examining the dagger in a way that seemed as if she recognized it but could not quite place its origin. Then, Cove saw her attention shift to her shadowmarked hands, and finally, to her reflection in the mirror.

Cove sat on the edge of the bed, moving a plate of food toward Ravenna, and found herself fidgeting with her fingers. "They'll come to get you this evening," she said. "They plan on using the throne room." Ravenna poked at her lunch but did not take a bite. She said nothing, and her silence was beginning to make Cove nervous.

"Are you sure you can do this?"

"What is there to be sure about?" Ravenna asked, eyes darting up to Cove. "I have no choice. Degare will not be the first man I've killed. I've killed many for less." Cove felt her eyebrows lower as she wondered just who Ravenna was talking about. She thought Degare was the most death-deserving man that had ever walked the lands. He—who had killed hundreds and caused the death of thousands—was surely even more deserving than Andreas had been. Sudden guilt overtook the room, and Cove looked to Ravenna and began speaking before she realized that the guilt was her own. But maybe her words were what they both needed to hear.

"None of this is your fault, Ravenna." *None of this is your fault, Cove,* she tried to convince herself. "You were born into this world of darkness and never shown the Light." *But your eyes have seen, Cove, so why are you behaving as if you are blind?*

Why are you looking elsewhere for help? "It was bound to consume you sooner or later." She swallowed as she felt the Light reaching for her once more, begging for her trust. "All you can do is hold onto that ember within your soul," she said. "The one that I can feel. I can feel the Light working within you." The Light was surely with her, if she was the Dove. It was gently tugging—gently pursuing—as it would until her last breath. Until that ember grew into an unquenchable fire of faith. Cove needed to remind her of that as much as she needed to remind herself at this moment. "*That* is you. Not the darkness."

Mirren came to Ravenna's chambers that afternoon to call on Cove for assistance once more. Jara was being quite needy after her meeting with the king and required a hot bath and a feast of sorts to be strong and ready for the spell. All afternoon and into the evening, Cove and Mirren waited on her every request. When it came time for Jara to perform the spell, Cove followed her up the dais in the throne room, hands trembling, gripping a platter of meats, cheeses and red wine in case the witch grew faint.

Apparently, this spell took much power, and because she was to complete it alone, without the help of a clan, it was risky. She had been careful to preserve her strength. The throne room was empty aside from a few soldiers, another random servant, the king with his staff, and the witch. One of the dark-haired Despiri soldiers stood near the king's throne at his left, and Cove wondered what his title was. Mirren was in the kitchens preparing Jara a special meal for after the spell, and

Cove was growing nauseous with fear. She wished she could take a swig of the wine.

Cove rocked back and forth on her feet as they awaited Ravenna's arrival. Her eyes were fixed on the massive wooden doors, waiting for them to uncage the Dove. *This better work,* Cove thought. The wine glass began clattering on the tray as she shook, but she took a deep breath, stilling it at once. Elias could have calmed her, if he were here.

She missed the peace that seemed to follow him everywhere. She had only felt a hint of that here in this kingdom once, with Zephaniah. *What had become of him? Where is he now?* She had not heard him in the torture chambers but once. *Had they gone too far?*

She hoped not, but then she thought maybe that kind of demise would have been better than life in this darkness.

When the heat of vengeance filled the room, Cove knew Ravenna was coming.

The doors opened, revealing two guards and the Dove between them. Her face was that of determination. Eyes full of promise, eyebrows settling over them, casting them in shadow. Her hair had not been brushed but had escaped her braids in a mess of frizz. Her hands were clenched tightly in front of her, shackles tight on her wrists. Her body was covered in yellowing bruises—only a few were still purple. She wore the same brown dress she had been in for days—the one they had placed on her after her other one had been shredded at the whipping post.

The back had been left undone while she underwent treatment, but now it was laced up and stained with blood, old and new, as the scratchy fabric rubbed her wounds raw again.

With each of Ravenna's steps forward, Cove's heart plummeted a little further into her stomach. Cove winced as the guards kicked the backs of Ravenna's knees, making her fall forward. She choked out the sudden need to defend her and focused on calming her own breathing before they got caught for conspiring together. Cove wore a mask of indifference, but her hands still shook as Ravenna was forced to bow before the king.

As he spoke, she could hear the cruel smile on his lips. "Ravenna, my dear." He held out a hand. "Come forward." Cove had not been near the king but once, but she would know him by the sheer darkness that poured from his veins. She had never felt such heaviness on her soul as she did in his presence.

Ravenna rose to her feet and stepped forward. Cove counted each step, trying to keep her mind clear. *One. Two. Three. . .Seven. Eight.*

The king met Ravenna at the bottom of the dais, offering her a hand up. His hands shook with illness—not fear. They shook like Sebastian's had, and for a moment, Cove missed the King of Oriana. He had never been trustworthy, but at least he was not Degare.

Jara sliced both the king and Ravenna's palms above a golden bowl, allowing the red liquid to drip into it, and then added one drop of her own. Cove narrowed her eyes as she watched. Ravenna's face was beginning to flush, and Cove noticed her swaying where she stood. While the witch was distracted, Cove did her best to muster the calmness she always felt from Elias—to recreate it and offer it up to Ravenna. Cove had not practiced such things, and as she envisioned a wave of peace and willed it toward Ravenna, she was not sure if it worked. When Ravenna's chest rose and fell in relief, she thought maybe it had.

Cove wondered if she or Ravenna was more nervous for the spell to begin. *Surely, Jara will not notice the minor changes I made to the spell. This has to work.* When Degare's power shifted to Ravenna, there would be a moment of shock. Degare would be weak, and probably dazed, and Jara would be caught in a stupor of confusion. That was when Ravenna and Cove needed to strike their prospective targets. Ravenna would reach for the dagger beneath her skirts and kill Degare while Cove swiftly moved in on Jara from behind with a knife from the kitchens. Cove gulped. She was about to kill again. This time, it was calculated.

When the two most immediate threats were extinguished, Ravenna's attention would shift to the soldiers in the room. Cove would aid where she could, but with no water in the room and no experience in fighting, she was sure to be little help. To help in any way, Cove would need to focus in a moment she was sure to be panicking. *For Elias,* she reminded herself. *You can do this.*

Jara's peculiar chants tore Cove from her spiraling thoughts. Quickly, Cove turned her attention to Ravenna and watched closely for any signs the spell was working. Ravenna shifted on her feet but remained otherwise focused on the king and the witch before her. *Cold. Calm. Calculating.*

Cove's body went rigid as she recognized the part of the spell she had altered. She could not tell if the other words were those she had read before, but this part she knew. She remembered the sounds the characters made and how they looked scrolled on the paper in the witch's chambers. *This is going to work,* Cove assured herself.

There was a shift in the room around her. She realized Ravenna was beginning to feel something. Cove swallowed, eyes darting between Ravenna, the witch, and the king. *Get ready to strike.*

The king's face blanched, and the witch clawed at her chest, panting for air between chants. *It is working. Just wait for the final word.* Cove reached into her apron and wrapped her fingers around the knife.

The king collapsed onto the floor, still gripping his staff. Cove's breaths became rapid, she backed up a step and paused. *Stay focused. For Elias.*

As the final word left Jara's lips, she turned to the king. Cove waited for her back to turn again so she would not see her readying for attack in her peripheral vision. The knife was hidden in Cove's grip in the pocket of her apron, but then she left it to steady the trembling plate with both hands. *Be calm. Collect yourself.*

Ravenna was swaying where she stood, but the plan was spinning behind her eyes.

"My power. It is gone," the king rasped. "She took it. She *took* my power!"

Jara looked between the king and Ravenna, and with the witch's hand gripping the fabric of her dress at her chest, she held herself upright using the nearby table. Atop it was the golden bowl of blood, now black. Jara seemed too calm as the king continued. "Fix this, or your clan will never see their homeland," he raged.

Jara looked as though she could care less about his words, and instead, fell to her knees as she continued gasping for air. *The spell truly had made her weak. She will not be hard to kill, afterall.*

As Ravenna crouched over the king, and Jara made no

move to stop her, Cove steadied her hand and reached for the knife. The dark-haired Despiri that stood on the dais with them was panicking, trying to determine his approach. He paid Cove no mind as he kept his attention sharp on Ravenna. *Would he kill her before she had the chance to kill his king, even though she now held all the power the king so desired? Would he risk his life to spare Degare's?* Cove perceived his sudden fear in the uncertainty of Ravenna's capabilities, and she was not surprised at his cowardice. Everyone had fear, but not everyone was brave. Bravery was being afraid and stepping forward anyway.

She wrapped her fingers around the knife. Ravenna did the same with her dagger. The king's soldiers were quickly approaching behind Ravenna, and Cove was growing uneasy as she waited for the perfect moment to lunge forward at the witch. Ravenna blinked as if her eyes were losing focus and pointed her dagger at the king.

"Please. Don't kill me," he pleaded. Ravenna laughed, and it was cruel and wicked, and Cove wondered if the shadowmarks on her skin had darkened the Dove's soul more than she'd realized. Cove inched forward toward the witch, movements so minute no one would notice.

Ravenna's confidence did not waver, but Cove could tell that her strength was beginning to. She was becoming unsteady, and the pink in her cheeks had paled. The power was rooting its way into her body, making a home for itself like a parasite. *Quickly, Ravenna. Quickly,* Cove wanted to say. But something was wrong. Ravenna was not moving.

Do it now, Ravenna.

Still, Ravenna did not move. She hovered there, examining her hands. She rose to her feet and backed up a step. *What are you doing?* Ravenna moved forward with the dagger again, as if to stab him.

"No," the king begged from where he still lay.

Ravenna halted, and Cove watched as the dagger fell to the ground at Degare's plea—*as if she had to obey him.* At the witch's smirk, Cove realized that was exactly what was happening. Ravenna was not on Cove's side—she was on the king's.

Cove bit back a loud cry and dropped the platter onto the stone, meats and blocks of cheese bouncing at her feet as she fled, spilled wine staining the skirts of her dress. *It had not worked. You failed. You failed Elias.*

You never should have tampered with that spell. You fool. Had it been her mistake, or had the witch been one step ahead? It did not matter. Either way, Cove knew she never should have turned to dark magic. Not when the power of the Light was at hand. But to trust in his plan required a strength she had lost with Elias.

Cove had made many mistakes in her life, but this one was perhaps the most irreversible of them all.

What was Ravenna now? A weapon? Some sort of slave to the king's every wish? How would she ever usher the Light back into Arresia? With all that power—both the king's and that of the stone—who could stand against her?

Cove's mind jumped to Leith and his army of Embers— full of the Light of life— which would soon be marching into this kingdom under his orders and with the hope given by his empty promises. If they came here, Cove knew they would die.

So, she fled to the beach where a flock of ravens awaited her and sent her first message to the Shadow.

Do not come. Your little Dove is too far gone.

ACKNOWLEDGMENTS

My gratitude overflows.

First and foremost, thank you Jesus, for your unending love, for turning my heart of stone into a heart of flesh. For giving me the breath of life. Your hands have drawn me out of many waters, and now my hands will write these stories to share that hope with others.

Thank you to my husband, who has supported this dream from the beginning, who is my *calm* and a steady voice of reason when anxieties and doubt begin to creep in.

Thank you to my family and friends, for listening to me babble about this series for years now and for supporting me with excitement through the process.

To my editor and proofreader, Chelsey: I am so incredibly grateful for you. You have spent countless hours studying the notes and outlines for this series, editing, listening to an insane amount of voice texts, and making sure everything is as close to perfect as it can be, all while uplifting me with words of encouragement and becoming a close friend.

Elaine, fervent supporter and friend, you've been one of the firsts to read each of my books, and your love for this story motivates me to keep going. Oh, and thank you for allowing me to bombard you with songs for the cinematic playlists.

My deepest appreciation to: my alpha and beta readers, for helping to shape this story into what I dreamed it could be.

Lastly, thank you from the bottom of my heart to those of you who have supported in any way, whether that be through an Instagram message, comment, share, or by reading these books. Your support does not go unnoticed.

ABOUT THE AUTHOR

Abigail Brier is the American author of the epic fantasy series, *Til Kingdom Come.*

Aside from writing, Abigail enjoys quiet time in nature, bird watching, flower gardening, and spending time with her family in the midwestern United States. She finds herself very busy with her many creative hobbies, which include painting, design, and photography. She can often be found sticking post-its on the walls or working on her laptop to the background noise of cinematic music or worship songs, snuggled up with her cats and dogs.

Abigail's love for storytelling blossomed when she was in middle school. She started (and abandoned) many stories until she came to the idea for the *Til Kingdom Come* series. In the midst of grief, she was reminded of the hope she has in Jesus, and this story became an outlet for her to share the good news with others. She began pouring little pieces of her own story into her characters, many times unintentionally, until the story came to life. If readers take away anything from this series, Abigail hopes it is this:

There is light in the darkness. There is hope in despair. There is joy in the midst of grief. There is redemption when you feel irredeemable, and you are loved beyond measure.